To Marie,
Enjoy the adventu...
Thonie T...

WITH MALICE AFORETHOUGHT

Also by Thonie Hevron

By Force or Fear

Intent to Hold

This is a work of fiction. Names, characters, and incidents (other than those based on historical events) are the product of the author's imagination. Real places and locales are used to enhance the fiction and lend historical significance only. Any mistakes in the representation of same are those of the author and are not meant to be regarded as fact. Any resemblance to persons living or dead is entirely coincidental.

Copyright © 2017 by Thonie Hevron

All rights reserved. No part of this publication may be reproduced, distributed or transmitted in any form or by any means, including photocopying, recording, or other electronic or mechanical methods, without the prior written permission of the Author, except in the case of brief quotations embodied in critical reviews and certain other noncommercial uses permitted by copyright law. For permission requests, email Thonie Hevron at the address below:

badgec65@gmail.com

Published by Thonie Hevron

Book & Cover Design by Carol Ruskin,
csruskin@csrdesignco.com

ISBN-9780999095546

Printed by CreateSpace, An Amazon.com Company

Printed in the United State of America
10 9 8 7 6 5 4 3 2 1

WITH MALICE AFORETHOUGHT

A Nick and Meredith Mystery

Thonie Hevron

Acknowledgments

This book would have looked entirely different if I hadn't made Mike Brown, read it. As with all my stories, I'd outlined it. I sent it to Mike to check its accuracy. Mike is a retired captain from Sonoma County Sheriff's Office, and former homicide detective. When he told me, "It couldn't happen like that," I knew I had to start over. Sigh. What happened isn't unusual—this is a much better, especially authentic book. Mike did the job that Nick and Meredith hold throughout the story. He even gave me some great ideas for side stories. Always available to answer questions, his patience knows no bounds. Thanks, Mike!

Tim Dees, the legendary writer and trainer in criminal justice procedure helped immeasurably with guns, their terminology, and practical usage. John Schembra, retired Pleasant Hill police sergeant was an early reader and helped me "get it right."

For advice on ranching life, Joan Carey Marshall, of Ekalala, Montana, on the Montana Board of Veterinary Medicine and daughter Kerri Marshall, painted a vivid picture so I could translate it into words. Colleagues, law enforcement veterans and authors themselves, John Wills, Pete Klismet, Mike Black, from the Public Safety Writers Association helped with task force info as did Mike Worley, author of the Angela Masters Mysteries.

Jeff Justice, Detective Sergeant at Rohnert Park Department of Public Safety helped with gang info and Phil Lamaison, also from RPDPS supplied me with radio tech help.

As with both my previous books, my critique group played a vital role. Andy Gloege (as yet, unpublished), Fred Weisel (author of Teller), Billie Settles, (author of The Thing in the Attic)—thank you for your moral, technical and critical support. Billie Settles and Charlie Ellicott for helped editing the manuscript in varying stages.

My sincere gratitude to Carol Ruskin, formatter and graphic designer extraordinaire for putting this in such an attractive package with a great cover!

Last but certainly not least, A huge thanks to my family—my husband, Danny, our kids, Dan, Melisa (and Eric) and Robbie. Thanks for being my support group and number one fans!

THE SANTA ROSA PRESS DEMOCRAT | July 7, 2016

News Release: JULIE JOHNSON

Fire destroyed several vehicles and two outbuildings late Wednesday at a remote hunting camp in the Geyserville area west of Lake Sonoma, Cal Fire officials said.

A caller at 8:53 p.m. reported a single column of smoke rising from the hills west of the lake, sending fire crews on an hours-long search for fire, emergency officials said.

The Sonoma County sheriff's helicopter helped locate the fire. The first crew arrived at the site at 2 a.m. after traveling about 11 miles down a rough dirt road that winds through the hills of timber, tan oaks and madrones, Cal Fire spokeswoman Suzie Blankenship said.

The property is part of the Wickersham Ranch Road Association. An owner couldn't immediately be reached Thursday.

The fire burned 2.3 acres and destroyed two outbuildings, one housing a Jeep and another apparently used for storage, as well as three old RVs, Blankenship said. Three fire engines, two inmate hand crews and one dozer was at the scene throughout the night and early Thursday morning, she said.

Blankenship had no further details about where the fire originated or what might have caused it.

You can reach Staff Writer Julie Johnson at 521-5220 or julie.johnson@ pressdemocrat.com.

CALIFORNIA PENAL CODE SECTION 187

187. (a) Murder is the unlawful killing of a human being…with malice aforethought.

CHAPTER ONE

Monday, May 18, late morning

Jake Cavanaugh parked his sixteen-year-old ATV under a buckeye tree. Dang motor was as old as he was. Salvador Escobedo, his buddy, pulled up next to him as a dust cloud engulfed them both. In the late spring afternoon, dust was a constant companion on a dirt road in the Dry Creek Hills.

Without the jarring noise of the ATVs' engines, the silence was profound. Jake looked around, feeling like a piece of him was missing. Just the noise, he thought. He nodded toward the road ahead. "We walk a mile further and we can see them."

"Walk?"

Jake shook his head at his friend's dumb question. "If we take the ATV's they'll hear us. They're like, in stealth mode. You know?"

Salvador cocked his head with doubt. "Oh yeah? How do you know that if they're so stealthy?"

"I saw some of them sneaking down a trail day before yesterday."

"How'd you know they were sneaking? Maybe—"

Jake nodded with a knowing glance. "Oh, they were sneaking. All hunkered down so nobody would see them."

"But you did." Salvador squinted against the late morning sun. "Why are we here again?"

"I wanna see what these guys are up to."

Salvador's dark eyes bored into Jake's. "And you care, why?"

With an impatient chuff, Jake answered. "They've been coming and going on the fire roads. Nobody up here uses these rough-ass roads unless they have to, like, for feeding livestock. There's no livestock up here."

"How do you know? You've been here just a week."

"They leave tire tracks, asshole. Now, you coming or not?"

Salvador shrugged and pushed himself off the ATV. "K, I'm game. You still haven't told me why you give a shit"

The tic-tic-tic of the cooling engine broke the silence. Jake wasn't sure he could put it into words. "They're strangers and this is my family's land. Grandpa wouldn't take kindly to squatters." Jake pulled out a worn four-inch .22 revolver and stuffed it into his back pocket. "Besides, maybe I can get myself out of trouble. If I can tell Grandpa where these squatters are living, he might figure out I'm not a juvenile delinquent."

"You want to redeem yourself with your Grandpa?"

Jake shrugged. "After Dad's version of the fight at school, I don't think the old man trusts me." He shrugged again, facing the truth by saying it for the first time. "Dad already thinks I'm a loser but Grandpa has always—well, you know, trusted me." Jake pulled out the revolver, flipped the cylinder and eyed the bullets. He nodded. Loaded with .22 rounds.

Salvador whistled a low tune. "This is like an old-school western movie." He looked over the hills. "How much land is your grandfather's?"

Jake followed his friend's gaze. "We've been on our land for the last hour. The boundary is the creek up ahead."

Salvador's face scrunched. "Wait. These guys aren't on your land, then."

Jake sighed. "Not exactly. But they're in my neighborhood."

"Oh man," Salvador whined. Jake's friend liked to play it safe. That's why Grandpa liked Salvador so much—like, he'd keep his grandson out of trouble. But Sal wasn't a wuss. Just last week he got in a fist fight at school. The Junior jocks had pushed him too far.

"Don't worry. We won't get in shit," Jake said. Knowing Salvador wasn't reassured, Jake pulled water bottles from the tool storage box on his ATV. He tossed a water to his friend and took a long pull of his own. It was going to be hot. He already felt the spring sun burning through his cotton shirt.

A mile there and a mile back. That shouldn't be a big deal. He emptied the water and nodded to his friend. He wanted to get back to the ranch before his Grandfather returned from Santa Rosa. Time to walk.

***

The boys slowed going uphill. Jake's ball cap was drenched with sweat, and he wished he'd worn his Stetson instead. The tops of his ears were already fried.

The insects' songs resonated in the hills surrounding the boys. It was the only noise except for the soft thump of their boots. Jake felt at home here. His happiest memories were of summer heat, sweat and a splash in the stock pond. Yeah, his house in Tiburon was flashy, but Grandpa's place was comfortable. He could put his feet up at Grandpa's, smell dinner simmering on the stove, and eat on the living room couch. Every summer since he was seven, Jake had come to Sonoma County to help his Grandpa with the family ranch. The rules were easy: respect. Respect his grandpa by working the way he was told. Respect the land and the animals. They were fortunate to have a part in something larger, grandpa had told him. He'd loved every tough, dry, splintery moment of it.

Now someone was pushing Grandpa's limits, though the old man didn't know it—yet. Jake would fill him in tonight, after he got all the facts about these squatters. A simple reconnoiter and he should have enough information.

Ten minutes down the road, Salvador asked, "What if these guys see us?"

"Shut up." Jake worried that they'd be discovered. He was sure the guys had moved into an abandoned camp. Another half a mile—

They walked side by side as they came around an S-turn. There, in the middle of the road, stood a man a few years older than them. Dressed in olive drab fatigues, an ammo belt cinched his dingy brown T-shirt. A soldier? Yeah, a soldier. With a rifle strap dangling, the young man pointed a slim semi-automatic rifle at them.

The muzzle swung from one boy to the other, then the young man aimed it at Salvador's chest. "Stop," the man croaked. "Stop."

The boys froze, not so much from the order, but from fear. The guy's hands were shaking. Fuck. Jake heard his Grandpa's voice echo in his head: A scared animal is a dangerous animal.

"What the fuck?" Salvador jumped sideways, the muzzle following him.

"Shit," the soldier spat, looking like he'd trapped a mountain lion by mistake. "Get back." The soldier motioned toward Jake with the rifle.

"Wait," Salvador yelled, diving into a ditch.

The soldier's attention riveted on Salvador.

Jake wasn't sure who his friend was telling to wait. But while the soldier's attention was off him, he dug into his back pocket and pulled out the revolver.

"No, you stop," Jake's voice rose higher than he'd intended. Sweat made his grip slippery. "You stop," he said again, louder.

"I'll shoot your ass," the soldier screamed, spitting in his panic. A sudden blast came from his rifle and a puff of dust erupted from the dirt two feet away from Jake.

The discharge startled Jake, making his index finger clutch the trigger. Exploding from his grip, his shot wasn't as loud. But his brain's inability to digest the violence rocked him backwards as he saw the soldier drop the rifle. A look of disbelief spread across the man's face as blood oozed from the hole in his forehead. He dropped to his knees then fell flat on his face, raising a small cloud of dust.

From the ditch, Jake saw the whites of Salvador's eyes. "Whew," he said, over and over, as if he didn't trust himself to form a full sentence.

The shock took hold of Jake's brain and squeezed. What had he done? The enormity of it closed in. His head felt like it was in a vise. "Is he dead?"

Salvador crawled from the ditch and scrambled to the body. He kicked the automatic rifle out of the soldier's reach. Jake barely heard the firearm tumble down the side of the hill. Leaning over the body, Salvador pressed two fingers against his neck.

"Fuck." Jake thought how odd it was that he whispered. "Is he dead?"

"I don't know." Salvador straightened, shrugging. "I can't tell. I see 'em do it on TV."

Jake shook himself back to reality and stood next to Salvador. He held his fingers against the soldier's neck like his Grandpa taught him to do on calves, but felt nothing. Jake swallowed hard and turned the body over. Dirt-clotted blood clung to the soldier's face. His surprised eyes had grown milky. Jake was sure. "He's dead."

"I can't call 911." Salvador jabbed at his phone. "No service."

Jake knocked the cell phone from his friend's hands. "Don't." He didn't want a phone call to bring more crap. His mind reeled with the possibilities. How would his Grandfather react—he'd be disappointed, for sure. Then, what his father would say? And there were the cops. He'd already been in enough trouble. He didn't need more.

His mind made up, Jake picked up Salvador's phone and handed it back. "Sorry," he said. "I'm going to push him over the side, off the road. We'll throw some dirt on top. No one will ever find him."

"Are you fuckin' kidding me?" Salvador shouted.

"No."

CHAPTER TWO

Tuesday, May 19, mid-day

Raymond Cavanaugh didn't appreciate squatters, dope growers or anyone else fouling the land. Cavanaugh Ranch property or not, he aimed to look into the rumor he'd heard. He had to know what he was up against. Out here, you couldn't go calling the sheriff every time someone dropped a cigarette butt. His neighbor had mentioned something unusual but hadn't had time to check on it. Up here, people looked out for themselves and their own.

The late spring sun scorched through the woven straw of his nicely broken-in Stetson. He savored the view while keeping an ear open for man-made noises. Hearing none, he relaxed and watched the green-gold oat grass carpeting the rolling hills wave in the afternoon breeze. Twenty miles to the west, the cool ocean fog gathered to temper the warm terrain now glowing with sunlight. A red-tailed hawk screeched in the distance, its long call punctuated by the steady plodding of rock-hard hooves against the dirt. Sound traveled freely over these hills with no ambient noise to dilute it.

Behind him, Jake's horse sneezed.

"Noisy up here, ain't it?" Jake wouldn't expect an answer.

Cavanaugh's heart swelled as he swayed along on his reliable old sorrel, Rocket. He pushed the horse to the edge of the dirt road, where he could sit and gaze at the hills. He loved it up here. Away from the frenetic suck of the world below, the stillness of the Dry Creek hills calmed him to the core. The sweet melody of nature surrounded him. He was happy to share it with the person he loved most in the world, his sixteen-year-old grandson, Jake.

A smile worked its way to Cavanaugh's lips as he recalled his grandson's arrival last week. The wary set of Jake's shoulders, the lines on the boy's forehead, told him what he needed to know. This early in his annual visit to his family's remote Sonoma County cattle ranch, shadows still lay behind Jake's eyes. It would take a few more weeks until Cavanaugh could ward off the ghosts that inhabited his grandson's world. Soon, Jake would remember, as he had every summer, that he was important to someone, someone who counted. Since the boy turned seven he'd spent his summers at the ranch far from the heavy burden of his parents' expectations.

Cavanaugh worked the kid like he had at the same age. Jake was always willing to do the job, no matter how dirty. Cavanaugh was pleased with how well-suited he was to ranching, and how much he seemed to love it.

Today, they had just enough time for a ride. Chores came before fun. Those done, Cavanaugh used the ride to check on the report of squatters he'd heard from Manuel Vila, his neighbor who helped out at the Cavanaugh Ranch.

When the trail forked, Cavanaugh draped the reins against Rocket's neck, steering him to the shorter route through the meadow. Vila told him about some trouble in the hills—a pair of steers were missing with evidence of slaughter, gunshots heard, and strange vehicles on the dirt roads. It was rumored the trouble came from an abandoned parcel of land five miles to the west. "Keep your eyes open, boy—for man or beast."

He was called "Mr. Cavanaugh" by most, and "Cav" by only those who were invited to do so. Only one person called him "Grandpa."

"I know, Grandpa." Jake had heard the warning before.

"Uh huh. Did you see the ground chewed up where the boars have been rooting around back there?"

"Um, no."

"Uh huh." Cavanaugh kept moving, his deep voice fitting into the rough countryside. "Vila said he found a sheep carcass yesterday. He thinks it was taken down by a big cat." Mountain lions had a tenuous grip on the balance of the food chain in these hills. When predators began killing livestock, a rancher had no choice but hunt them. Cavanaugh could easily qualify for a depredation license.

Jake grunted.

"Pay attention." Cavanaugh left it at that. He'd check the little canyon beyond the ranch property line. It wasn't his land, but it didn't matter. He suspected it was where the human-type trouble came from that Vila told him about. And, as always, he'd watch for marijuana growers. Up here, it was a matter of survival.

Cavanaugh's mount was savvy enough to snort out trouble. Rocket was an old ranch horse with a thorough education in cutting cattle from a herd. Cav's son—Jake's dad—had used him for a bit of penning and some high school rodeo when was younger, but these days, a relaxing trail ride into the hills was as much as either Rocket undertook. For work, Cavanaugh used either a younger horse or an ATV. Some days, he wondered if they should have both been put out to pasture—then dismissed the thought. Rocket still had plenty of git-up-and-go. For that matter, so did he—for a sixty-five-year-old.

Old Rocket was a hell of a horse. Yes, sir. Cavanaugh smiled at the silly little cowlick between Rocket's ears. He leaned over and patted the horse's neck. A good boy.

Beside Cavanaugh Jake rode Denver. The twelve-year-old Quarter Horse gelding had been his grandson's birthday gift four years ago. "A man should have his own horse," the rancher had grumbled, handing over the reins. Jake rode Denver, a working horse, every day during the summer. The rest of the year, the animal went back into the string.

On the trail, the horses' muscled haunches powered up and down the hills, their ears swiveling like radar dishes scanning the terrain. When Rocket flushed a rabbit from the underbrush, both horses watched with interest but no alarm.

They dropped into a dry creek, the horses picking their way around bowling-ball sized stones as they crossed to the other side. Then, a bone-jarring lunge up the steep slope brought them to the far side of a scrub oak-bordered meadow. Cavanaugh bumped his calves into Rocket's flanks, bringing him into a gentle lope and they rambled along a game trail that crossed the field.

Jake caught up. "Where're you going, Grandpa?"

Cavanaugh was surprised to see his grandson frowning. "Up beyond those trees."

"Hold up." Jake pulled Denver to a stop and Cavanaugh halted beside him. "The ranch property line runs along this fence, right?"

Cavanaugh eyed him.

"Who owns the land on the other side of the trees?" Jake asked.

Cavanaugh shrugged. "Probably a bank."

"There's nothing over there but an old fire road. It hasn't been graded in a while."

How would Jake know? "Where does it go?"

"Nowhere." Jake looked away, at the heel of his boot. "Salvador and I took the ATV out there yesterday. There was nothing for miles."

The rancher stirred in his saddle, his temper warming his face. "Jake, I've told you before to be careful out here. There's all kinds of——"

"Aw, Grandpa, I had your old wheel gun with me."

Cavanaugh held his angry reply. Jake could get into trouble in plenty of places out here. But he hadn't, so Cavanaugh would go easy on the kid. God knew the boy got enough grief at home. Last week, his father over-reacted to another such situation—no real trouble, just the possibility. Jake had been yanked from his school and friends and dumped up here in the middle of nowhere. It had to be a shock for the boy.

Cavanaugh rubbed a sweaty hand on the denim covering his thigh. "If you're going to live up here, you have to learn that this isn't Disneyland. The bobcats don't have names." His voice strained with his effort not to shout. "If you want to take over this operation, you have to think ahead. If you'd rolled that ATV, you could be stuck out here for hours, if you're lucky enough not to get injured." Not to mention bad people hid in these hills in years past. "There's all kinds of danger up here a gun won't get you out of." Cavanaugh nodded to the hills.

"I know, Grandpa." Jake's jaw set.

Cavanaugh read, 'You don't trust me,' in his eyes. When did the boy start shaving? Now he's pissed. He'll get over it. "I'm riding out to the road."

Cavanaugh studied his grandson's face. Jake squinted, his lower lip quivering slightly. This was wrong. The kid was lying about something and displaying an edge the old man had seen years before in Jake's father. Maybe he should have been tougher on him.

Cavanaugh leaned over the saddle horn, stretching his lower back. "Stay or come with me. It don't matter." The leather squeaked as he sat back and nudged Rocket into a lope.

The horse's rhythmic clomping drowned out Jake's protest. When the kid caught up to Cavanaugh his face was flushed, his freckles faded.

Something was eating at Jake.

They'd slowed through the trees, both eying the terrain. Cavanaugh reined up just before they got to the road. Jake was right. It had been years since the road was last graded. Deep ruts told of rivers of rainwater washing down the path of least resistance. However, some traffic had been on it. From his saddle, Cavanaugh made out the tire impressions from Jake's ATV trip yesterday—along with a half-dozen other tire tracks.

Rocket sprung up the incline to the road and then sauntered on in a cloud of dust.

"Grandpa!" Jake's voice was a whine that sounded like his father. But the boy turned his horse and followed.

The two rode on for an hour, the road meandering through rolling hills. They were alone under an azure sky so vast it seemed to swallow the earth. Still irritated by Jake's irresponsibility, afternoon's familiar comfort slipped away. He paid attention to his grandson.

Cavanaugh glanced at his watch "It's getting late," he said. He rounded a curve, a shallow bank dropping from one side, an oak-studded knoll rose on the other. Intending to turn back, he wheeled Rocket around to face Denver.

Denver spooked, his front legs shooting out in a stiff refusal. Cavanaugh watched Jake sit back and ride it out. With a high-pitched squeal, Denver tossed his head, throwing his center of gravity backward. His front legs scraped at the air, reaching for balance against the weight that drew his rump down to the dusty road.

Jake slipped from the saddle like a wet towel. Landing on the edge of the road, the kid rolled from his hip smoothly like his grandfather had taught him. His body teetered at the edge, then slipped down the embankment. Soft earth crumbled beneath his weight as he skidded to a stop five feet below. Cavanaugh couldn't see what had stopped him, but he was in one piece.

The rancher lunged, grabbing Denver's reins. He nudged Rocket to the edge of the road with Denver trailing behind, squealing again and pulling away. The reins snapped from Cavanaugh's hands.

"Damn," the rancher snorted, keeping an eye on the kid. Was that a boot Jake had tripped on? Whose was it?

Cavanaugh spun Rocket to pick up Denver's reins again, and yelled over his shoulder, "You okay?"

There was no answer for a long moment. Cavanaugh's nerve endings began to tingle with dread. When it came, Jake's unenthusiastic, "Yeah," didn't convince him.

Cavanaugh dismounted and walked to the edge of the road, his gaze on his grandson. Jake was safe. Maybe getting dumped from the saddle had wounded his pride. No. Jake slapped the sandy soil off his jeans with his ball cap, keeping his eyes averted from Cavanaugh. No, there was something else. The young man straightened, then stiffened. He looked at the ground behind him.

The rancher looked past Jake to a man's scuffed work boot jutting up from the dirt. This boot had halted Jake's slide down the slope, when the kid's shirttail hung up on the heel. The boot stuck out of the earth at an unnatural angle, attached to something. A lump under a thin layer of dirt and rock—the reality jolted through Cavanaugh.

A corpse.

He'd seen bodies before. Khe Sanh, Quang Tri Province, Viet Nam, April 1968.

"Get away from there, boy." The command tone of a combat-hardened Army lieutenant reverberated in his chest. Adrenaline powered through his veins, suppressed through the long dormant discipline of a soldier. He swung from the saddle and handed the reins to Jake.

The dirt was mounded with more haste than caution. The stench of rotting flesh struck him as he got closer. A shredded a brown T-shirt barely covered a distended abdominal muscle covered by dirt and flies.

Cavanaugh stood for a moment, lost in another age. Then, he turned haunted eyes on his grandson. "S'pose you can't get cell service out here."

Jake stumbled over the words. "No, Grandpa. Not 'til we get back to the ranch."

"Get on up here." He tossed Denver's reins to his grandson. "We'll call the Sheriff from the house."

CHAPTER THREE

Wednesday, May 20, morning

"Congrats, Nick. You deserve to be sergeant." With his signature Italian enthusiasm, Lieutenant Ferrua pumped Nick's hand in a sweaty handshake. "Come on in and have a seat."

Nick Reyes stood in Lieutenant Gil Ferrua's office—the man in charge of the Detective Bureau—Violent Crimes Investigation: (VCI), Property Crimes, Narcs, Domestic Violence/Sexual Assault, Crime Scene Investigation (CSI) and the Coroner's Unit. Reyes tried to settle into the office chair, a place intended to be uncomfortable. People didn't linger in the Lieutenant's office. Nick had to work at getting along with him, and there was always a specific purpose for a detective to be in the office. Nick didn't think congratulation on his promotion was a good enough reason.

The Lieutenant smiled, hunched over his clasped hands on the cluttered desk. His office was a study in chaos. Files, cables, and batteries were piled on every horizontal surface. A wall displayed a big Sonoma County map. Ferrua smiled, his head bobbing with practiced gusto. "Yeah, your promotion is a real good thing. Nice to see the brass can get it right sometimes."

"Thanks."

"So, you must be wondering why I asked you in here." Ferrua stopped smiling.

"Yep."

The Lieutenant's face slipped into an all-business mode. "You know Leahy is going out next week—getting snipped—a hernia. I've kept him on—" Ferrua's fingers made air quotes. "—a modified light-duty status since he found out he has to have the procedure. I didn't feel it was safe to have him in the field. Something could easily happen to make his condition worse."

Nick was impatient with Ferrua's need to set a foundation for his decision. Too much explanation was part of the Lieutenant's indecisive command style. Get to the point and leave the justifications behind.

"On to part two of why you're here." Lieutenant Ferrua took a deep breath. "I'm sending you on a death investigation. You'll be acting VCI sergeant, calling the shots at the scene. Some old rancher found a half-buried male in the hills west of Lake Sonoma up in the boonies. Shot through the head." He rubbed his chin. "You'll need a new team. Take Willis because he's on call and his partner has court."

"How about Ryan?"

"Yeah, Ryan, too. She doesn't have a partner." Nick had been her partner until last week when his promotion had been effective. "Yeah, Ryan and Willis will be your team."

Working with Meredith made Nick's pulse jump. But there were risks. "Does Leahy know?"

Ferrua held his hand up to halt Nick's protest. "Not yet. I wanted to get you moving first."

Nick stood. "We'll be out of here before he finds out."

"It's for his own good, even though he won't see it that way." Ferrua shrugged. "Patrol is already up there. Keith Ormiston is the deputy securing the scene."

Nick's interest flickered to life like a Boy Scout blowing on a spark to start a campfire. "What do we know so far?"

Ferrua smiled, relaxing his shoulders. Nick was hooked. "The reporting party is a rancher who was out yesterday on horseback and found a partially buried human body. He told dispatch there was a hole in the skull. I want you three up there—like now. The crime scene folks will be right behind you. The nearest paved road is several miles away, and the access is a fire road. The only way in is to walk."

"Or on horseback."

Ferrua nodded automatically, then smiled when he got it.

"Here's where you're going." The Lieutenant stood, pointing at the center of the map. "The body is west of Lake Sonoma by several miles. The RP said take Rockpile Road to the split up here, where there's a turn off to a fire road. The crime scene's about two miles up. Ormiston marked the way with rocks." Ferrua's pudgy fingers moved to the right, past Lake Sonoma. He stabbed at a thread-wide line indicating a road. "The RP lives here. 2650 Cherry Creek Road, the Cavanaugh Ranch. Well over an hour from the scene."

"Could it have been an old Indian grave?"

Ferrua scowled. "That's Native American, and no, there's a bullet hole in his head. It sounds like the body hasn't been out there long."

"I'll have dispatch call the RP and tell him to meet us at the road, then I'll be en route." Nick glanced at his watch. "We'll be on the road in twenty minutes and should get there before the RP."

Ferrua's head bobbed. He slipped his hands in his pockets. "When you get back, you'll fill in for Leahy until he returns from his medical leave, then go back to patrol rotation, probably graveyard." His eyes fixed on a pen laying on his desk. "By the way, if you need them, there are resources up there for you, like a place to write reports and catalog evidence." He paused. "Kind of innovative, when you think about it."

"What do you mean, resources?" Nick's bullshit sensors alerted. Ferrua wasn't an innovative thinker. "We'll use the sub-station at Lake Sonoma if we need to."

Ferrua waved Nick's thought aside. "No, the sub's shut down for the rest of the week due to a rodent infestation."

Nick waited.

"The Northern California Marijuana Eradication Team will be up there at an old World War II radio site. They're using it as a base for operations." Ferrua squinted at Nick.

"World War II what?"

Ferrua threw up his hands, like everybody but Nick knew this. "During the war, the military built radio repeater and radar installations all up and down the coast. This was the farthest they built inland. Anyway, they were all abandoned after the war but the government held on to this one, God knows why. A couple years ago, the Feds gave it to the State. Department of Justice (DOJ) and Northern California Marijuana Eradication Team—Nor Cal MET—got grant money to fix it for use as a base for their summer sweeps in northern Sonoma and Mendocino Counties. DOJ is the lead agency, with locals rounding out the dance card."

"What does this pot base have to do with me?" Nick felt his blood pressure rising. He wasn't sure what to expect, but he was sure he wasn't going to like it. "If I need someplace to sit, I'll use my car."

"Now don't get excited." The lieutenant put a hand on Nick's sleeve. "It's an experiment. Because it's between the body and the RP, the captain thought you might use the base during the first hours of the investigation. At least for today. You can get some paperwork done without a two-hour drive back to Santa Rosa."

"Whose idea was this?" The thought of intruding on another agency's mission irritated Nick. He wouldn't want anyone near his own operation. Fucking Ferrua had been out of patrol so long that he'd lost his sense of what was real.

Ferrua sighed. "This order came from Sheriff Flannery. I guess we'll save a few bucks by combining resources. We'll throw some cash at Nor Cal MET for supplies. It saves us mileage, saves you time."

Nick shoulders relaxed. "I can't see we'll use it." He turned to leave. "Why the hell does the sheriff think we need this kind of help?"

Ferrua shrugged. "I think he's got a grant in the works for a project with the MET people. He wants us to look like we're a cooperative agency." Ferrua smiled with his best press conference expression. "—which, of course, we are."

Nick worked to calm himself before getting back to his office. It was never simple, just doing the job. The bosses sat behind desks back at the Main looking at graphs and stats. They had time to dream this crap up while he and his team were in the field, battling the clock, the suspect, and other unknown factors. He blew out the annoyance. There was always something.

But this time, Nick would have more on his mind than the investigation and stepping on allied agency toes.

Meredith.

CHAPTER FOUR

Wednesday, May 20, morning

"Ryan, wait outside," Lieutenant Ferrua snapped.

Meredith grabbed her small backpack and slung it over a shoulder. As she passed him, Sergeant Donald Leahy's face was so close she could feel the heat coming off his red skin. She closed the door behind her, leaned against a wall outside Lieutenant Ferrua's office and exhaled with relief. Open or closed, the door made no difference as the two men's voices rose. The coroner's office across town could probably hear them.

"I don't give a rat's ass if she was hand-picked or not," Leahy snapped. "Isetta and Willis are next up. Why the hell can't Isetta drive himself up to the scene after court?"

Meredith hated being discussed like this. They reduced her to an object to be tossed around the office, with no regard to her value in the organization of VCI. She never felt superior to the rest of the unit—nor had she felt any less than them—she carried her weight.

"Reyes wants her, and she's available now." Ferrua's whine sounded like a plea.

Damn Ferrua, why doesn't he stand up to that asshole, she wondered.

"We need to get up there ASAP." The lieutenant presented his case to his subordinate. "By the time Reyes and his team arrive, it will be three more hours at least."

"The victim isn't going anywhere."

"Bullshit. You know as well as I do time is critical." After a pause, Ferrua's voice cracked. "What's your objection anyway? I'd think you'd be glad to get rid of Ryan for a while."

"Don't be such a fool, Gil." Leahy's voice dropped, like he'd passed the point of no return. "She doesn't deserve the special treatment she gets-from everyone around here."

"Special treatment? What the hell are you talking about?"

"She didn't get this promotion on merit. She got it because some obsessed judge pulled strings to keep an eye on her."

Leahy's words stung Meredith. Part of what he said was true—she 'd found out just before the judge had tried to kill her. Her shrink called it erotomania, a type of mental disorder where the affected person had delusions their victim is in love with him or her. Meredith had fought the judge—with Nick's help—because the lieutenant had been too spineless to hold the judge accountable. The sergeant wouldn't listen to her. It had ended badly—the judge was killed by his own man using her gun.

"I don't play favorites like you do, Gil. Ryan has to earn respect in this unit."

She hated that this conversation could be heard in the VCI office. Although she thought no one knew about the judge's interference, she'd been working hard to prove she deserved the position. She'd hustled through her cases and helped anyone else who needed it. In fact, she and Nick had the highest number of closed cases in the unit, second in arrests for investigations.

"Look, the Sheriff likes her. She does her job well and makes him look good. We treat her fairly. Period. She gets assignments like everyone else." She heard the springs in Ferrua's chair squeal. "That's all, Don."

The door swung open. As Leahy stormed out, he bumped into Meredith and stopped, his face flushed. "Hurry up and get your shit, Ryan. You're going north with Reyes." He pushed past her without waiting for an acknowledgment.

Ferrua and Leahy's squabble would make working in VCI more difficult. Leahy disapproved of women in his office and had never concealed his aversion to Meredith. When she was first assigned to Violent Crimes Investigation, Nick had told her she embodied what Sergeant Leahy hated in women: she was independent, motivated, and logical. At the Sonoma County Sheriff's Office, Leahy was known as a misogynistic good-old-boy who ruled his unit absolutely, nudging the department's rules of conduct boundaries at will. Rumors persisted Leahy had something on the Sheriff enabling immunity from losing his job.

Ferrua did what he could to cope with the sergeant, standing up to him every now and then. This was one of those times, and Meredith regretted wishing her lieutenant would grow a spine. She was especially sorry she and the whole office had witnessed it. She'd given up trying to get along with Leahy.

She was happy to be out of the office, even for a day. In the wild hills of Sonoma County, her next adversary would surely be more identifiable than Leahy. No matter what she felt about him, he was her boss. She had to work to his satisfaction. It was his unreasonable expectations that wore her down. Though he was rough on her, Meredith behaved with the respect she showed every other sergeant. She was pretty sure that only worsened his animosity.

She hoped he would be on sick leave for a few months while he recuperated from his surgery.

CHAPTER FIVE

Wednesday, May 20, morning

Highway 101 traffic thinned the farther north they got. The morning sun cast a golden glow on suburban businesses, housing, and then to backyard horse ranches and vineyards. Most people, even locals, appreciated the beautiful Sonoma countryside. Yet Nick grew irritable with the silence in the car. Willis chatted, being sociable. At about the Windsor City Limits, the uncomfortable silence between him and Meredith shut Willis up.

Nick didn't know what to say to Meredith, unless it related to work. She'd withdrawn when his promotion had been announced. She snapped at him, too, which wasn't her normal MO. So, he kept away from her. His thoughts followed a familiar path—an impression arriving as a half-heard whisper. After looking at it from all sides, the idea changed into something unrecognizable. In the end, all his notions vaporized with nothing to show for his efforts.

What the hell happened to his life?

Nick's recent promotion to sergeant was about the only thing that had gone as he'd planned. Early on, he'd been arrogant enough to plot out a detailed future. His marriage to his beautiful wife Angela seemed perfect. He'd even picked out his daughter's first car—a metallic blue 1967 Chevy Chevelle Malibu, two-door, eight cylinder, and manual transmission. But, in a few short years, his life turned upside down. His marriage was over, his daughter buried. With those losses went all his dreams for a perfect life.

So how did he move on? He had to take one reality and replace it with another. There was a hole in his heart where his love for his daughter lived. And now Angela was with another man—she was already carrying his child. A part of him thought he should be happy for her, but there was too much hurt for such altruism. He was alone, and he didn't like it.

Angela had been gone over six months before she asked him to come to Mexico. He figured he'd grown accustomed to a solitary life, but when she called, he ran to her. He couldn't help himself. It didn't take long before he realized she wanted his help not his love. Mexico proved that.

If he could fool himself about Angela, what other "cast in stone" delusions did he have?

The one thing that wasn't a delusion: there'd always been Meredith. She'd always had his back.

And now? He couldn't put words to the thing that kept him at a distance from Meredith. It hurt to see her every day, but being away was painful, too. They'd crossed the line in Mexico. That one kiss had felt like a promise. He trusted her—she'd saved his life—but he couldn't risk being hurt again.

In any event, their days as partners were over. He would forever be fearful of losing her, on the job and off. If they never saw each other again, this, this—kiss would be between them. He sighed. As soon as he cleared this case, he'd grab his promotion and escape to the anonymity of graveyard patrol.

Nick couldn't explain to Meredith why he'd taken the sergeant's test. He hadn't wanted to leave Meredith behind in VCI, but he still had a career he cared about. Although he loved VCI, he'd been there for three years and was beginning to feel restless. And, despite what he'd told the administrators on the sergeant's oral board, his career goals had grown a bit hazy since his daughter's death. That devastating event made him re-evaluate his life and re-arrange priorities. This was an ongoing course for him.

He felt like an idiot for putting the space between him and Meredith. If only his wariness would relax for him to talk about it. They were still friends, weren't they? Certainly, they weren't lovers.

It dawned on him that there was an expiration date on a woman's heart. Mere would move on, eventually, if he gave her no encouragement. There was no comfort in that thought.

Turning off at Canyon Road and heading west, Nick scanned the distant hills. Stitched with neat rows of grape vines, the green was so vibrant it had a life of its own. The air was still for now; later in the afternoon, a chill from the ocean would creep in.

Dry Creek Valley was a hidden gem in Sonoma County. Family vineyards blanketed the valley floor, often with a Victorian or Craftsman farmhouse as a centerpiece of the property. Oak groves and pines dotted the surrounding rolling hills swathed with ripening oat grass. Farther up, scrubby French Broom illuminated roadside slopes with their invasive yellow flowers. A pair of black-tailed does grazed in a marshy divot. Everywhere Nick looked, there was life.

It was good, here in Sonoma County. Even out here in the wilderness. The stirrings of renewal thumped in his chest. Maybe things would get better.

While he loved his job, his impeccably timed promotion enabled him to admit that Violent Crimes Investigations was wearing on him. Sergeant Leahy was a stone bastard of a man, ruling like a dictator, inflexible and vindictive enough to get one of his detectives hurt or worse. And, Nick hated the way the sergeant treated Meredith—giving her the shittiest jobs, ordering her to bring him coffee, type reports and other duties he wouldn't have made a male perform. She'd told Nick that she'd play her sergeant's silly games his way—for now. She didn't need him to be her knight in shining armor. She'd choose her battles.

It wore down the rest of the team to see a peer treated so badly. But Leahy was an equal opportunity asshole—he spread the misery around—only different from what he dished out to the sole woman in the unit. The team seemed to think of Nick as the real leader, and a buffer between them and Leahy. It had become a burden trying to keep the peace.

The field, though, was something else. Interviews, culling evidence and circumstance, building a case from nothing but a mess like a soup sandwich—he thrived on it. Banging on doors, a foot pursuit, and the satisfying click of handcuffs snugging around the suspect's wrists—catching bad guys was the culmination of all the hard work.

That was what he loved.

CHAPTER SIX

Wednesday, May 20, mid-morning

With Willis in the front passenger seat Meredith curled up in the back, pretending to nap on the drive up Highway 101. Nick drove, his mind-numbing cowboy music blaring. Who ever heard of a Mexican listening to Country and Western music? When the signal weakened to static, Nick turned off the radio. Thankfully, Willis had given up on conversation.

Meredith had other things on her mind. Like moving to the small condo she'd recently bought in Petaluma. Escrow closed the sale of her Forestville property, but the timing had been off closing at her new place. Downstairs needed mold treatment, drywall replaced, and re-painted, delaying her move-in date another week. With her few possessions in storage, she'd bunked with her best friend Christie for a month. Having her living space in limbo tilted the balance in the rest of her life.

Doctor Kathie Servente was tops on the list of burdens she wrestled with. The psychologist had asked some provocative questions. Yet, she wondered whether all this therapy was productive. It seemed every time she met with Doctor Servente she walked out with some new nagging question. Meredith progressed from worries about moving to her last session.

"Meredith, what do you want from life?" Servente stared at Meredith until she made eye contact.

Gawd, this was irritating. She searched for words and knew what she came up with was inadequate. "I just want to be happy."

"So, tell me what that looks like. Is it a family? A husband, two and a half kids and a Chevy in the garage?" Servente twirled her pen between her fingers. "What about your career? Blending a family and career?"

"It's not an easy question." Meredith knew she was evading. She wasn't even buying time to think of an answer. She didn't have one. It was that simple. She didn't know what happy "looked like."

"Okay, let's back up a bit." The therapist leaned forward putting herself in front of Meredith. She never broke her stare. "Define happy."

Meredith released an impatient breath, looking away. "So sixth grade."

Silence was a technique Meredith had learned for interviewing people. Humans needed to fill a silence. Yet she found herself speaking to fill the void. "It's when life is good—you like your job, have a partner who is equally committed to you—"

"When you say 'partner' do you mean a work partner or a domestic partner?"

Meredith's irritation grew as she spit out the words with little thought. "Both, I suppose."

Servente leaned back, her eyes wide with mock surprise. "Both? Do you hear your answer, Meredith?"

"I have to think about it," she snapped. "I can't vomit out a Brady Bunch answer."

"There is no right or wrong answer." Servente scribbled on her pad, then looked up. "You come up with your own definition. It's not 'one-size fits all.'"

"Hmm."

"What about your father? How does he fit into your life?"

What the hell? *My father*? Why is she butting her nose in there? As far as Meredith knew, he was still rotting away in a convalescent home in Rohnert Park. Meredith looked past Servente's shoulder to a spot on the wall. "He doesn't."

"Are you sure?"

Was she sure? Would she be open to a relationship? Maybe, but only if her father wanted it. She had long since given up trying to be a daughter. The last time she visited him, he said he didn't want to see her.

Family? Father? Husband and kids, or career?

She was at a crossroads, where her decisions would chart a course for the rest of her life.

Crap. She didn't have to decide right now, did she?

CHAPTER SEVEN

Wednesday May 20, mid-morning

Raymond Cavanaugh left a note for his grandson. Jake was out feeding the stock. The rancher figured he'd be gone most of the morning and into early afternoon. After the call from the Sheriff's Office he'd wrapped up his bookwork, hopped into his truck and headed out to meet the deputy.

The roads around Dry Creek always surprised visitors. There were plenty of fire trails and dirt roads in varying conditions, but the main thoroughfares were smoothly paved and maintained. They were to meet on one of those roads, at a turn-out just below where he and Jake had ridden yesterday.

Until two weeks ago, he hadn't been sure whether Jake would spend the summer with him. Cavanaugh had been sitting in a cantina in Playa Blanca when he got a call from his son, Steve—Jake's dad.

"Dad, Jake's in trouble."

Cavanaugh had dropped his Modelo to the pine table. "What happened?"

Steve launched into his explanation. "Well, it's not as bad as it could've been. Jake's been hanging around some low-lifes from the Canal area in San Rafael who think they're tough guys."

"Go on," Cavanaugh prodded. Steve milked the drama out of every situation. Cavanaugh was growing tired of this conversation already.

"Some of his new 'buddies' broke into a house and tried to steal guns."

"Tried. So they got caught." It wasn't a question.

"Yeah."

"And Jake? Was he in this crew?" Impatience flooded through him. *Tell me what the hell happened.*

"Well, no," Steve drew out the last syllable. "But he was the one who told these idiots where the guns were. You should never have taught him how to shoot."

Cavanaugh snapped, "How the hell did he know where there were guns?"

"He says he just happened to see them at a friend of a friend's house."

"Do the cops know?" Cavanaugh took a gulp of his beer.

"Yes. They've questioned him. I got a lawyer. He doesn't think Jake will be arrested."

"Okay."

"Dad, I'm looking for a little support here." Steve's voice rose to a whine. "I need some help. We've got to get him away from these thugs, particularly that Mexican kid, Salvador."

Cavanaugh's pulse quickened. "How do you plan to do that?"

"Amy and I were thinking—"

"Yes?" He knew what was coming. He wanted to hear his son ask him for help. Steven had never wanted assistance before when Cav had offered, but it was different now, wasn't it? With a police record—mere contact—Jake had the potential to ruin Steve's social standing. In a small town like Tiburon, people would know.

"You're making this hard, Dad."

"Hard? Son, I just buried your mother after a three-year battle with ovarian cancer. That's hard."

Steve began an answer, but Cavanaugh cut across his son's comment. "Look, I'm tired. I needed a break, so here I am in Costa Rica, swilling beer and eating *camarones*. Now cut to the chase."

"I get it," Steve's voice was stiff with disgust. "We won't bother you anymore. Don't worry about us."

"I won't, Steven. Not one little bit." Cavanaugh straightened in the chair, readying himself for another huge commitment. "Because I'll take Jake. I'll go back to the ranch, plant him there with me and work his ass off. He'll go to school in Geyserville until he graduates in two years and turns eighteen."

"Thank God." Cavanaugh heard relief in his son's voice. "I didn't think you wanted to help."

Cavanaugh allowed himself a little smile. "I was getting tired of hearing you whine."

CHAPTER EIGHT

Wednesday, May 20, mid-morning

Meredith studied Nick as he glanced at the directions on the mobile digital terminal—the sheriffs' computer mounted on the dashboard. After turning onto Dry Creek Road, he accelerated up the grade. Willis tipped the screen and read out loud, "Follow Dry Creek to Rockpile Road for a mile. Turn to Sproul Road then pull off at the shoulder where you see the patrol car."

Meredith wondered at Ferrua's eagerness to get her out of VCI—even temporarily. After his promotion, Nick was designated to cover short-term supervisor absences until his permanent patrol slot opened. For now, she was paired with Angus Peters whose partner, Emil Anderson, was on light duty with a shoulder injury. Peters was a good guy, a critical-thinker kind of detective, but their working relationship was barely manageable. It was hard operating with someone else after having the best partner she could imagine.

Meredith mulled over what she knew about today's case. A homicide: a partially buried corpse found in a remote area of the hills west of Lake Sonoma. The initial report indicated a gunshot wound to the head. That didn't mean the gunshot was the cause of death. She'd seen a few people survive head wounds, so she kept her mind open.

But, a new case up in the hills near Lake Sonoma made her nervous. She was a city girl; although she liked the outdoors, she hated spiders and varmints. Especially possums. Nasty, snarling creatures. Then, she shrugged mentally. If she could survive a jungle in Mexico, like she had a few months ago, she could manage her own backyard. Besides, she was ready for a break from Leahy, no matter how short. When Nick left, so had a lot of VCI's appeal. A fresh view of the department would do her good—although the corners of her subconscious prickled in dread over the potential for danger.

She wasn't used to feeling like this—in fear that she might freeze.

Getting out of the office might be a good idea. With any luck, she'd be so busy she wouldn't have time to think about her relationship with Nick or the fear.

She wasn't sorry to miss tomorrow's session with Doctor Servente, either.

CHAPTER NINE

Wednesday, May 20, mid-morning

The detectives parked behind the patrol SUV on a long, shale-covered shoulder under a pair of scrubby oak trees. Nick and Willis got out of the car and stretched after the long ride. Meredith tucked her water bottle into a backpack and slipped it over her shoulder. All three detectives donned sheriff's windbreakers and ball caps against the morning breeze as much as for identification. Grateful she'd found a pair of comfortable gym shoes in her locker this morning, she leaned on the car waiting for the two men.

Nick stuffed a portable Motorola radio into the nylon holder on his belt and hung his Sheriff's Office identification lanyard around his neck. "The RP should be here in ten or fifteen minutes." Nick used verbal shorthand. RP stood for "Reporting Party." Along with phonetic alphabet codes, such as "Nora" for N, cops had to be concise on the radio. Taking up too much air time could prevent other officers from reporting in. As in most workplace settings, acronyms found their way into daily conversation.

Willis glanced at his sergeant. "Where're you going?"

Nick tugged on the bill of his ball cap. "To scout the trail to the fire road and see how rough it is. Be back soon."

"Okay." Willis leaned against the car next to Meredith as Nick disappeared up a slope into the trees.

After the sound of Nick's footfalls subsided, Willis said, "He's moody today."

"Hm." Meredith made what she hoped was a non-committal sound. "He's thinking about the case."

Willis leaned toward her, sliding his sunglasses down his nose. "You, too?"

"Moody?"

"Yeah," His bright blue eyes studied her. "Hey, do you have something going with the Sarge?"

She couldn't help when a tiny sarcastic laugh escaped. "No, nothing going on. We're not even partners anymore."

His eyes widened. "Oh, that's how it is, huh?"

"No, that's not how it is." She pushed herself off the car and faced Willis. "Nothing between us, Joey." Why hadn't she noticed how beautiful his eyes were before?

"Oh yeah? Well, looks like I touched a nerve." He shoved his glasses up the bridge of his nose with an index finger. "He piss you off?"

She hated that she couldn't see his eyes. He was a cop stereotype, muscle-bound and arrogant, but damn, he had the most beautiful blue eyes.

Where was he going with this? She groaned and leaned back on the car, feeling sullen. She didn't want to talk. What the hell would she say? She shook her head. "Drop it." She pulled the brim of her ball cap over her eyes, low enough that she could just see him.

When he smiled, it was with white teeth so straight she could picture the braces. He pulled his glasses off and slipped them onto the back of his head in a move she suspected he practiced before a mirror. "It's good to get a sense of the playing field."

"Playing field?" She felt her face flush.

"You get the idea. I can see by the expression on your face." He flashed a thin-lipped smile.

"And what makes you think you have a chance?"

The sound of an aging diesel engine cut through the surprised silence. Thank God, Meredith thought. Saved by the truck.

A late-model, dust-encrusted red Ford dually pulled in behind their car. The tall, sinewy driver in a sun-faded red plaid shirt, unfolded from behind the wheel. Meredith thought of a wary rattlesnake uncoiling as she watched him get out, his eyes taking in everything. Here was someone who knew what life was about.

She pegged him for his mid-sixties, kept fit by a life of hard work. Bareheaded, he was someone who spent much of his time in the sun— his forehead was pale; the skin below his nose was the color of tanned leather. His expression gave nothing up, no smile or grimace. She wasn't sure which way he was going to go. Would he cooperate? Was he pissed off about having to drive all the way out here?

Meredith shoved herself off the car. As she approached him, one hand held up her badge, the other outstretched. "Mr. Cavanaugh? Detective Meredith Ryan, Sheriff's Office. Thanks for meeting us."

Cavanaugh leaned into the handshake, his eyes narrow against the dappled sunlight. "Ma'am."

"This is Detective Joey Willis. Sergeant Reyes will be here shortly."

On cue, Nick appeared at the top of the incline, skidding down the rocky trail to the cars.

Meredith announced, "Sergeant Reyes, this is the reporting party, Mr. Cavanaugh."

Cavanaugh took Nick's hand.

Pulling off his sunglasses, Nick got right to it. "Mr. Raymond Cavanaugh? Thanks for coming out. I understand you called last night to report finding a body."

"I did." Cavanaugh straightened, flexing his shoulders. To Meredith it looked like he wanted to be anywhere but here. Understandable.

"Can you tell us what happened?"

Cavanaugh slipped his rough hands into his pockets. "Yeah. I was riding out here yesterday on this old firebreak up a-ways. My horse spooked and I saw a boot stuck up in the dirt. Didn't have any cell service, so I came back to the house to call you folks."

Nick's mouth splayed in a frown of understanding. He pulled off his ball cap and squinted at the rancher. "Any chance you'll come up to the site with us? I'll have more questions after I see where you found the body?"

Cavanaugh glanced at the trees, where Nick had first appeared. "It's a long walk."

"Yes, sir."

The rancher thought a moment then went to his truck. He grabbed the straw Stetson from the hat rack, then closed and locked the door.

CHAPTER TEN

Wednesday, May 20, late morning

The morning sun ticked its way up to full power. As Nick led the others closer to the crime scene, the road got rougher, filled with more gravel and rock. The shape of the land graduated from oak-studded hillocks undulating around verdant meadows to craggy cliffs that grudgingly supported a grove of digger pines, scrubby tan oak and low-growing madrone. A few fragrant buckeye and laurel trees provided intermittent shade. As they walked, a wall of loose rock rose on the other side of the track, then bent back on itself as the road curled around.

A handful of marble-sized rocks rolled down the wall's face.

The elevation rose so slightly, Nick barely noticed. He walked along the uneven shoulder of the road, noting a trail of irregularly outlined prints in the dirt. From the deputy, Ormiston, he figured. The footprints indicated Ormiston had avoided stepping on tire tracks. Nick was satisfied; the deputy had thought ahead well enough to not obscure potential evidence in a crime. Ormiston was one of more than 275 sworn deputies in the Sonoma County Sheriff's Office. Nick hadn't met him, but his caution with a crime scene was a good first impression.

Nick walked with Cavanaugh at a steady pace, with Meredith behind and Willis bringing up the rear. He was glad to have her on his six. Stable and disciplined. Yet, an outside-the-box thinker, always offering ideas Nick hadn't considered. Perfect attributes for a good partner.

Except he was a sergeant now, and she wasn't his partner.

Cavanaugh had dropped behind. Nick slowed. "Mr. Cavanaugh, where did you get onto this road?"

The rancher glanced sideways, cocking his head toward a dull thud. Three muffled pops followed. Everyone stopped, looking up toward the sound—the top of the hillside.

Cavanaugh shouted, "Watch out! Rock slide!"

A rock the size of a Volkswagen sailed down the slope, followed by a billowing rooster tail of dust. A cascade of smaller stones came next, like chicks following a hen. Slowly, at first. Then, it was on top of them. A fist-sized rock slammed into Nick's hip with an unnatural thump. He felt the shock of impact, but no pain. Nick grabbed Cavanaugh and pushed him uphill and out of danger. The rancher sprawled onto the road. Nick reached for him while Meredith grabbed Cavanaugh's other arm. Half-dragging the rancher, they made it past the edge of the tumbling slide. They dropped to their knees, choking from the dust.

Willis skidded to Meredith's side. He coughed. "You okay?"

Nick's jaw tightened as Willis put his hand on Meredith's shoulder.

She didn't seem to notice and answered with an automatic, "Yeah." Her attention was on the rancher as she twisted sideways. Cavanaugh's face drained to the pale color of his straw hat. "Mr. Cavanaugh?"

The rancher's muscles seemed to give way. He dropped to the ground with a sigh and rolled over against Meredith. "Give me a minute."

"Are you hurt, sir?" Meredith rolled onto her butt, making her shoulder a more comfortable place for him to lean.

"Nah, I'll be fine." He rubbed his eyes.

"Joey, Mere? Any injuries?" Nick's brows drew together.

Willis stretched. "I'm good." He offered his hand to Nick, pulling his sergeant to his feet.

Both men turned to Meredith and Cavanaugh. After taking a silent assessment, Meredith answered, "I'm okay. We should check Mr. Cavanaugh for injuries, though."

Meredith gently settled the rancher against a boulder.

Nick laid a hand on the rancher's shoulder. "Mr. Cavanaugh."

The older man glanced aside. "Yeah, I'm fine." He leaned forward, trying to get to his feet.

"Wait a minute, sir." Nick held him against rising. "Take an inventory.

Your head?"

Cavanaugh seemed to snap out of his shock, his eyes finding Nick. He nodded smartly and said, "Head's fine." He stretched his arms and legs. "I'll live." He gathered himself to stand, but took Nick's outstretched hand. "Just a little pissed it took me so long to get out of the way."

"Don't be too upset, Mr. Cavanaugh," said Meredith. "Your warning probably saved us all.

Nick waited for the rancher's breathing to slow. The exertion had taken a toll. The way the old guy fell, Nick was sure he was hurting somewhere. How were they going to get him to the car? Jeez, they hadn't made it to the body yet.

The slide covered the roadway behind them. Dust settled over the rocks, tree branches, and clumps of grass that had careened over the road's shoulder and spread down the slope. Even now there was an electric quality to the air, charged as if the threat was still active. The musty smell of long-buried earth surrounded them.

Nick watched a final rock roll past him, over the edge and out of sight. No way were they getting back to the car the way they came.

He glanced uphill at the sheer cut in the hillside and wrote off that as a possible way out, too. "Either of you guys have cell service here?"

Willis and Meredith both checked their phones. "No."

Nick felt for the portable radio on his hip. His fingers met shards of thick plastic. Pulling it out, he inspected the smashed housing. That's why he didn't feel any pain when the rock hit him. He frowned as he shoved the radio into his jacket pocket, checked his watch and decided. "Sorry, Mr. Cavanaugh. I hadn't meant for you to get stuck at the scene with us. Your safety is my responsibility so now it looks you don't have a choice. I can't afford to leave one of my detectives here to sit and wait until the cavalry arrives."

Cavanaugh raised his eyes, his expression fathomless. "I'll go with you."

Nick nodded at the rock slide. "We're not getting back the way we came. We'll walk in to the scene, and hope we can find a place where the deputy's radio works."

"Hey," Meredith shoved her phone back in her pants pocket. "How about I take a little hike up this hill and see if I can get a cell signal?"

Nick said, "Take Willis with you."

Meredith waved her sergeant's idea aside. "No offense," Meredith glanced at Willis, then back to Nick. "But I can make it faster alone. Shouldn't take more than thirty minutes to get up there."

Nick checked his watch. "Okay, be back in an hour. If you're not, we'll come looking for you." A silly warning, he thought. Someone had to stay with the old man. For her own good, maybe he should make her take Willis. What if she fell and broke a leg? No, he'd tried before, making her do what she didn't want to. It hadn't been pretty. And, she was right about being able to travel faster alone. For all the noise she makes about being in the wilds, she handled it better than she gave herself credit for.

And she called herself a "city girl."

Meredith tied her windbreaker around her waist, pulled her long brown hair into a ponytail and stuffed it through the hole in the back of her ball cap. She scrambled up the rocky incline and was gone.

CHAPTER ELEVEN

Wednesday, May 20, noon

The slope greened to a lavish late spring carpet and Meredith dodged swampy marsh grass that grew in spring-fed basins. She passed brash yellow Scotch Broom and scrubby brush and shivered, creeped out about ticks. It was too early in the season for ticks, wasn't it? She hated bugs. And snakes. Were there snakes up here, too?

Conifer-lined crevasses cut through the low points between knolls. On either side, the hillside was a broad swath of grass, open for what seemed a half a mile. No cover, little concealment.

Focus. Think about the case. The steady uphill climb provided time to consider the crime. There were some weird aspects to this case. First, it was too remote for a body dump; the murder must have occurred close by. Second, it made no sense to bury someone next to a dirt road. Why hadn't the shooter shoved the body off a nearby cliff? There were plenty of ravines out here where a corpse would never be spotted.

Was the homicide tied to a grow operation? Most of the crimes she'd heard about in these hills were connected to marijuana. Personally, she could never work up any enthusiasm over enforcing misdemeanor pot laws. Some grows were legal, with the proper documentation. But an untold number of residents of the culturally and politically liberal Northern California coast sold pot to people from out of state. In Humboldt County, cannabis was a major part of the local economy. Here, every election ballot voted in more leniency to marijuana legislation. Her brother, David, a musician, had often used pot. She didn't care, unless its sale or possession hurt someone. But, that was the problem. People did get hurt.

In the most recent incident, a pair of Kansas residents came to Sonoma County to buy their marijuana and killed the man they bought it from. Drug dealer or not, he didn't deserve to die.

People got hurt.

Doctor Servente's throaty voice from last week's counseling session intruded into Meredith's thoughts, taking her in another direction where people got hurt. "What are you worried about? The *Federales* forcing you to give up your gun, or the guy in the basement who tried to strangle you?" The doctor's platinum gray hair shook as her gaze riveted on Meredith.

"I don't know. Both, I guess." In Mexico, she'd done what she had to. She'd killed the bastard in the basement. But somewhere deep inside her, she wondered if there was another way to survive. She figured this was a normal reaction. "The real issue was hesitating, then giving up my gun."

Servente leaned toward her, with earnest sincerity. "The *Federales* would argue your hesitation was a good thing, wasn't it?"

Meredith was silent—it was a question she couldn't answer yet. Servente waited.

After a minute, the doctor continued. "The bad guys weren't bad guys at all. They were Mexican Federal Security Forces who interrupted your search so you wouldn't blow their cover." The psychologist sat back. "Seems to me that's good situational awareness. Some instinct told you not to shoot. Had you ignored it, you could've caused massive casualties—including you and your partner."

"It's a cardinal rule not to give up your gun. Now, I worry about failing my partner every day I go to work." Meredith was exhausted by the hopelessness she lived with daily. She could avoid predictable tactical situations, like serving arrest warrants, always aware of the possibility of something dangerous. But, that was part of her job. If she couldn't get over this fear, she had no business in law enforcement.

Absorbed in her thoughts, she caught her toe on a rock and stumbled. A thought jarred loose. Maybe she should throw in the towel. Quit. Quit being a cop.

And do what? She had to make a living. Her husband, Richard's death the year before left her with shaky finances. She could teach. She was credentialed, but had no classroom time. Could she get a job teaching Physical Education like she'd planned in college? It would be safer—no one's life on her hands, no working graveyards in the rain, no tyrannical sergeants—no more nightmares.

Quit?

CHAPTER TWELVE

Wednesday, May 20, early afternoon

Meredith climbed to the nearest high point, a rock outcropping. She turned to see the trail behind her and caught a view that took her breath away. Miles to the west, a blanket of fog draped over a ridge near the ocean. To the north, wisps of fog clung stubbornly to the coastline, but her discerning eye noted the mist burning off as the sun's rays grew warmer. To the east, a gray smudge on the horizon suggested the top end of the agricultural Sacramento Valley—Colusa, off Highway 5. The gray turned to brown as she turned southeast to the East Bay Area—Oakland and Berkeley. The rain had stopped weeks ago with no more in sight, and a layer of smog hung above the southeastern hills. Another turn, and she had an expansive view of the coastal hills. Pillars of steam from the Geysers, a geothermal power plant, to the east served as a landmark. She took a moment to absorb the beauty of the tree-covered slopes and the light terpene haze in the air. She remembered the vapors given off from conifers from near her home in Forestville. What seemed a lifetime ago was less than a year.

Steep inclines and rugged brush that lay before them was too challenging for an injured Cavanaugh. For that matter, none of them could traverse this terrain.

No visible way around the slide.

She raised her phone, hitting the "home menu" button. Nothing. No service. She turned, and tried again. After the third try, she sighed. Nothing. The phone was a paperweight.

Meredith trotted back down the hillside. She'd been gone an hour and she thought she'd seen a glimmer of relief in Nick's face as she approached.

After her report, Nick said, "We walk."

Cavanaugh mumbled, "We could do it easy with horses."

Hiking at a slow pace, they let Cavanaugh determine the stride. Meredith worried the old man was hurt and too stubborn to say anything. She walked beside him when the trail allowed, listening for changes in his breathing. He was a determined old coot, though. While he didn't move fast, he moved steadily. She admired his stamina. In fact, she liked him. Period. His aloof manner might put some people off, but Cavanaugh said what was necessary, no more. Her father was kind of like that, and it was something she appreciated about both men—one of the few traits she valued in her father.

With a twinge, she realized she'd talked more to Cavanaugh in the last two hours than she had to her father in years.

The road ahead was quiet. The surface moisture from the morning fog dried. Several sets of tire tracks and the deputy's footprints goaded them onward, promising a story. The day was breathless under a sky so blue it gleamed like a precious gem. The terrain meandered from ravines sliced from hillsides to grassy knolls. Ten minutes later, the road leveled and hiking became easier.

Nick dropped back to walk next to Cavanaugh, avoiding Meredith's gaze. "Can we get started on some questions, Mr. Cavanaugh?"

The brim of the rancher's Stetson dipped.

"Does this road go to your property? Where did you access it?"

Nick strained to hear the answer. "This road follows the ranch property line up to the dried-up creek back there." His chin pointed over his right shoulder. "I left from the house and we parked—"

Meredith and Nick asked, "We?" at the same time. They glanced at each other, then looked to the RP.

"Me and my horse." Cavanaugh squinted at Nick like he was a fool. "I parked the trailer about a mile west from your deputy's car, then we rode north on a dirt road nobody saw fit to name. It's the ranch boundary. I hadn't been over there for two, maybe three years. We rode on and came across the body about an hour after passing the spot where you guys parked."

Behind them, Willis groaned. "An hour?"

Cavanaugh's smile was thin. "A slow walk, a gradual elevation rise."

"What time did you find the body?"

Cavanaugh sighed. "About four p.m., I guess. The sun was throwing shadows across the trail on the way back."

"How long did it take you to get home?"

The rancher considered this. "An hour at a lope back to the trailer, with a thirty-minute cooling out period, an hour to the house. It was just before sunset when I put the gelding away, almost seven-thirty."

"Then you called 911 from your landline at home?"

Cavanaugh nodded. "A little while after I reported it, a deputy called me from his cell phone to pinpoint directions to the body. I talked him to it until the call dropped."

Nick spoke over his shoulder to Willis. "The deputy walked part way back to call dispatch and confirm the location. He returned to the scene overnight, keeping the body protected from predators."

"Nice duty," Willis muttered.

Meredith had a thought. "Have we had contact with the deputy since he made the call?"

Nick shook his head. "No. There's no cell service and the radio is out of range."

A shiver of dread tracked down her back. She was glad she wasn't in Ormiston's place. She didn't like the idea of guarding a corpse in the wilds of the county without any means to call for help.

Help against what? Marijuana growers? Probably not; the deputy would be stationary. His responsibility would be to keep the body intact against wildlife. Scavengers were a likely hazard. Around here the worst were wild pigs, coyotes, and mountain lions. She shivered again, recalling an American Lit class in college where she heard a quote from someone she couldn't remember. "Only two things to fear in the wild—lightning and humans." What a crock.

She missed concrete.

Nick continued his interview with Cavanaugh. "Tell me how you found the body."

Cavanaugh licked his lips. Meredith was about to offer him some water but caught Nick's glance. It said, not now.

"My horse spooked. I wound up on the ground and saw the boot. It was attached to a leg." He pulled off his Stetson, ran his fingers through his wavy gray hair, and slid the hat back into place. "I saw plenty of that in Southeast Asia." Something about the way he answered bugged Meredith.

"Did you check—" Nick began.

"What—" Cavanaugh stopped. "—to see if he was alive?" The rancher shook his head as if ridding himself of the images. "No way. The critter that dug him up made sure he wasn't."

"So, you can identify the body as a male? You must have seen more than a boot and leg."

Cavanaugh started moving again, the slightest hesitation in his gait. It was his right hip. "He'd been shot in the head. The coyotes went for the soft parts first. He hadn't been out there for long, maybe overnight." He eyed Nick. "But, he was dead."

Nick glanced at Meredith. "Ryan, will you take some notes?"

She scribbled in her notebook as Nick fired off his questions. She added her own observations about the rancher's account after noting Cavanaugh's first comments about his timing and finding the body. She didn't add that he was lying about how he found the victim.

"Where was the grave in relation to the road?"

"About five feet from the edge." Cavanaugh kept his answers simple.

They walked for another few minutes, Nick glancing around at the hills surrounding them. "Who comes up here?"

"Other than the odd hunter wandering out of bounds, no one. There used to be a hunting club up here a few decades ago, but it's long gone." Cavanaugh followed Nick's gaze. "The road that leads to this old track dead ends somewhere up there. A couple of months ago, I was riding along my property line, checking fencing, and noticed it from above. Dropped on to it from a narrow path—a game trail. I wouldn't have found it today if you hadn't been there. In the old days, this was gravel. The county came along and paved some of these country lanes in the '80's when they had more money than good sense."

"No one out here feeding cattle or sheep?"

"I don't have any stock out this far." He paused. "Matter of fact, there's no one out here. My ranch is farthest west until you get to Galloway Springs—almost to the coast."

"So, who owns the land where you found the body?"

Cavanaugh shrugged. "A bank, I guess. Folks walked away from their homestead and left it before debt was popular."

Nick was silent, his head bent. Meredith knew he was visualizing the scenario the rancher described. "Have you seen anyone else on the property?"

"I don't get out here much. I work closer to home."

Willis pushed toward Cavanaugh. "Have you heard any rumors about the place?"

"Rumors ain't my business." The rancher's jaw shut, the flexing muscles saying, "This trail just ended."

Willis had found a way to piss off the old guy. Meredith had a feeling Cavanaugh's cooperation had bottomed out. Oddly, it ramped up her respect for the man. He didn't care what the deputies thought. He stated his truth, popular or not.

Except he was lying about something. A guy like Cavanaugh would know anything weird going on in the adjoining property, wouldn't he? And how he found the body—that didn't add up.

CHAPTER THIRTEEN

Wednesday, May 20, early afternoon

Raymond Cavanaugh stepped up the rocky slope, one foot in front of the other, dreading what waited for him at the end of this hike. He didn't like what he and Jake had seen yesterday—a human being who had died by violence. A body unearthed, and gnawed on by a wild animal.

He wondered about the corpse—a hunter? He hadn't seen a firearm or a bow but the man was outfitted in woodland camos. Cavanaugh felt menace, even with the corpse in its present condition. He couldn't explain it, but he'd learned long ago to respect his hunches. Besides, who would bury a body out here?

At the site and back at home after he'd called the sheriff, Jake's behavior was off, like bad meat. Jake wasn't squeamish and yet, under these bizarre circumstances, he acted odd. Ranch life, even part-time, hardens a man to the sight of dead animals. So why was he so antsy?

Jake knew the body was there. He had tried to steer Cavanaugh away. He'd been keen enough that it troubled Cav. Only one way he could've known. This meant nothing but trouble until he had it out with his grandson.

Cavanaugh didn't much like this business of cooperating with the authorities. He didn't consider himself a law-and-order man, but he wasn't dishonest, either. Jake's behavior put him in the uncomfortable position of misleading the police. Jake said he didn't know anything about the dead guy but Cavanaugh didn't buy it. He hoped to hell the boy hadn't done something bad enough to foul up his future.

Last night, standing in the kitchen, Cav punched in the Sheriff's Department's phone number. The look of panic on Jake's face stunned Cavanaugh.

"Do we have to do this, Grandpa?" Borrowing one of Cav's own favorite expressions, he'd continued, "It's none of our business."

The rancher jabbed the call-end button. He stared at his grandson. "You're wrong. It may be miles from this house, but this is my neighborhood—ours, now. What goes on here matters. There's a dead man in the ground. Somebody cares about him, somewhere. Right? Whether it's a pot-grower or some other criminal, I want to know how he got there."

"If it's a pot grower, the last thing you want to do is get involved." Jake's freckles paled. "They're into vendetta stuff, you know. They'll come after us."

"You're wrong." Cavanaugh answered, "If it is them, they don't want trouble any more than we do." He wondered what scared his grandson so bad.

"What'll the cops do, anyway?"

The rancher held his temper. "Their jobs."

"Cops don't know shit," Jake sputtered. "They'll mess everything up."

Cavanaugh's voice deepened to a mad-dad tone. He squared off with his grandson. "You know more than you're telling about this." It wasn't a question.

"No," Jake answered, staring at his shoes.

Cavanaugh started punching numbers into the phone again. "I'm calling the cops."

The 911 dispatcher answered as Jake bolted from the room. Did he reach into his pocket for his cell phone? Cav couldn't tell.

The boy had been upset, no doubt about it. Cavanaugh hoped Jake would do the right thing and come clean. But it would have to wait. Meeting with the sheriff's deputies meant Cavanaugh would not make it home until later. He hoped his grandson would remember to feed the livestock in time for evening chores.

CHAPTER FOURTEEN

Wednesday, May 20, early afternoon

The sun's glare burned Nick's nose to a cherry red color. His gaze rotated between the road at his feet, the route in the distance, and the hills around them, making his neck ache. A packed dirt track, glazed by a layer of dust, twisted in front of them. One side rose in a steep incline, bare of vegetation until the earth curled into a knoll at the top. The other dropped into a craggy ravine dotted with coyote brush, manzanita, and poison oak. In the sky a quarter mile in the distance, a cluster of vultures drifted on layered air currents. Nick hoped he was getting close to the body site.

Besides the vultures, there was plenty to see. Tire tracks looked a day or two old, narrow like those of an ATV. Hoof prints meandered from side to side across the road, bisected by the ATV prints. It could almost be the tracks from two horses. Nick walked in the deputy's boot treads at the shoulder, ten feet from the evidentiary prints. It gave him hope the crime scene would be intact.

Cavanaugh cleared his throat. "We're coming up on it. Around the next bend."

Meredith and Willis hustled to Nick's side. She whispered, "You want me to look it over first?"

Annoyed Willis hadn't volunteered, he waved her away. "No, we'll just go in."

Meredith dropped behind without comment. Nick glanced back at her frown. Dang, he'd pissed her off. What had he done?

Nick counted on Meredith to watch Cavanaugh. She seemed to prefer the rancher's company to his, anyway. The old guy was keeping up, although breathing heavily at times. Meredith would alert Nick if they needed to stop for a rest.

The road wound to the right, past a sharp rocky cliff. The shoulder dropped four feet then plateaued out to a shelf, where a dark-colored lump of clothing rested. Nearby, a crew-cut, well-muscled deputy lounged on a mound of granite. Ormiston.

The deputy nodded at them, stood, and walked around the bundle to Nick. He introduced himself.

"This is the RP, Raymond Cavanaugh." Nick motioned to the rancher.

"Thanks for coming out, Mr. Cavanaugh." Ormiston said with a polite smile over a handshake.

Nick cut the greetings short. "You have a radio that works?"

Ormiston reached for the portable strapped to his duty belt and handed it to Nick. "Yeah, I turned it off after it was clear I couldn't use it out here. It should still have some juice."

"Where were you when you lost the signal?"

The deputy shoved his hands in his pockets. Smudges of fatigue sat under his eyes. "Just after I caught this road—a long way back."

"We can't go back that way." Nick sighed. "A rock slide blocked the road about a half-mile from our starting point."

"No shit." Ormiston looked to the top of the hills. "I thought I heard rumbling. What the hell happened?"

Nick rubbed his eyes. "I'm not sure. I heard three pops, then the mountainside came down. We can't get back overland, either."

Ormiston's bloodshot eyes widened. "You think someone did it on purpose?"

"It's occurred to me." Nick's lips pressed into a thin line. He cast a quick glance at Meredith, who caught and held his gaze. He hadn't said anything to her because he didn't want to alarm Cavanaugh. Nick was sure she'd heard the same. He wasn't sure Willis had noticed. He looked back at Ormiston. "Have you had any trouble?"

The tired deputy answered, "Nah," and stepped back to give Nick a full view of the body.

"Looks like a coyote got to him. He's pretty chewed up." Ormiston pointed to the paw prints.

After snapping on his latex gloves, Nick noted the time. He observed the scene. The mound had shallow holes and small piles of dirt where an animal had dug up the body. The victim was a male in his early twenties with shaggy brown hair, his milky eyes wide with surprise. His stocky build was clothed in a shredded brown T-shirt, olive green camo fatigues and worn brown work boots. The head was half-buried, but the bullet's entry created a visible hole on one side of his forehead. A thin trace of dried blood and dirt lined the wound. As Ormiston had told them, a carrion-eater had torn open the victim's lower torso. Flies swarmed over intestines. The air reeked with the smell of rotting flesh.

"CSI won't get out here for a while, so I want to look at what we have—a partially buried body of a white male. Age, possibly in his early twenties," Nick called out. "Ormiston, what time did you find him?"

"I got up here just after dark. It was 9:20. I scared off an animal, but couldn't see what it was. Maybe a coyote." The deputy rubbed his eyes. "No, I didn't check for a pulse. His guts were hanging out so he was good and dead." His face reddened as he glanced at Cavanaugh. It wouldn't do to speak disrespectfully in front of the RP.

Willis spoke up. "I'll take notes."

"No, Ryan's already started. No photos until CSI gets here. And stay off the road and away from this area." Nick pointed to the corpse and began his observations: time, approximate temperature, weather, terrain and overall conditions. He named everyone present and articulated his reasons for proceeding before the CSI's arrival.

Focusing on the ground, Nick found more footprints that pounded out a path around the grave. Then, he worked his way back to the edge of the road and another jumble of impressions. He pointed to a pair of shoe prints. Damn, he wished CSI was here to work their magic. The two senior guys were knowledgeable and experienced enough that Nick trusted their work. Two feet from the edge of the footprint patterns, he squatted. At a small mound of dirt, he used the pen to unearth a lump of material.

A spent bullet; its tip flayed open after being mashed into the ground. "Look for a shell casing."

After a moment, Meredith said, "Got it."

"Diagram where you found it and where this slug was buried."

"Yes, sir."

"And put it somewhere it won't get contaminated."

"Yes, sir."

What the hell was that kind of answer? Sir? She'd dispensed with "sir" after her field training nine years ago. She's still pissed. Get back to the body.

Despite having cameras in the detectives' phones, Nick couldn't take pictures of the scene. If a suspect made it to trial, all evidence including photos must be preserved in the original condition for the defense to see and examine. That meant if he took a cell picture, the phone must be deemed evidence at that point and the defense has access to everything in it. Although this was designated a VCI-only phone, the defense would be able to see phone numbers from witnesses or victims of other investigations, including confidential informants. To avoid this, CSI handled crime scenes. The defense would have less to exploit in the chain of evidence at trial.

Backing from the body, Nick scanned the road. Again, circling methodically, he pointed out more prints. With a flat sole and heel looking detached, they were clear imprints of cowboy boots. Nick pointed to them and remarked, "These look like Mr. Cavanaugh's."

"Yeah," Cavanaugh said. "I walked from here to here." His finger traced a line from the road to the body.

The other imprints were heavy lugged work-boots soles. A tiny splatter of dried blood droplets created coffee-colored stains on the ground. Nodding to it, he said, "Ryan, sketch this boot print." Nick glanced at the grave, then back to another lugged sole impression. "These look like the victim's."

"There's another pair of prints." Meredith squatted, pointing to a patch of disturbed earth four feet in front of her. "There could have been a struggle."

"Or these are the shooter's foot prints from moving the body." Nick stayed at the road's shoulder to keep his footprints out of the immediate crime scene. "Looks like the incident began here." He scrutinized his surroundings as he listened to what the evidence told him. "One bullet and one shell casing." He glanced at the corpse. "The round should be in the victim's head. This slug could've gone wild."

"Still just one casing." Not from a revolver. Maybe two guns.

"Whatever was used, the guy's deader than a doornail." Willis said, stating the obvious.

Nick quelled his irritation at the detective. When he finished observation of the area, he returned his attention to the setting. This was an unusual crime scene because of its remoteness. Sketches, measurements and photos would be done when the evidence techs got there. CSI was usually not far behind him, but with the landslide, there would be delayed. Nick suppressed his normal efficiency to think outside usual practices. He had to project the possibility of a trial and appeals process as he looked at the victim. It only took a seed of doubt in one juror's mind to lose a conviction. Catching a bad guy and keeping the bad guy can sometimes be two very different things.

Waving away the flies, he looked at the loose dirt on the camo-printed fabric. "One round in the head. I don't see any other injuries. The trauma to the torso appears post-mortem from a carrion-eater. From the tracks, maybe it was a coyote."

Deciding to take a huge chance on disturbing the evidentiary opportunities, Nick bent over the corpse and patted the pockets. He pulled out a small brown leather bi-fold wallet dampened with body fluids. The contents were unremarkable. A California driver's license under the name of James Easley. Nick said the name out loud. "He's from Bridgeport."

"Where's Bridgeport?" Ormiston asked.

"Mono County, the back side of Yosemite," Nick answered.

"A little far from home." Meredith squinted. "Wonder what he was doing over here?"

"Robbery wasn't a motive. He's got more in his wallet than I do." Nick counted $136.00 in cash. "Wait," he said, pulling out a dark colored identification card. "Volunteer—Amgen Tour of California." He looked at Meredith, searching her face.

Her mouth twisted in a thoughtful expression. "Seems a stretch for a guy like this from the mountains to volunteer for a bike race in the burbs hundreds of miles away."

Nick felt the same prickle. He filed it in his mental file cabinet, hoping all the scraps of information would fit together to form a complete picture. He turned from the puzzle forming in his mind. He needed more pieces, the sooner the better.

"Anything else?" Willis strained to look over Nick's shoulder at the wallet's contents.

Nick's latex-encased fingers felt two folded pieces of paper tucked in a credit card slot. With his thumb and index finger, he pulled them out and unfolded the paper. "It's a map. Here," he handed it to Meredith. "Hold this." His attention returned to the card. "Damn. He's a card-carrying member of the Covenant Family."

"Who?" Willis asked.

Nick looked past Ormiston to the hills behind. "You should be reading the intel bulletins. They're domestic terrorists—paramilitary survivalists. They believe the U.S. government is out to dominate the world and wipe out Christianity. They plan to overthrow Washington."

Meredith sucked in a breath. "Like anarchists?"

"Yeah, but worse. The Covenant Family has a militant branch, an army. In recent months, they've been migrating from Arkansas to Susanville, in northeast California. ATF and the FBI know about them. I read an article in the latest Southern Poverty Law Center bulletin. They have a reputation for recruiting parolees, especially skin heads and white supremacists. They're reported to be moving arms into California."

"A great jumping off place to get into the prison system—so close to Susanville Prison." Meredith shook her head.

"What're they after?" Cavanaugh asked the critical question.

"Their goal seems to be to at least disrupt government, ultimately overthrow it. These guys are tied to the Oklahoma City bombing, and they're affiliated with the Aryan Nation."

"What are they doing here?" Meredith asked.

"I don't know." Nick twisted in a 360 degree turn, glancing at the hills. "My guess is they're here to train, maybe for a specific mission. Maybe hiding weapons, cooking street drugs for cash, maybe." He shrugged and turned back to the body.

Willis waved a hand around. "They can train here with no looky-loos. Who's going to see them?"

"Crap," Meredith shouted. "This is a map of downtown Santa Rosa. See," she pointed to intersecting lines. "This is where Highway 101 crosses over Fourth Street. Railroad Square on one side and Courthouse Square on the other. They're obvious, even without the street names." She shoved the scrawled map under Nick's nose, jabbing a finger at the scrawled abbreviations. "RS for Railroad Square, CS for Courthouse Square. Here's the highway, and a date—tomorrow—in the corner."

Meredith handed the paper back to Nick. He looked at her. "This could be directions to the Redwood Gospel Mission on Morgan Street. It's—"

"I know where it is," she snapped. He referred to a homeless shelter and soup kitchen on the west side of Highway 101. One of the first things a cop learned in Sonoma County was that when an individual's identification card gave the address of 600 Morgan Street, Santa Rosa, it was the mailing address for an itinerant person. It's where they picked up their mail.

Her eyebrows drew together in a look that said this was something important. Back up. Re-think this. She might have something. Based purely on Nick's trust in Meredith, he handed the card back. "Put it in an evidence bag." He looked away, adding, "Please."

Meredith flipped the paper over. "There's more. Here's the route from Court House Square to Sonoma Avenue and Brookwood." Her eyes widened as she glared at him. "That's Santa Rosa PD."

"Jesus," Nick took a breath. "Makes you wonder why he's got this sketched out." He knew he sounded like a jerk, telling her to do what she was already doing. "Hang onto this."

"It'll be in my pack with the bullet and casing," Meredith said.

In a second, Nick's urgency to find this man's killer grew. Ideas clicked in his brain, firing into incomplete thoughts like lightning rods that showed him where but not what. This was more than the random homicide of a hayseed survivalist.

When Nick was a rookie, he used to believe detectives didn't give a damn about victims like Easley. Some got what they deserved. Live by violence, die by violence. In time, he learned the opposite to be true. Maybe Easley's death wasn't a blow to society but every murder victim deserved the truth. Nick's role had evolved into what he considered a weird place. Finding and arresting the killer—it was his job. He worked hard, as if every victim was the Sheriff's daughter, and let God and the DA make the judgment.

Besides, it was really cool to get two bad guys out of circulation.

But Nick was realistic about his victims. This guy, Easley, made Nick's shit-bird radar hum. Where there's one of these assholes, there's usually more. And this man's friends weren't going to take it kindly that someone murdered their pal.

Unless his pals killed him.

CHAPTER FIFTEEN

Wednesday, May 20, mid-afternoon

Meredith reviewed her notes. Satisfied she'd captured the facts, Meredith tucked the pen into her backpack, along with the evidence bag with the map.

Nick was also finished with his observations. He and Ormiston discussed their next moves. "You realize you're going to have to stay until CSI and the coroner get here. It will take them a while to figure out they have to come in from the coast." Nick looked at the forlorn deputy. "It will be hours before you're relieved."

"Yeah, yeah." Ormiston shrugged, indifferently. "These bad guys come sniffing around, a uniform should be here to tell them to back off." He glanced to the west, as if he could picture his relief marching in overland. Then, looking from Meredith to Willis, Ormiston asked, "Any chance you'll leave me one of these two for back-up in case the shooter returns?"

"Willis." Nick pointed to Joey. "You stay here."

Nick reached out and handed Willis the car keys, hoping to be back in civilization before Willis got back to the department sedan.

Meredith was relieved. She hated the idea of sitting in one place for God knew how long, standing guard over a corpse on this rapidly warming afternoon. "Hey. I have some energy bars in my pack. You guys hungry?"

Ormiston's eyes opened wide. "Oh, yeah." He ripped off the plastic wrapper and ate half the bar in two bites.

"You look much happier now." Meredith smiled. She handed one to Cavanaugh. The rancher scrutinized the snack with a look of doubt.

Ormiston toasted her with the empty wrapper. "Thanks." Willis frowned as he ate.

"Here's our plan," Nick began. "We walk west on the road until we find someplace we can call or radio to the Main for extraction." Nick glanced at Cavanaugh. "The Main Office."

"You leaving me here, too?"

"No, sir. You'll come with me and Detective Ryan. Chances are we'll get out of here first. These guys have to stay here to keep predators from damaging the body."

Meredith tied her windbreaker around her pack and hitched the rig onto her back. The yellow block letters, "Sheriff," splayed across the width. She said, "Ready," and she, Nick and Cavanaugh set off down the road.

It occurred to Meredith that she'd traveled with Nick a lot, with every form of transportation. Patrol car, plane, and a lot of hiking. No trains yet, but you never knew. And a boat—and there it was again, the memory of that steamy, lingering kiss on the smuggler's boat to Mexico. She couldn't forget that moment, no matter how hard she tried.

With Cavanaugh beside him Nick trooped on, Meredith following. Letting the old man set the pace was thoughtful. She'd known Nick for eight years and his quiet kindnesses still touched her.

Nick. He was a man unlike any other—at least in her life.

The afternoon sun beat down on them. She'd be sunburned, for sure. She'd have to remember to put sunblock in her pack. Even with the potential for an encounter with dangerous militia men, the monotony of putting one foot in front of another began to take its toll on her alertness. Meredith's mind drifted to last week, a conversation she'd had with her best friend, Christie.

***

The plump young blond was Meredith's brother's wife. They'd become fast friends when Christie married into the family, introducing David to stability. He hadn't been in love enough to give up his itinerant life as a musician. When he was murdered by a psychotic judge, they'd been in the middle of a divorce. With so much turmoil surrounding them, the two women found strength in each other.

"Where's your partner?" From her living room couch, Christie looked up at her friend with a directness that didn't allow for evasion.

Nick.

Meredith had been folding laundry when the question came. She groped for the right words. Christie was her best friend but she hated saying them out loud. She owed her the truth.

"I haven't seen much of him since we got back from Mexico. I told you he got a promotion."

"I remember. You also said he never told you about taking the sergeant's test."

Meredith smoothed a cotton T-shirt with the palm of her hand. She took her time answering. "It sucked to find out from the lieutenant."

"Did he say why he didn't tell you?"

Meredith's face warmed. "He didn't want to jinx the test."

"Really? He's that superstitious?" Christie's eyes widened with doubt. "Or does it mean you're bad luck?"

"He wasn't lying." Meredith didn't try to mask her hurt. "But there's more to it. His mother is ill—she has Parkinson's Disease. His sister is an RN and is caring for her in her home. Nick's giving her money to help. He said the raise will help with that."

"So, that doesn't answer why he didn't tell you." She cocked her head. "Oh yeah, jinx." Christie's eyes narrowed as she slammed her laptop shut. "I thought you told each other everything. What did he think was going to happen when he got promoted?"

"He knew that it would change everything." Meredith threw a pair of jeans back into the heap and leaned back into the couch. "Everything has changed already."

"What are you talking about?"

"In Mexico, we—we kissed."

"No shit, Meredith?" Christie's eyes sparkled with salacious curiosity.

"Would I lie about that?" Meredith avoided her friend's gaze. "We were on the boat and there was a moment—"

"What happened?"

"The friggin' Mexican Navy showed up."

Christie covered her mouth with her hand but couldn't contain her laughing. "Really, Meredith? You're the only one I know who could—"

Meredith waved away her friend's giggles. "You don't get it, do you? Everything is different now—he'll always worry about me and me about him. It'll be like being in high school, for God's sake." Disappointment welled in her chest. She rubbed her eyes so Christie couldn't tell she was getting emotional.

"Oh, honey," Christie said, walking over to her. She slipped an arm around Meredith's shoulders. "It doesn't have to be like that. You're rational people. You can deal with this."

Meredith shook her head. "No, he's made his choice. He wedges people between us so we won't be alone. I can't fight the job—and I don't want to."

Since the promotion, Nick had diligently cleared their cases. Yesterday, the department sent him to an in-service so there was little for Meredith to do. She helped the other detectives with their workloads and closed out most of her own reports.

Who would she work with? Would Leahy or Ferrua split up another team and put her with a more experienced detective, or would she be training Nick's replacement as her new partner? She hated having things like this up in the air—decisions that would affect her future were being made by the sergeant who despised her and a lieutenant who didn't have a spine. She should expect the worst.

"How do you know how Nick feels if you don't ask him?" Christie tucked her blond hair behind her ears. "Honest to God, Mere. Sometimes you are so stubborn."

"I'm not stubborn." It annoyed her when Christie caught her being hard-headed. "I don't think he wants a relationship. I mean, he avoids me and doesn't make eye contact unless he has to. I'd have to be an idiot to miss those cues. He doesn't want to be near me."

"You have the emotional intelligence of a fifth grader." Christie knew what she was talking about. She was a fifth-grade teacher.

Meredith shook her head. "You're wrong. I can see the obvious." She glared at her friend. "You're complicating this."

"But he kissed you. That doesn't happen unless he has feelings for you."

"Ancient history—months ago. We were in the middle of some high-tension drama."

Christie's hand flew up to protest. "Just an excuse, girlfriend. In your line of work, there's always the potential for drama."

***

Walking up the dusty trail, Meredith pondered Christie's words. Maybe she should give Nick a chance to explain himself. They'd been such good partners and friends. When he'd kissed her, it had changed everything. She would take the moment back if she could return to the way they were. She missed him. And even though he was with her, he wasn't.

There he was up ahead, tall and sweaty and handsome as hell. She couldn't imagine her life without him.

What did she have to lose?

The angle steepened as tree-shaded ferns walled both sides of the road. Cavanaugh's breathing rasped. "Nick, let's rest a moment," Meredith said.

The rancher dropped to a fallen tree limb. Behind him was a moss-covered rock wall in a shape like a grotto, almost a cave, damp with dripping water. Both sides were obscured with dense thickets of coffeeberry.

Meredith pulled a water bottle from her pack and handed it to Cavanaugh.

Nick stared down the road. "I'm going to find a way up this hill. Maybe I can get radio reception." He nodded to a sharp escarpment ahead that rose to block the view of the road.

She watched him march off, irritated that he left her. "We'll wait right here," she called after him. Meredith sounded snarky.

To hell with Nick. She plopped down next to Cavanaugh.

"Nice of you to stay and take care of the old guy," Cavanaugh said, smiling in a half-apology.

She sighed, thankful he wasn't chatty. That would have gotten on her nerves. They would be together for the rest of the day. Maybe the night, depending how long it took them to find cell service or get into radio range.

Maybe Christie was right. What if Nick had feelings for her? How wrong could she be about him? What about her feelings? How would she react if Nick wanted to have a romantic relationship? Did she want that? Was she over her husband's death? It had been so long she couldn't picture romance, particularly with Nick. Did she want to—?

"You married, Mr. Cavanaugh?"

He looked at his calloused hands. "I was."

"Ah," she acknowledged his simple answer. He didn't want to talk, either.

"Divorced?"

He glanced to the trees and scrub across the road. "Naw. She passed on three months ago."

"Oh, I am sorry." She kicked herself for pushing him for her own agenda—trying to glean an insight into this man-woman thing. Gawd, she could be selfish.

"I wasn't any good at it. Marriage, I mean." He straightened, patting his breast pocket. "Wish I had a stogie."

She smiled, glad he didn't have one.

"She did all the work—birthed babies, raised them to be good people, made sure they got an education. I did the easy stuff. I worked the ranch, fought in the war, put food on the table. Too busy to let her get close." Cavanaugh looked at her and smiled, a glint of humor and mischievousness cracking his craggy face.

Her shock must have shown. He chuckled. "I've had three months to figure all this out."

Meredith sighed. "I hope it doesn't take me much longer."

"The Sarge giving you some trouble?" He looked in Nick's direction.

She was surprised he'd guessed. "I'm not sure if it's him or me, to tell you the truth."

He squinted, searching her face. "You'll figure it out." He looked across the road again. "You can call me Cav."

They sat in silence for ten minutes before they heard rocks sliding from the hill into the grotto. Nick scrambled down, jumping over a soggy ditch and landing behind Cavanaugh with a thud.

"Quick, back into the bushes. We've got company coming."

CHAPTER SIXTEEN

Wednesday, May 20, afternoon

Cavanaugh moved faster than Nick thought possible. Meredith was behind, following the rancher into a dense coffeeberry shrub. She pressed in front of him, her hand on her Beretta as they pushed against the damp wall.

Across from them Nick tucked behind a bush and watched the road. A half dozen men trudged toward them, each dressed in varying colors of green and brown camos. Without a cadence, they were a bad imitation of a military parade. They still presented a formidable picture. Every man carried an automatic rifle, an AR-15, a M-14 or a shotgun along with holstered side arms. The jumble of clothing and weaponry said they weren't real military. And, the murder victim would have fit right in. These guys must be the Covenant Family. What the hell were they doing up here?

When he'd first spotted them on the hill, he knew they'd have to be interviewed. It was reasonable to assume they were connected to the victim, based on their clothing. But the idea of making contact evaporated when he spotted the guns and the paramilitary posture. They looked much more menacing than the report he read. Nick had to assume they would be hostile. Covenant Family had a history of being resistant to law enforcement. Because they were skinheads or militia, he had to wait for a few more deputies for support. When he could, he'd ask Ferrua for a team. Against these heavily armed men, he and Meredith were hopelessly outnumbered.

He, Meredith and Cavanaugh had to get moving toward civilization while avoiding the militia. He had things to do: get Cavanaugh home safely, CSI to the body, and follow-up interviews. All this would have to wait until he was in a stronger position. For now, he couldn't risk being discovered by these jerks.

Damn, it was getting muggy up here. Must be the moisture from the waterfall. Nick was sweating, worrying about what could happen.

Through the leaves, he saw Meredith, her face set the focused, professional expression he knew so well. She was alert, aware of everything around her.

Then, men's voices. The soldiers were coming closer.

CHAPTER SEVENTEEN

Wednesday, May 20, afternoon

Cavanaugh settled against the rock wall, dampness seeping through his shirt. The female detective shielding his body felt like overkill. She didn't know he could take care of himself, but he'd let her do her job.

When her head turned, he saw her profile. Her eyes took in the same thing he'd been taught so many years ago at Navy SERE Training—Survival, Evasion, Resistance and Escape. Alert for movement, anything unusual. She had it, he thought. She was a warrior. A fine sheen of perspiration sat on her upper lip. Tension, which would be normal. She'd mixed it up before.

He watched her face, taking in her beauty. No, beauty wasn't the right word. With no make-up, she wasn't glamorous, but striking, athletic. He'd always found that look so attractive. When he was young, so few women felt free to be athletes. Though his wife wasn't a warrior, she'd been an athlete—on the tennis and swim teams in high school. Up until the day he'd lost her, she'd had the same quality Meredith had—a dynamic energy that refused to be restrained.

Raymond Cavanaugh bet Detective Meredith Ryan gave her sergeant a run for his money. Cavanaugh lost his smile as he heard boots shuffling in an untidy rhythm.

Not military-trained personnel.

CHAPTER EIGHTEEN

Wednesday, May 20, afternoon

The soldiers plodded up the road. From alongside, a lanky man with bad posture snapped at them like a drill instructor. The men cradled their firearms as if they were precious cargo or an extension of their arms. Certainly, they were not the precise posture of the United States military. Unshaven chins, prison tattoos, pony-tails and tobacco chaws were dead giveaways. A teenage girl with ear buds could have heard them two miles away.

They came from behind. He'd put money on them setting off the rock slide.

These guys were Covenant Family militia, like his victim. Nick shook his head with dismay over the unreliable radio problem. Hoping that Ormiston and Willis stayed safe, he worried about the CSI's protection. If he'd had access to department resources, Nick would have called the SWAT team to form a perimeter around the crime scene to protect personnel as they processed the site. Processing took several hours or more.

He would pressure Ferrua as soon as he could make a call. This area was unsafe.

Their slow pace added to Nick's frustration. He wanted them out of the way. He had a job to do. Finally, after Nick counted eleven soldiers, the leader stopped outside the grotto. Through the leaves, Nick made out the outline of two men, ten feet from the where he stood.

"Damn it, Ramey." The leader shouted like a real Drill Instructor. "Get your ass moving."

"I'm coming. I'm coming," whined a younger voice, puffing with exertion.

"Not fast enough. Get up here."

"Whatsamatter, fearless leader? You afraid the team will leave without us?"

"Shut up." The DI hissed.

"They won't leave. They need us."

"You don't know what you're talking about."

"You're crazy, old man. Everyone knows there's a mission coming up."

At the DI's sputtering, Ramey continued. "You can't plan a mission like this and think people won't talk. Why did we just blow up a hillside? To block the road and keep people away, that's why." Ramey had flamed out at the DI with his frustration. He kept up his tirade. "Hell, there's nothing to do up here in Bum Fuck Egypt except minding other people's business."

"Shut the fuck up."

"This is my business."

"You don't know what you're saying."

The leader's face was turned from Nick, but the guy named Ramey was squaring off, furious again. "I believe in the cause. But I don't believe in getting killed for no reason."

A shoe scraped against the dirt. Then, with a thump, Ramey was down. Nick saw a camo jacket and the leader's shoulder twisting with each vicious blow. Nick fought the instinct to barge in and help Ramey. The soldier grunted repeatedly.

So much for protect and serve.

The beating was over in a minute. The leader grumbled, "Get up."

Ramey staggered to his feet, holding his bloody ear, and stumbled away. The leader followed.

Nick waited until the footsteps faded, then two more minutes before he stepped out into the open. On a rock in the afternoon sunlight, a tiny droplet of blood glistened where Ramey had been beaten.

Meredith and Cavanaugh joined Nick. She brushed leaves and spider webs from her shirt and he thought about how much she hated bugs. Especially spiders. Yet she'd buried herself in the bushes to shield the ranch-er. Pride filled Nick. She'd been his partner, the best partner he'd ever had.

"Thanks for the concern, Detective Reyes." Cavanaugh dipped his head in a tribute, "but I can take care of myself."

Nick felt it was his job to explain Meredith's actions. "Sir, at the mo-ment, you're in our custody. It's our obligation to keep you safe." He slipped off his windbreaker and stuffed most of it into his pants pocket. It felt good to be out of the cavern's oppressive heat. The light breeze cooled his skin.

"Custody?" Cavanaugh's eyes widened.

"More like our care, sir." Meredith explained. "You're not under arrest nor being detained." She frowned at Nick.

"Right. And now, we have more problems than we started with." Nick squatted, studying the muddle of footprints. "These prints are the same kind of soles as the murder victim's. The corpse was wearing a camo jacket, too."

"They're the Covenant Family?" Cavanaugh sneered after the soldiers.

Nick rose, watching the man's face. "I was hoping you'd know, for sure, Mr. Cavanaugh. These are your hills."

Nothing. The rancher's expression gave up nothing. "Never seen 'em before." He kicked a rock aside. "You can bet they're gonna be mad their buddy's been killed." He eyed Nick with a piercing stare. "And I damned well ain't in nobody's custody."

CHAPTER NINETEEN

"I don't know what membership card they're carrying, but a few things are obvious." Meredith cleared her throat. "It's an organized paramilitary group with an imminent operation. One of them said something about 'planning a mission like this.' They're not here on vacation."

"Exactly." Nick's lips pressed together tightly. "It looks like we have a change of priorities. We still walk west until we can call for help, but we stay off this road. The most important thing is to find a place with a signal ASAP. It means we hike the hills." He squatted before Cavanaugh, who was resting on a log. "Are you up to it, sir?"

When Cav answered, Meredith saw a shadow of a smile. "I'm with you, son." The rancher looked at Nick. "In fact, there's an abandoned World War II radio tower not far from here. At the top of a good-sized hill. It'll take some time to get there, but you might get line-of-sight radio reception from there."

Oh yeah, that place Ferrua mentioned. Nick checked his watch. "Then let's move out. It's five o'clock already. I'd like to get airlifted out of here before dark."

Following Cavanaugh's direction, the group hiked up the incline shrouding the grotto. The slope was steep and rocky, but erosion had cut a clear path of unevenly carved steps.

Meredith listened to Cavanaugh's wheezing. "Cav, you okay?"

He straightened. "I'm fine."

She caught his eye and smiled. "My first name is Meredith."

Cavanaugh smiled, seeming pleased at the familiarity. He looked up the hill. "The rest of the way is rough, but not as steep as this. I haven't been up here in years—decades."

Nick led with a slow, steady pace. Cavanaugh was second, and Meredith behind.

They followed a game trail that twisted through the knee-high grass, then dropped into a dark, tree-shielded ravine. Their feet tested each step against the creek bed so progress was slow. Each touched the person in front to follow. The slope rose again when they reached the edge in less than five minutes.

They'd made it to a grass-covered plateau. Nick scrambled over the ravine's lip and waited under a dead oak split in half. Bleached limbs lay rotting on the ground. Meredith boosted herself onto the turf. As she stood, she tripped over a branch and fell against Nick.

He twisted and wrapped his arm around her waist, catching her before she went down. His touch was electric. She couldn't help herself, she slumped towards him in a moment she wanted to last longer. Her face flushed.

Then, she pushed away. "Sorry," she said.

"Mr. Cavanaugh," Nick cleared his throat softly. "How long until we find this place?"

"Right quick." Cavanaugh took Nick's offered hand and pulled himself up. "We'll find a gravel road leading to the gate over there." He nodded to the next hill.

"Gate?" Meredith shouldn't have been surprised "Are we going to have to break in?"

"Probably," the rancher said, slogging up the grassy slope.

"We'll worry about that when we get there." Nick snapped.

Why is he so irritable, Meredith wondered?

The hills were in shadows, as the light slowly drained from the sky. A slim crescent moon had risen over the hills to the east but offered little illumination. A darker gradient of gray arose before them, encircling the hill's crest. The distant ocean meant a cooling air temperature. A breeze came up—enough to ruffle the tall grass.

Nick signaled a stop with his hand. His voice was just above a whisper.

"Mr. Cavanaugh, you stay here. Ryan and I are going to check this fence out."

Meredith dropped her pack next to Cav. Making sure her Beretta was secure in her belt holster, she pulled on her windbreaker. She wanted the SHERIFF identifying letters on her back. Nick did the same.

It was a fifty-foot hike uphill to the top. The property looked abandoned. Weeds grew indifferently at the base of the galvanized chain link fence. There were no sensors or glass insulators on the barrier, so it wasn't electrified. The lack of razor wire at the top told her the builders were more interested in keeping animals out than spies or saboteurs.

Meredith turned on her phone. No service.

Nick leaned into her. "Cavanaugh said there's a gate close by. Let's find it." A breeze caught the scent of his aftershave and sweat. She held her breath.

Nick trailed a hand on the rough metal strands as he moved along the fence, stepping sideways to avoid clumps of grass. In another twenty yards, they reached another shadow, deeper than the fence. The gate.

Nick found the lock that clinched a chain together. No spider webs, no dust.

This place wasn't abandoned.

The unmistakable sound of a round ratcheted into a chamber cut through the late afternoon. A gravelly voice shouted, "Put your hands on your head."

CHAPTER TWENTY

Wednesday, May 20, late afternoon

"We're Sheriff's Department," Meredith shouted. Beside her, Nick raised his hands and dropped the flashlight.

Meredith looked over her shoulder at a solitary shape.

"Keep your eyes forward, bitch," the man ordered, tension pulling his voice taut. "I said, hands on top of your head."

"We'll do what you say, but we're cops, dude."

"Shut the fuck up. Get down on your knees."

Meredith sucked in a breath as if she was going underwater. She dropped to the hard-packed earth. Marijuana grower? Stupid redneck?

Nick thumped to his knees beside her.

In seconds, the man was behind them, straddling both their legs. "Girlie, with your left hand, show me your creds."

Meredith yanked on her badge ID. The lanyard had tangled around her collar. She tugged on it again, trying to break it free.

Behind her, a blow, a groan, and a body thudding to the ground.

Meredith rolled to her right, her glance seeking out the assailant. Nick went in the opposite direction. Her hand covered her Beretta as she tumbled over. She rolled to her feet, the gun in her hand pointed to where the voice had come from.

Cav. She swung the barrel away from him, then turned toward Nick.

"Sheriff's Department," Nick announced again, in the same isosceles position as her. Knees bent to a slight crouch, arms straight, a two-handed grip on his Glock, the gun was pointed down toward the bulky shape writhing on the grass. The man rolled to his side, protecting his head from another assault. Meredith saw the block letters, "DOJ"—Department of Justice—on his windbreaker. Bureau of Narcotics Enforcement. Crap.

Raymond Cavanaugh stood behind the man, chest heaving, while his hand clutched a bat-sized tree limb.

Meredith holstered her gun and was on top of the DOJ guy laying on the ground. Nick used his foot to knock the gun from his hand. She wrestled the man's beefy arms behind him to snap on handcuffs.

His voice muffled in a clump of marsh grass, he shouted, "Fuck you guys! What the fuck are you doing?"

"Feel different on the other side of the gun, dude?" Nick's voice was deep. He was pissed. She was, too. What the hell was this guy doing, sneaking up on them, then drawing his gun?

Meredith rolled him over and sat him up. The man carried his bulk in his chest and arms. His head was so big Meredith couldn't see his neck. "Where's your ID?"

"On a chain around my neck," he glared at her. "Like yours."

She pulled the dangling ID toward her. Nick shined a flashlight beam in the fading sunlight so she could read it. "Lieutenant DeGraffenreid?"

"Lyle DeGraffenreid, De-Graf for short. Accent on the 'De'" He spit the name out.

"DeGraf, from the Department of Justice, —Bureau of Narcotics Enforcement, California Department of." Meredith looked to Nick, who clicked off the light.

"So DeGraf, what are you doing here?"

"I could ask you the same thing." DeGraf snapped.

Meredith walked behind the man and unlocked his cuffs. "Now back off, big guy. We're all on the job here."

She couldn't see DeGraf's expression as he rubbed his wrists. "Are we?"

Meredith tugged at her ID. She grabbed the flashlight from Nick and switched it on, pushing the badge under his nose. "There, Sonoma County Sheriff's Office, like we said." She nodded to Nick. "This is Sergeant Nick Reyes."

DeGraf glanced behind Nick to the old rancher. "And who's this, Deputy Dawg?"

"Got the better of you." Cavanaugh's words were sharp. The rancher chucked the limb and turned. One animal showing scorn to another.

"I'll ask you again: What are you doing up here?" Nick was losing the battle to keep his temper.

She could almost hear the gears clicking in DeGraf's head. He shifted into a fake, good-ole' boy tone with a tenor that set her teeth on edge. She'd known nothing but trouble from guys like this, mostly in her early years as a deputy.

"I came out here to open up this old radio tower compound—like I do every spring for the past five years. We've been using it in the summer as a base of operations for our Marijuana Eradication Task Force."

"How long have you been up here?"

"I'll tell you what." A pause. "Let's go on up to the compound and I'll fill you in." Meredith half-expected him to light up a stinking old cigar. "I got food, if you're hungry," he added as an enticement. "It's starting to get cold and you all will need—"

Nick interrupted him. "You have radio or phone service?"

He waved the thought aside. "Sure, no land-line, but we got a radio."

"We'll follow you." Nick turned and touched Cavanaugh's elbow. "C'mon, sir. We'll get something to eat and find the fastest way out."

CHAPTER TWENTY-ONE

Wednesday, May 20, twilight

DeGraf led them to the gate. Discernible in the shadows, the gravel road tracked off in the opposite direction. Was that a car down the road? Where had it come from?

Meredith slapped DeGraf on the shoulder. "Hey, the car yours?"

They stopped and stared where she pointed. A 1990 silver Jeep Cherokee sat in the middle of the road a quarter of a mile away. DeGraf must have been here a while, or they would have heard the car approach.

"Yeah." His tone was flat.

Nick asked the question on her mind. "What's your car doing down there?"

"The road I took washed-out during the winter. I decided to walk it before I get the jeep stuck". DeGraf's frame slumped in an "I give up" posture. "I had to take a whiz." He looked from Nick to Cavanaugh. "Fuck you guys." Bending over the lock with a key in his hand, he snapped. "I was taking a leak when I heard you guys talking. I decided to walk up and see what was going on. That's when I saw you." He yanked on the lock and flung the gate away from him. "Satisfied?"

Yuck, she'd cuffed him.

Without waiting for an answer, DeGraf turned and headed for the Jeep. The engine made a tinny sound as he stopped at the gate, reached across the passenger seat and opened the door. "You want a ride or you feel like walking uphill?"

Meredith, Nick and Cavanaugh wasted no time getting in. Nick took the front passenger seat. Meredith shoved heavy cardboard boxes from the back seat to make room for Cavanaugh and herself. When the Jeep passed through the gate, she jumped out, closed and locked it.

DeGraf clunked the gear shift into four-wheel drive, and the Cherokee's transmission ground all the way up the gravel road. The engine was so loud they didn't try to talk. At the summit, the road dropped into a shallow basin. On a ledge at the far side, a pair of radio antennas poked toward the sky. Below, a half dozen cinder block and corrugated metal sheds circled the basin. In the middle sate a large Quonset hut. A single-masted antenna with dishes mounted along its length, the hut was the prominent structure. A bean-shaped propane tank set on the perimeter stored the compound's energy source.

The Quonset hut was the only building that could contain more than two people. This must have been a radio repeater site at one time, but it looked abandoned. The doors were chained and padlocked, damage to siding had been left to corrode, and a crop of errant weeds sprouted behind buildings. Scrubby brush dotted the basin's edge around the structures.

Yet, it looked like it had been used in recent years. The center area was free of weeds, although the bare dirt was windswept with disuse. This place was kept up, even if only seasonally.

DeGraf thumped his transmission out of 4-wheel drive and parked in front of the hut. He jumped out and unlocked the door, shouting, "Pick up a food box from the Jeep and bring it in."

Meredith slowed Nick and handed him a box. "Take one in with you."

His frown told her this wasn't one of those times he appreciated her leadership skills. She gave Cav a box, took one for herself and followed everyone inside. Nick dropped his on the kitchen counter. The box had, "SCARO" written with a thick permanent marking pen. A flap loosened at the top, so Nick pulled up all four folds to re-close it. Curious why he was poking around in DeGraf's boxes, she looked around his shoulder.

"Hm, reflective vests and ball caps with 'Amgen Tour of California 2016' stenciled across the crown. Why the hell would DeGraf have this stuff?"

DeGraf entered the kitchen behind them, his arms laden with grocery bags. "Oh, that box is for my buddy. He needs it for some volunteer shit he's got going this weekend. Put it in the corner by the TV, will you?"

"Sure," Meredith offered with false enthusiasm. DeGraf was off before she lifted the box.

When she returned, Nick was across the hall in a radio room on a portable radio. Empty rows of built-in racks lined one wall. In its original construction, radio equipment had been stacked here. But now a small shelf held a charging station with two rows, of two ports each, for portable radios.

DeGraf noted Meredith's interest. "Sounds like he's talking to my dispatch in Sac. He could use his phone but using the radio won't drain his battery."

Nick was trying to give directions to Dispatch but the transmission faded intermittently. She caught the frustration in his voice.

DeGraf dropped a box on a counter. When the flap flew open, Meredith saw a well-used Motorola mobile two-way radio, the kind that had been appropriated from an old police car. It sat on top of a six-port portable charger and four handsets. Cavanaugh brought in a box, saying, "Last one."

Meredith scanned the main living quarters. The inside walls were sheet-rocked and painted the familiar institutional green. On one side, mattresses rolled up on a half-dozen pipe and wire cots were stacked against a wall. An open bathroom door was close by. Along the far wall sat a kitchenette with a small stove, sink and refrigerator behind a serving counter. An exterior door was tucked next to the fridge. She ticked it as an access point. A dinged-up dining table surrounded with mismatched chairs sat in the kitchen area. Three sagging sofas bisected the middle to create a living area. A tube-style TV and VHS tape player on a drooping press-board television stand completed the decor.

Meredith walked over to the dining table. Pulling out a chair, she smiled to Cav. "I'll get you something to drink."

Cavanaugh dropped into the chair and Meredith saw him rub his eyes. He was tired—and surely hungry.

DeGraf had all the boxes open, sorting through the supplies. Meredith took a bottle of water and some Safeway cookies over to Cav.

Cavanaugh downed the water in a few gulps. Nick joined them and took the bottle Meredith offered him, sinking into the chair next to Cav. For the first time, Meredith noted lines of exhaustion around Nick's mouth and eyes. She pushed the cookie box toward him.

"Did dispatch give you an ETA?" Meredith opened her own bottle and drank several gulps. She was hungry, too. Her glance took in the apples DeGraf had in a carton on the serving counter.

"They're going to have Ferrua call my cell. I told them to make it a priority." He tapped the 'on' button on his phone. "I'll tell the lieutenant to have Henry One fly the CSIs in with some SWAT guys to protect them. That will take care of Ormiston. Willis will manage the crime scene until I get back. I told dispatch to send food and water in the helo." He paused to eat a cookie. Crumbs fell on his lap as he grabbed another.

Gawd, he was something, even tired.

When he stood, the cookie crumbs rolled to the floor. "Hey, DeGraf. When are you going back down the hill?"

DeGraf shoved a pair of cans in a cabinet. He turned, his face twisting into a stink eye. "I suppose you want to get back tonight."

"Well, yes…" Nick began.

DeGraf cut him off. "No way. I'm not going down these dirt roads at night." He turned away. "Tomorrow. I'll take you down first thing tomorrow morning."

Meredith exhaled, realizing she'd been holding her breath. She wished Ferrua would call, so Nick could tell him about the militia—or whatever they were. It had to be a priority. As for her, going down the hill tomorrow was soon enough. Now, she wanted to eat something and grab some sleep. She was sure Nick and Cav felt the same way. She stood, intending to set up cots from the corner.

The door flew open and a short, bristly man stepped into the room.

CHAPTER TWENTY-TWO

Wednesday, May 20, early evening

"Hey," The man said. Then his mouth made an 'o' shape, but there was no surprise in his eyes. "Sorry, DeGraf. Didn't know you had company." He stood on the threshold, a messenger bag hanging from his scrawny shoulder. The stranger was a pale man in his forties, with a head of wavy copper hair and an intense gaze.

Nick's hand rested on his Glock.

"Jerry!" DeGraf hollered from the kitchen. "I wasn't expecting you until tomorrow." DeGraf wiped his hands on his jeans as he walked from the kitchen to greet his friend. "C'mon in."

"Aw, no, Lyle." He cast a sheepish look at Nick. "I don't want to bother you. I'll come back tomorrow." He made no move to leave.

Nick's hand remained on his gun.

"Don't be stupid, Jer. You're here now." DeGraf pulled the skinny man inside and closed the door. He addressed the detectives. "Nick, Meredith, Mr. Cavanaugh. This here's Jerry Steiner."

Steiner lifted his hand in a cheery mock salute.

DeGraf continued. "They're Sonoma Deputies, Jer." Nick saw Cavanaugh rise in anticipation of handshaking. But Nick had to know—who was this guy who showed up in the evening at an allegedly abandoned radio tower site?

He leaned toward Steiner. "And you are?"

"Ah, I'm an amateur radio operator." Steiner's voice had a deep, almost commanding tone in a contrast to his mousy appearance. "I'm a member of Sonoma County Amateur Radio Operators, SCARO for short. I volunteer to keep our antenna in order. Come up here every spring—"

DeGraf cut over Steiner's answer. "Don't worry about ol' Jer. We been pals for some time."

"How did you know to come up—?" Nick wasn't buying it. Something was off about this guy.

DeGraf exploded. "Oh, for God's sake. I called him when I got the date I was going to be here." The DOJ man's face reddened in the waning light. Someone flicked on an overhead light. Nick was a foot away from De-Graf, and beginning to think he would have to fight his way out of this.

But DeGraf backed down. "We came up here the last couple of years so he can take care of his radio shit and I can make this base usable for the summer."

"What kind of operation?" Meredith asked from behind Nick.

"A task force—Nor Cal Marijuana Eradication Team." A sly smile spread across DeGraf's full lips. "Now whaddya say we sit down and fill each other in on our jobs?"

Steiner walked to the kitchen and hollered. "You know why I'm here. So I'll rustle up some dinner. There ought to be something we can eat in here." He glanced at Meredith, mouthing, 'whoops.' "Don't want to step on any toes. You can do this if you want, Miss."

"Uh, Deputy Ryan isn't a cook and just so you know, she's a better shot than most of us." Nick stifled a laugh as he sat at the dining table. "You go right ahead."

A glance at Meredith revealed a small smile. She was so touchy these days. She'd lost much of her sense of humor in the past few weeks and he didn't know if she'd find this funny. Relieved, he turned his attention to DeGraf. "You first."

"The task force comes up here a couple of times during the season. We travel all over the northwestern California counties, and sometimes our cases require us to stay in the area several days or more. I like to have places established where we can go that duck below the radar. Local motels are sometimes part of the problem, so we try to avoid them. This place is out of the way, but the remoteness serves our purposes."

Nick asked, "There are more of you?"

DeGraf paused to take a drink from a bottle of Budweiser Steiner placed on the table in front of him. "My guys will be up tomorrow. You'll know them if you see them—they're the only ones goofy enough to drive around in a state pool van." He raised his beer to Jerry Steiner, who was moving from box to box in the kitchen. "In the meantime, Jer and I enjoy a game of poker and have been known to hoist a few."

Nick listened as DeGraf chatted. He watched Steiner slip from the kitchen and scan the living area. He went to the corner that held the box of Amgen Tour stuff, opened the box, looked then closed it. Hoisting it to his chest, he was out the door with a speed that contradicted his easy-going demeanor.

"Your turn," DeGraf said, dropping his bottle on the table with an enormous belch.

Nick cleared his throat. It was his turn to tell DeGraf about their case but he'd keep it vague. "We're investigating a homicide. Mr. Cavanaugh here, discovered the body. He had the bad luck to be with us when we got trapped on this side of the hill after a rock slide."

A car door opened and closed, then Steiner sauntered back in.

DeGraf sat up. "No shit? A rock slide?" From a beat-up briefcase, he shoved papers around. "Hey, Jer. You have a map of the North County area?"

Steiner shook his head.

DeGraf pushed his friend around and shouted. "Yes, you do. It's in your back pocket, dumbshit."

Steiner's face reddened as he reached for it. He looked at it like it was written in Chinese, then pulled it out. "Uh, look at that."

DeGraf unfolded it and spread it on the table. It was a topographical map of the City of Santa Rosa covered the distance up to the Mendocino County line. He studied it for a moment then stabbed the center with an index finger. "We are here. Where's the road blocked?"

Nick studied the map, found what he was looking for and showed DeGraf. The only way that connected with Rockpile Road forged a circuitous path around the hills. Nick pointed to another line on the map.

"What about this road? It looks shorter."

Cav stood and looked over DeGraf's shoulder. "It would be if a good chunk of it hadn't washed out four years ago."

"Guess we'll be going down the hill on the coast-side tomorrow morning." DeGraf smiled, looking pleased with his superior knowledge. "You'll be ready early?"

Nick's lip curled in frustration. There was something else. "You know anything about a paramilitary group camped out in these hills?"

DeGraf waved the thought aside. "Probably those guys on the abandoned property about ten miles west of here. Why?"

"Our murder victim was outfitted in camos, like a hunter, only not. On our way, about a dozen guys dressed the same way came down a road not far from here." Nick glanced at the map again, his gaze falling to the downtown Santa Rosa area. The roads surrounding Railroad Square to Courthouse Square were traced in blue ballpoint ink, to form a rectangle. Another line followed Sonoma Avenue to Brookwood. Steiner's map had the same landmarks as Easley's, the dead guy.

Steiner stood listening. When Nick glanced at him, the radio technician slid a half dozen pre-packaged sandwiches on the map and dropped paper plates and napkins on the table. "Soups on."

Resisting the urge to grab Steiner and shake him, Nick stood and called Cavanaugh over. Meredith picked out a sandwich and handed it to the rancher.

Nick couldn't let this go quite yet. He caught DeGraf's attention again. "We overheard something about an imminent mission."

"Mission?" DeGraf squinted at Nick. "Any ideas what?"

"No, we couldn't get anything more. But it sounded like trouble."

"It sure does." DeGraf bit into the sandwich. Mashed tomatoes squirted out the bottom. "You gonna alert your people?"

Nick nodded and wondered when the hell Ferrua was going to call.

CHAPTER TWENTY-THREE

Wednesday, May 20, early evening

At the table, Raymond Cavanaugh chewed the mushy white bread and whatever was in between. He didn't look, figuring if he just ate, no matter what swill it was, it would give him fuel to operate.

Though DeGraf had promised to get him home soon, Cav didn't trust it. Neither did the detectives. In reading Reyes' body language, Cav saw the young man didn't put much faith in DeGraf. But he was especially wary around Steiner. The girl didn't miss anything, either. She kept to herself and listened to the conversation between DeGraf and Nick. She also kept an eye on Steiner.

She's one tough cookie, he thought. Glad she's on my side. Reyes, too. And I'll bet she's a better shot than most. The rancher smiled to himself, thinking how like him they were. He was suspicious of strangers, too. It wasn't automatic for him to have faith in a person because they were police. In his book, you had to earn his confidence. Reyes and Ryan had; DeGraf had not. Steiner was a question mark, therefore unreliable.

CHAPTER TWENTY-FOUR

Wednesday, May 20, early evening

Meredith didn't understand. "Why can't you call him directly?"

"Dispatch said he was in an interview with a homicide suspect."

"Wait, the only reason someone would interrupt an interview is for an emergency." She probed his bloodshot eyes. "This qualifies. I mean, we don't know what the 'mission' is, but these guys aren't planning a Boy Scouts Jamboree."

"You're right," Nick sighed. "I already tried, but his phone is off."

It was Meredith's turn to sigh in frustration. "What about calling dispatch to have someone interrupt him? Or better yet, get hold of the Watch Commander?"

"Already tried. The Watch Commander is with Ferrua." Nick's jaw muscles flexed. "Someone will get through to them soon. Until then, we'll have to sit tight."

"This ridiculous bureaucracy is obstructing communication—the very thing it's supposed to encourage." Meredith shoved away the gooey mound of wheat bread, her appetite gone. "Are we still leaving tomorrow morning?"

As Nick nodded, she bit her lip in frustration. She needed to do something more than wait around. She stood, picking up dirty napkins from the table. The others were eating. After dumping them in a trash bin, she pushed the door open and stepped outside. She looked behind her and noticed Steiner's ferret-like gaze following her. Creep.

Faint orange and pink streaks lingered on the horizon. If she looked hard enough she could see them disappearing. The sun was dropping fast, the purple shadows of evening veiling her world. The darkness made her feel alone.

An urgency crowded her busy mind, but she couldn't put her finger on the nature of the alarm. Her thoughts jumbled together with her instincts about the DOJ agent and Nick. She'd kept her worry about him as compartmentalized as she could. She'd have to wait until morning to sort that out with him. Until then, she'd focus on watching DeGraf and Steiner.

Meredith leaned against the siding of the hut, the heat of the metal warming her against the cool air of the evening. A breeze touched her skin. She shivered.

What would she do differently, if she'd been in charge? Find out what damage the militia has planned? How to do that? Find their camp and sneak in? What a stupid idea. No, Nick handled it the best way—for now. She couldn't fault his professional judgment. It was his personal life that was messed up.

What if she told him how she felt about him? That couldn't happen—she didn't know how she felt. There weren't words in her vocabulary to express the excitement she felt around him, or the fear of letting him closer. What if he wanted a relationship? What would he say? She couldn't guess. On one hand, he kissed her—out of the blue, after preaching that partners never got involved.

Well, they weren't partners now. What would she have to lose by telling him she loved him? There. She'd said it. Even to herself, it sounded strange. But there it was. Could she trust herself? So far, her relationship with men had been disastrous. Her cold and distant father, an unfaithful husband, a criminally deranged judge, and a malicious boss would have put anyone off men. But Nick was different—wasn't he?

The door swung open and Nick stepped out. He glanced at the sky, as if he was happy for the distraction of the evening. Then, a mechanical smile crossed his face as he leaned against the wall next to her. He cleared his throat. "Are you okay?"

"I'm fine, just tired." She turned to look at him. "That radio geek gives me the creeps."

A smile lifted a corner of his mouth. "Yeah, me, too." He continued, "I got hold of Ferrua. He's routing Henry One to pick us up after the CSI team is dropped off."

"What's their ETA?"

"Less than an hour. We'll meet them in the meadow at the front gate." He glanced at his watch. "DeGraf said he'd take us down there in his car. He's got the key to the gate, anyway."

"It will be good to get Cav home. He's been a rock star through this whole ordeal."

"Yeah, he has." Nick shoved his hands in his pockets. "We leave in thirty minutes."

She glanced at him, wondering if he was dismissing her. On his face was his usual business expression—shut down, blank. To hell with that. She pivoted and stood nearly eye to eye with him.

Now, a hint of surprise crept into his face. He hadn't expected a confrontation. She was acting boldly, she knew. This was as good a time as any.

"Nick, I'd like to talk…"

"Wait." He reached toward her arm then pulled back. His head turned sideways. "Listen, it's the chopper." He looked at her, "Get Cavanaugh, will you?" The whop-whop-whop of rotor blades cut through the air in the distance. CSIs would be off-loading their team and equipment.

Crap. She'd been so close to telling him. Now the Sheriff's helicopter, Henry One, was coming and she'd have to wait.

Nick nudged Meredith. "Cavanaugh."

She went inside to gather Cavanaugh and her backpack. Nick trailed behind her.

Cavanaugh and Meredith waited outside for Nick. The quiet meadow atmosphere began to vibrate with the humming of the helicopter, a half mile away. A minute later, the pitch of the engine changed, and the droning began to fade. Not sure what it meant, she went to the hut's threshold, looking around for Nick.

She found him standing inside on his phone. Concentrating on his conversation, he noticed her, then beckoned with a finger. Putting the cell on speaker, he held it so they both could hear.

Lieutenant Ferrua's voice crackled with tension. "We got a request to assist Coast Guard with rescue of a charter boat out of Bodega Bay. I mean to tell you, this stretches us to the max. The helo has been re-routed out there and I hear H30 from the CHP is enroute to the coast, too. Sixteen souls aboard. And we got a messy assault out in the Valley. I need you and your team to get back ASAP and handle the assault."

"If you called off Henry One, how do you expect us to get back?" Driving was dangerous on dark, dirt roads, and it would take hours. Aside, Nick told Meredith. "He re-routed Henry One to a coast rescue." He tapped off the speaker and put the phone to his ear as she whispered back. "He could call out Leahy to run the Valley case. He's not officially on the injured list." That way, Ferrua would be off their backs—at least, for now.

The depth of Nick's smile touched a chord in her chest. He liked her idea, though it meant they weren't getting out tonight as planned. He put his hand over the mic on the phone. "No doubt he volunteered us. I'll deal with Ferrua, then. We can't depend on help from him."

With his nod, she sighed quietly, sorting out how she felt about staying here. Meredith walked away as he offered her solution to the lieutenant.

She filled DeGraf in, then went outside.

Cavanaugh stood, his spine straight, looking at the azure sky as it deepened to cobalt. When she reached his side, he said, "I heard enough to know we're not going anywhere tonight."

"Yep. We're not as important as a multi-casualty rescue."

"You're right. We aren't. Even if we are in the middle of another hot mess."

CHAPTER TWENTY-FIVE

Wednesday, May 20, evening

A faint breeze ruffled Meredith's chestnut colored hair as Nick stepped into the night. She stood under a porch lamp with Cavanaugh, her highlights glistening under the glare. Too bad she wore it up in a ponytail for work, Nick mused. It looked best swinging free below her shoulders. Nick liked her hair loose like that.

Meredith scowled at him. "I told Cav the situation."

"Cav?" Nick wondered where this familiarity came from. The old guy obviously liked her. Everybody liked Mere. Nick admired the way she talked to victims, with compassion and empathy balanced with a professionalism. He respected how she put people at ease—a talent Nick didn't have.

Still, it wasn't like her to trust someone so fast.

"So, what's the plan, Sarge?" Her lips twisted into an awkward grin.

When she addressed him by his title, she acknowledged the distance between them. In front of someone else, this would be her professional demeanor. Normally, she would use the same kind of formality with a reporting party, too. Cavanaugh must have told her to call him by his nickname. Nick suspected intimacy didn't come easily for the old rancher. Meredith would know that, too.

"Back to the original plan. DeGraf will take us down the hill in his Jeep at first light, drop Mr. Cavanaugh at his place." He looked to the rancher. "Then, he'll take us to the Main." Nick didn't try to mask his annoyance with Cavanaugh. He couldn't understand why he reacted that way? Because a stranger had come to know Meredith's value, and invited her to become closer?

Cavanaugh gave a nod. "I'm going to get some sack time. See y'all in the morning."

Shit, Nick thought. *I can be such an asshole.* An apology would give the situation more importance than it deserved, so he let it go.

Meredith turned to watch Cavanaugh go inside. She looked at Nick, her arched eyebrow visible in the glow from the porch light. "What? Am I too close to a civilian, Boss? Putting me in my place, Sarge?"

Uh oh. He hadn't planned to be so transparent. *Crap.* He sounded like a high school drama queen.

"Mere," he began, using the shortened version of her name. The one that conveyed their own intimacy. But the words he needed didn't come.

She faced him, her jaw set. "Mere, what?"

"It's just—" He started to say something, meaningless words that were a place-holder for silence. Of all people, she would see through trite phrases. *What did he want to say?*

"I'll tell you what." Her lips thinned. "You don't like it when someone else gets close to me, even if the guy is old enough to be my father." She squinted, leaning closer to him, like a cook sniffing out a bad smell. "You're jealous and you won't admit it. And you don't know what to do."

"Jealous?" He sputtered, the word's taste sour on his lips. *Jealous?*

"Yes. You care, but only when it's convenient. You keep it hidden deep down inside." She lowered her voice to keep the words between them. "I'm not important enough for you to compromise your career. Or even to work at finding a way out of this mess." He knew exactly what she meant by "mess."

"No, Mere." *Was she right?* He couldn't answer that. Since their time in Puerto Vallarta, he'd pushed her away. He'd been confused about seeing Angela, his estranged wife. He'd built walls against emotional troubles. A failed marriage made him a poor choice for a mate.

He'd trusted Meredith's offer of help with a family matter in Mexico when his soon-to-be ex-wife had called. Angela had asked for his help to negotiate a ransom for her brother. When they realized the kidnapping had nothing to do with money, Nick and Meredith were embroiled in a cartel turf war. Meredith had struggled alongside Nick. She'd fought, killed for his family.

Was the problem simply his long-held rule that partners couldn't have a relationship outside the job? Well, they weren't partners anymore, were they? No. Now it was worse—she was his subordinate. He gave the orders. A classic scenario for Sexual Harassment Training, this was a hands-off situation if there ever was one.

"No, you're wrong." He touched her arm, afraid she would leave.

She shook off his grip. "Oh yeah. Prove it." Her shoulder lifted with a challenge. If he didn't do something, she'd walk. He couldn't stand for her to leave now. Think of something to say, dumb ass.

Instead, without conscious thought, he reached out and pulled her to his chest. He drank in her scent, the animal smell that was hers alone. "You're wrong," he whispered into her hair.

Rigid as his arms first embraced her, Meredith soon melted into his body. He felt her resistance fall away and a new, sudden eagerness spread from within, warming him.

His lips touched hers, and a shudder of excitement shot through him. Fighting an unfamiliar fear, he held her tighter, even as he was afraid to hold her at all. Her mouth opened and allowed him to move his tongue over her lips. He savored her taste, like salt and sand and acres of dry grass on a hillside. He loved the way she met him halfway, his lips against hers. He'd avoided thinking about them since Mexico, and for all the wrong reasons. This was as natural as breathing. He pressed her to him, harder, not wanting to spend another moment without her.

Christ, he wanted this woman.

The realization stunned him. Hands on her shoulders, he backed her up. Her eyes searched his face with an intensity; a happiness that pleased him.

The words came before he could censor them. "Dammit, Mere. I think I love you," he said.

CHAPTER TWENTY-SIX

Wednesday, May 20, evening

Meredith couldn't believe what she'd heard. Shock numbed her body. *He loves me.* echoed through her brain. Finally she could study his face without him looking away first. She saw something she'd never seen before. The hardness was gone, the mask was gone. Nick Reyes looked vulnerable, able to be hurt.

God, she didn't want to hurt him. She shook off his hands and took a step backward.

Is this what she'd wanted all along? Now, she wasn't so sure. She thought she'd loved her husband, Richard, too, and that had turned sour. Her father? Any love she'd had for him was long gone. But, she wasn't sure she was ready for Nick to fall in love with her. She had things to figure out before she could make a commitment. Didn't she?

Commitment? Holy crap, she couldn't think about that. What had she done?

Meredith turned, embarrassed at her response to Nick's kiss. Trying to think of what to say, her brain failed her. She felt like she was standing on a beach, the sand washing from under her feet into the surf. Her footing was eroding, upsetting her balance. It was frightening—stepping into something so new. Meredith felt the same paralyzing fear as when she had her finger on the trigger. Having her life turned upside down the past year was taking its toll. Was a committed relationship with Nick the missing puzzle piece that would complete her?

An alarm went off in her head. No man—even Nick—is the answer to my problems.

So, what is? Why not Nick?

Because something had happened after they returned from Mexico. Their relationship had changed. Then, at work she found out Nick had been promoted. The disappointment took her breath away, like the shock of plunging into icy water. He hadn't told her he intended to take the test—his own partner. It felt like a fundamental breakdown of the partnership they'd built. His failure to tell her hurt more than she cared to admit.

She'd risked her life and career for him, and he'd kept something so important from her.

Nick's hands grabbed her shoulders again. "Meredith. You're not sure?"

He set her at arm's length, his gaze searching her face. Was it hurt that made his jaw flex?

"I—" she began. She found it impossible to put a name to her feelings. She couldn't figure them out herself. But she wanted him to understand. Expressions tumbled through her brain, words to assuage his pain, but her voice failed. If he couldn't be honest with her, she had to tell him the truth. But what was the truth? She needed to sort her feelings out—was she sure she loved him? She thought so.

But what if she was wrong? What if her affection for him wasn't love? Could she spend her life without him? Before she figured that out, she had to get the betrayal over his promotion resolved, didn't she? A growing dread roiled inside her. She knew one thing—this scared her ten times more than facing a murderer.

"Mere?" Nick sighed, his shoulders slumping. "Where do we go from here?"

His words took a while to sink in. Her mind raced far from where she stood. She forced herself to concentrate. "I can't answer that—not yet." She couldn't look at him. She couldn't stay here one more second.

"Mere, there's no going back." The broad, magnetic smile spreading across his face dared her to stay; his eyes sure of his purpose.

She glimpsed it as she turned to run.

***

Lying in her cot, she yanked the woolen blanket off and turned to her other side. Sleep was miles from her busy mind. Nick filled her thoughts.

What should she do? Where could she go to find answers? Servente, the shrink? She thought about their last session.

"Let me get this straight: You think I feel guilty because I shot and killed a man who was inches from stabbing another deputy?"

Doctor Kathie Servente made a steeple with her index fingers. The psychiatrist's back was straight as she sat in a mocha-colored Eames chair with the requisite notepad on her lap. The room was tasteful—tan walls with a modern desk and matching credenza—but vanilla in its lack of personality. It was as if the doctor tried for a blank page to have her clients color in. "Doesn't that sum it up?"

Meredith's lips tightened frustration. "There's so much more to the story. I don't want to re-hash the details. I've been doing that for two months now. It hasn't gotten me anywhere."

Servente slipped her notebook and pen onto the table. "Yes, it's an oversimplification, but I want you to look at it from the world view." She leaned toward Meredith, her plain features displaying a comforting earnestness. "You have been involved in two life-or-death killings in twelve months. That is a literal phrase, Meredith. In both cases, the men would have killed you. In the first, you saved the life of another deputy."

Meredith had trouble turning the doctor's words into something she could work with. This was a summary of what she'd been living—nothing new.

"In the first case, a multi-jurisdictional team with no bias found you acted reasonably."

Doctor Servente sat back. She specialized in Post-Traumatic Stress Syndrome involving police officers. Meredith found the doctor's name on a list of mental health professionals offered through the department's Employee Assistance Program. She couldn't trust a therapist paid by the sheriff's department. A counselor might take a "fitness for duty" concern to the Administration. Being off work wasn't an option. By paying out of her own pocket, she hoped to hide these visits.

After several sessions to decide how far she could trust the shrink, Meredith took the leap.

A month earlier, she and Nick traveled to Mexico. She'd volunteered to help him with a family problem. The situation soon turned worse. The deeper they delved into the mystery the more trouble they found. Nick and Meredith had battled drug cartels, Federales, local police and even his own family to find the truth. Meredith had fought a man to his death, and had bruises and welts to show for it.

They returned on a Friday, and after the weekend off, were back at work on Monday. By then, her bruises had faded enough to cover with make-up. If Sergeant Leahy had known about their adventure, not to mention her hesitation under fire, he would have pulled her off the roster. She'd have been put on leave pending a Fitness-for-Duty evaluation.

It would have been the worst medicine for what bothered her. She couldn't stay home with this dilemma preying on her mind. She needed to stay busy. Working toward a solution, she avoided search warrants and apprehension details. She thanked God every day she hadn't gotten involved in a hot situation. She didn't volunteer for duty that would put anyone else at risk if she froze. But that wasn't good enough.

The doctor became the third person in the U.S. to know what happened in Mexico. Meredith was nervous about telling the story, and confiding in someone brought little relief. She and Nick had talked it over on the plane coming home, a distance emerged between them, added to her anguish. She needed Servente to offer a perspective that might help bring light to the shadows of their adventure in Mexico.

Nightmares of killing continued to haunt her. She had dreams where Meredith had no bullets in her gun when confronting the men she'd killed. Sometimes she couldn't raise her arms to shoot, and watched in horror as the men she'd killed wrapped their hands around her throat. She awoke gasping for air.

Doctor Servente rolled a pen between her fingers. "This last death was justified, no matter how you look at it. No U.S. agency would file charges. And I'm sure the Mexicans wouldn't prosecute you in the death of the cartel guard who'd held you hostage. He would've killed you, Meredith."

The detective sighed. Just because a shrink said it, didn't make it so. Would the Mexican Justice Department file charges if they'd known the truth about her role? But yes, it all sounded reasonable. After all, it was her career—she was a deputy, sworn to protect and serve. So why did she feel so awful when she did what everyone said was the right thing? Why, at the most crucial times, did she see the bloody impact of her bullet striking a staggering drunk? Like when she hesitated while she and Nick were ambushed, disarmed, and captured by the *Federales*? She had replayed the scenario in her mind over and over. She couldn't have done anything else. No one could have done anything else.

Then, Doctor Servente's last words hit home: "…the death of a cartel guard…holding you hostage…would have killed you." Meredith had choked him with her hands in a moment so intimate she could still smell him, feel his sweat slippery on her skin during the struggle. She'd strangled the life out of a man. His last breath had been in her face.

Thou shalt not kill….

She twisted in her cot, unable to find a comfortable place to sleep. The rehash of her last meeting with Dr. Servente brought no answers.

CHAPTER TWENTY-SEVEN

Thursday, May 21, before dawn

The waning moon gave Steiner barely enough light to move around. After walking the perimeter of the compound, he'd identified several weak points in the fence that would allow movement if he needed an emergency exit. He didn't want to kill these guys if he didn't have to.

He hadn't found any trace of James Easley, the sentry who'd gone missing. Steiner had been in these hills for over a year—long enough to know anything could have happened to Jimmy. One misstep could plunge him down a sheer cliff, a bobcat or wild boar could incapacitate a person to the point he'd become vulture food. This was the wild west, for sure, but not like the movies. He'd dismissed criticism he'd been too hard on Jimmy, always riding him, keeping after him. But the dumb kid couldn't remember shit. It was like he was frickin' senile or something. He was a passable soldier, but had to write everything down. In this operation, that was *verboten*. Still, he hoped Easley wasn't the murder victim the detectives were up here for.

As for the cops, there was a fine line between slowing them down and killing them outright. While he had no qualms about shooting cops, he knew it would court disaster for his plans. Cops always rally around their fallen hero, and cop killings would rain down a shit-load of trouble, fast and hard. He wasn't afraid of trouble, but had to keep things quiet until the operation began. Then he'd take on anything the cops could throw at him.

It was unnerving that they already knew about part of Steiner's plan. DeGraf would be taking them down the hill early in the morning. Steiner had called Lampson, his enforcer, on the satellite phone hidden in his Escalade. He'd told him to slow DeGraf's Jeep down—maybe flatten tires. That way it would be hours before they'd be in place to make a phone call. For now, Lampson would get someone in position. He'd let them know when the Jeep left, so his men would be ready for the ambush.

Steiner hoped Lampson had the sense to pick someone who could follow orders. While he'd trained and drilled most of these guys for over a year, most were far from the crack team he'd envisioned. The problem was discipline. Most of his men were decent shooters, good at hand-to-hand and general combat. But there were a half-dozen banjo-pickers in the Black Corps who didn't understand they couldn't do what they wanted. He'd have Lampson work on them—either they'd shape up—or they'd have to die. An exiled disgruntled militia man could alert the cops.

CHAPTER TWENTY-EIGHT

Thursday, May 21, before dawn

Still dark. Nick awoke, surprised he'd slept at all. He'd gone to bed in his clothes, thinking about Meredith. Under the rough wool blanket, he twisted and turned. He was discouraged by her reluctance. What was in their future?

After all they'd been through, what would happen to their partnership? He'd damaged it already by not telling her about the sergeant's test. She must have considered that a betrayal. Could he win back her trust?

If they got together, how would that effect their work? He tried to think beyond the thrill of the way she kissed him back. Work would be a challenge. He wouldn't be allowed to be her supervisor. Maybe they could work opposite shifts? The department frowned on relationships between deputies, but there were no rules against it. But douche-bags like Leahy could make their lives a living hell.

Not to mention Nick was no bargain as a partner. He already had one failed marriage and he was five years older than Meredith. He'd be thirty-four next month. He had his ghosts too. The loss of his daughter, Mia, would always claim part of his heart.

Nick had almost given up on the idea of a relationship with Meredith when the voice of his Academy PT Trainer echoed. "If it's not working, go back to basics and do something different."

Basics? Dating? Nah.

But courting? He wondered: how would he seduce this independent career deputy? No, seduction wasn't right. He wanted more from her than just sex. Romance? Flowers and champagne? Sentimental diamond-commercial expressions of love? Not his style, or hers, as far as he knew. Opening the door for her? Maybe. He pictured Mere barreling through opening her own door. But, respecting and listening to her? Didn't he already do that?

He did, didn't he?

DeGraf snorted, rolling over on protesting springs. No way could Nick get back to sleep. He sat up, glancing around. Meredith had dragged her folding bed across the room while Cavanaugh and Steiner clustered around Nick. Moonlight cast shadows through the high windows—the moon was fading.

Nick sensed, rather than heard, movement near the kitchen. Mere, Cavanaugh and DeGraf were all in bed. Steiner's blanket lay draped aside—the cot was empty.

Moving carefully to keep the springs from screeching, Nick reached under the balled-up windbreaker he'd used for a pillow and removed his Glock. He stood, gun in hand. Wearing his khaki pants but sock-footed, he crept the short distance across the slab floor to the kitchen.

Silence. No movement in the room. Maybe Steiner had gone outside.

At the kitchen entrance, Nick paused, his eyes trying to penetrate the darkness. A shadow next to the refrigerator? At the outside door?

Just enough moonlight brightened the entrance as he opened the door. He stepped out and walked ten feet from the hut. The night was silent. After a minute, the crickets started up and an owl hooted from a tree. Then, stillness again as nature held its breath at an intruder.

Nick walked along the lip of the basin, cussing under his breath that he hadn't put on his shoes. He tried to ignore the stickers poking through his socks as he walked back toward the Quonset hut.

A low noise, a voice, came from the parked cars. Nick padded toward it.

"I'm telling you, these guys make me nervous. DeGraf is manageable but I don't know about the others—" Silence.

The voice whispered again. "I don't want them messing up the weekend plans." Then, "You be ready for the race when I call. You know what they have to do."

Nick circled the hut and returned though the back door. He'd slipped the gun in his pocket and leaned on the counter when Steiner moved from the shadows back into sight.

"You're up early." Steiner's voice was hushed, an accusation.

Nick pulled out his Glock, but kept it alongside his thigh. "So are you. What're you doing?"

"Me? Uh, I couldn't sleep. I thought I'd go outside and watch the night sky."

"Uh huh." This guy was lying. "Get over here where I can see you."

"Hey, what the fuck's going on?" DeGraf thumped across the floor to Nick's side. He flicked on the kitchen overhead light and saw the Glock. "Put that thing away," DeGraf sounded like he was scolding a mischievous child.

DeGraf glanced from one man to the other. "What the fuck is going on?"

Steiner opened his mouth but Nick, holding the Glock, spoke first. "I heard something, got up to check. Found him coming in the back door."

"I told you. I couldn't sleep." Steiner put a flashlight on the counter. He spread his hands in a plea. "I wasn't doing nothin' illegal."

"Stand down, Reyes." DeGraf sputtered. "We're all friends here."

Nick wasn't sure why, but he knew the Department of Justice agent was wrong.

"Let's get moving, then. I want to get to the office." Nick turned and ran into Meredith. She, too, had her semi-auto in her hand, her face all business.

Meredith had his back. He should've known he wasn't alone.

CHAPTER TWENTY-NINE

Thursday, May 21, early morning

Jerry Steiner watched the goddamn cops leave, glad to see their tail-lights. DeGraf was easy enough to manipulate. This was one reason why Steiner hated to put an end to their symbiotic relationship. Steiner did the maintenance and electrical work on the base. In turn, DeGraf unwittingly gave him first-hand info on the task force's movements. Steiner was an expert information finagler.

The two men had a lot of laughs over the past two years, a beer and a deck of cards between them. He liked DeGraf, because the man didn't ask too many questions; had no clue he was being played. Plus, he laughed at Jerry's jokes. DeGraf thought the world revolved around himself. He was a second-string cop who missed the obvious, a victim of his own pre-conceived ideas.

Steiner was a good enough liar to make most people believe he was just a radio geek.

But these two deputies—Reyes and Ryan—weren't like most people. Certainly, they weren't as gullible as DeGraf. Steiner had seen suspicion in their faces. They were a threat to his Dry Creek hills operation. He dreaded the repercussions of messing with cops, but his timetable had to be protected. He was sure the sergeant—Reyes—had guessed he wasn't a radio tech. And the woman—she watched everything and said little. Steiner was leery of people like that.

The bitch cop wouldn't be dangerous much longer. None of them could be allowed to leave. They had to be stopped—at least for the next twelve hours. Months of planning, marshaling resources, humping all necessities into these fucking remote hills. There was too much at stake to keep their campaign a secret, but he had to protect it until the right moment.

Steiner had more riding on this operation than mere civil disturbance. His future with the Covenant Family—the stepping-stone to his larger plans—was at stake. Although it hadn't been his fault, his last two missions had failed. One because a loose-lipped soldier blabbed to the brother of a DOJ agent. The second because of broken-down logistics. Steiner had a plan that included Covenant Family leadership, although no one but Lampson knew it yet. For now, a group of elders "guided" Jerry Steiner as head of the enforcement arm—the Black Corps. The old fools had limited this mission to a pathogen that would sicken, rather than kill. Their logic held that killing a population they wanted to control wasn't productive. He'd disagreed, lobbying for some bacteria that would cause a more dramatic incident. In the end, he'd had to compromise. For the last time.

He'd hate to have to eliminate the elders too soon. They had influence, but the members of the Family listened to Jerry. He needed backing from the elders to keep his current mission financed for a little while longer. Then he would be free to do whatever he wanted. He was proud of his strategy.

Timing was critical. Events would go according to his design, even if he had to kill cops. He had a job to do and no one would stand in his way.

But first, he had to finish this part of the operation.

CHAPTER THIRTY

Thursday, May 21, dawn

From the back seat of the crowded Jeep, Meredith strained to see Steiner watching them leave. He'd followed them out and stood next to his midnight blue Escalade EXT pick-up as they loaded up. The Jeep crunched down the steep gravel drive. As they traveled behind a knoll, she saw him reach in his pocket. Cell phone? No, he wouldn't get a signal up here.

She nudged Nick's elbow to get his attention to Steiner, but the Jeep was already around the hill. Nick missed it. Bouncing on the pot-holed road, she leaned into his ear and told him what she'd seen. Being so close to him, she held tight rein on her feelings. This was work.

She shifted her attention. Watching DeGraf drive, his body loose and lazy, he looked like he hadn't a worry in the world. She wondered what the guy was thinking. Wary of his friendship with the creepy radio geek, she hadn't liked how he handled the situation at the gate. Although, she appreciated him driving them to the Main Office, she was glad their association would be over soon.

Cavanaugh was in the front passenger seat, silent and stiff. The rancher hadn't missed anything that was going on. He kept his thoughts to himself. Beside Meredith, Nick tapped on his cell phone. He turned and shouted, "Gil, can you hear me? Lieutenant Ferrua?"

With an exasperated sigh, he tried texting.

"Nice idea, but Ferrua doesn't text."

"Anyone else you can think to message?" Nick's forehead wrinkled.

"I'll try Maria in dispatch. If she gets the message, she'll pass on the info." Meredith pulled out her cell. "What do you want me to say?"

"Received unverified and unspecific threat by militia types in Rockpile Road area approximately five miles west of homicide scene. Possible target Amgen Tour. NFD." No further details.

DeGraf's voice was a growl over the noise of the engine. "Jeez, you guys are taking these clowns too seriously. They're a bunch of rednecks playing army, exercising their Second Amendment rights." He stopped the Jeep and wrestled the transmission out of 4-wheel drive. The gravel road had flattened out.

"You're wrong, DeGraf. I heard him on a phone this morning telling someone we could mess up their weekend plans."

"Aw, you're making more out of it than he intended. He's probably talking about a poker game. Besides, how could he get cell reception up here?"

"What about a satellite phone?" Meredith asked.

"Mr. Cavanaugh," Nick touched the rancher's elbow. "You're sure you don't know anything about these militia types?"

Nick leaned toward the rancher to hear his answer.

Cavanaugh shrugged. "There've been rumors for years. Until yesterday, I figured the neighbors had a case of Tea Party paranoia."

Meredith sat back, disappointed with Cav's answer. She stared out at the sheer cliff dropping off inches from the car. The slope plunged into a ravine that rose as sharply on the other side. There was little to break a fall to the creek below other than a tenacious bush or boulder. She pulled her attention back to Cavanaugh. Whether it was the Covenant Family or not, Cav knew more than he told.

"All the years you've ridden these hills, you've never seen anything like those idiots yesterday?"

He twisted toward Meredith, but didn't meet her gaze. "They'd avoid contact with outsiders, wouldn't they? I've seen traces, tracks on the road and so on, but I never knew they were here. Depending on the season, there's one kind of hunter or another on most of these roads."

She returned to her phone. As she tapped her message to Maria, Meredith leaned into Nick's ear again. "I think you're right. Our victim was militia, and that has something to do with their imminent mission."

Meredith returned to her cell to finish her text. She raised a thumb to push "send," but the deep throbbing of a motor broke her attention. She looked behind them, and her breath caught. A black Dodge 4-X-4 truck, studded and chained like a motorized demon, ground down on them. Its headlights stared like predatory eyes spotting prey. A heavy crash bar mounted on the grill made its intention clear.

The truck wheeled around to aim at the passenger side.

"Hang on," Meredith shouted.

CHAPTER THIRTY-ONE

Thursday, May 21, morning

Meredith mashed her thumb into the screen, hoping the text to Maria went, then dropped the phone to grab an arm rest with both hands.

The impact jolted her sideways, banging her head into the side window. Nick slammed into her while struggling to pull his Glock. DeGraf shouted, fighting to keep the wheel straight from the Jeep's dynamic energy. The car spun 90 degrees, tires scraping for purchase on the gravel until the passenger side faced the hill.

Still rocking and sliding, the monster truck slammed them again. Coming at them from the driver's side, Meredith glimpsed two pale faces in the cab. Men in their mid-twenties, in forest camo ball caps, with vicious smiles etched on their faces.

Meredith tightened her grip on the armrest and braced for another impact. The truck smashed into the driver's door. Cavanaugh cried out, "No," in fury. Nick fired his Glock out the window. The shots competed with the screams inside and the metal of the two vehicles grinding against each other.

The truck forced the Jeep sideways a foot, then two—towards the cliff.

"Fuckers are pushing us off the road," DeGraf yelled. He jammed the accelerator, trying to hold his ground even as the truck bumper caved in the opposite door.

The slope was almost vertical. A half-dozen burned tree stumps and scrubby bushes held a tenacious grip between shelves of rough granite. And the chasm grew closer. Meredith's heart pounded in her ears, making it hard to hear DeGraf's cussing.

The Jeep skidded sideways, a tire thumping over the edge. The axle scraped against the road's berm. Above the noise of metal grinding against gravel, Meredith heard DeGraf's refusal to accept defeat. He laid on the horn and kept his foot on the gas pedal, all the while shouting profanities.

She also heard the men in the truck hooting with vicious glee as the monster shoved harder.

Nick's fingers whitened around the grip of his Glock. With his other hand, he grabbed an armrest and yelled, "Hold on."

Seeing the worst was about to happen, Meredith breathed, "Oh God." How could this occur when her life was finally looking positive? Oh God, she wanted to fight this. She pulled her Beretta and aimed. Nick was in the way. She shoved the Beretta in her holster.

Then, the monster came toward them, delivering the first shattering blow. Thrumming with menace, the Jeep shuddered with the impact. Nick's Glock was even louder than the two vehicles. A rapid succession of shots, then nothing.

"Fuck," she heard Nick yell. The next second, he wrapped an arm around her body to buffer her from the impact. The truck grill mashed into the Jeep's windshield, splintering the glass.

"Oh God, I can't lose him now," Meredith's thought overtook the fear for her own safety.

After a stomach-wrenching jolt, DeGraf's SUV shuddered in a crab walk, tires unable to grab and stop the slide.

Suddenly, they were airborne. Seconds seemed like hours, until a rear tire struck an outcropping, then bounced. The back-end hit something hard, then the vehicle tipped upwards.

In a terrifying moment, Meredith saw DeGraf's bulk barreling towards her. His body snapped to a stop, an inch away, restrained by the seatbelt as the Jeep slammed onto something hard. The side windows exploded as the Jeep crumpled, accordion-style. With metal screeching and popping, the vehicle came to rest, enveloped in a cloud of dust. Sitting almost up-right, the windshield faced the slope they'd just catapulted over. The eerie seconds of silence stretched out as she realized the engine had died and the lights were out.

Every inch of Meredith's body hurt from the trauma of banging around in the Jeep's interior. She made a quick scan and found scratches and bruises, but found nothing of concern. Nick was wedged beside her, jamming her body against the chest strap. She blew out the breath she'd been holding and did a quick head to toe check on Nick. He looked okay. After feeling for her gun, she flexed her muscles. Her head began to throb and her chest hurt from the seat belt that had held her in place. Could've been much worse, but she'd ache tomorrow.

She strained sideways to see through the hole that had been windshield. Dust from their fall drifted up the hill, obscuring her view. A dangling tree limb broke loose and fell against the front bumper. The impact shook the car as it slipped downslope another ten feet. Like walking on a tightrope, any subtle shift of weight would tip the Jeep over and down the hill.

"Get out of here, but be careful," she said.

Nick grunted assent.

Cavanaugh exhaled a low gravelly, "okay."

DeGraf groaned, "I—I can't move."

Meredith forced her attention on the agent. Peering over his shoulder, she saw the steering wheel crammed against his chest. The dashboard pinned his legs. One arm twisted unnaturally above his head and blood seeped down his sleeve. She caught the sweet scent of anti-freeze and motor oil baking on a hot engine.

"Out," Nick echoed her order in a hoarse whisper. "Cavanaugh, you go first, then Ryan, then me."

Cavanaugh squeezed his way through the window with impressive agility. He landed on a ledge of granite. Grabbing a handful of tree roots from the slope, he steadied himself. Meredith followed by climbing over Nick. She slipped past the jagged edges of glass to the small flat shelf then turned to help Nick climb out. Grabbing the base of a coyote brush, Nick melded his body into the hillside and pressed her into the wall of dirt.

Metal screeched against rock in protest. The car wobbled, like an animal trying to get out of a trap. It tipped again toward the creek bed, one tire sliding down the granite lip. Suddenly, the Jeep cartwheeled over and rammed its way through the brush to the creek bed below. They watched, helpless to save DeGraf, still trapped in the vehicle. Meredith's scream vibrated through her body, but was unheard in the thundering from the car crashing downward.

Gravity crushed the cab with a deadly thump as the Jeep landed. Then, silence and another dust cloud. The noise vacuum left Meredith in momentary shock. She focused on the cloud of dust, leaves and tree branches wafting from the creek bed.

From above, men's voices—shouting. Meredith pictured men standing at the edge, taking stock of their work.

"No one could live through that shit," said one of the voices. "What a fuckin' end, huh? C'mon, let's get back."

Beside her, Nick whispered. "Got your gun?"

"Yeah," she said as she touched the Beretta tucked in her belt holster. She unsnapped the strap and gripped the gun as she looked upward. The bad guys had stopped their assault, but she was ready for anything. Would they climb down to confirm their kill?

Truck doors slammed shut. Tires ground against gravel on the road above them. They were leaving.

The survivors waited in silence for two minutes. Then, certain they were alone, Meredith looked around and stepped back. They were on four-foot ledge, most of it granite surrounded by dirt and leggy scrub brush. She stood at the edge looking up. Meredith thanked God for the bushes that had hidden their escape from the Jeep.

"You okay?" Nick squinted at her, looking like he dreaded her answer.

"Yeah," she replied, flexing her back muscles. "I'm fine."

They both looked at the rancher. Nick said, "Cavanaugh?"

He grunted, gripping the tree roots. His eyes were eagle sharp, his body rigid, energy crackling around him. She'd recognized an undefinable hint in his eyes. He'd been "in it" before and survived. She could almost see him as a young ground-pounder pushing through the Vietnamese jungle.

A dribble of blood trailed down his shoulder. Glass crystals were embedded in his red plaid shirt. He followed her gaze, then brushed the glass away. Meredith inspected Cav's shoulder finding a few glass splinters had cut through the shirt. She picked out as many as she could see. Scratches, really.

They stared down at the wreck, waiting for something she couldn't describe. No sign of life greeted them, no flicker of movement. This was the end of DeGraf. A shiver ran through her as the horror of the crash scrolled through her mind.

Meredith saw the debris from the Jeep left behind on the ledge. She brushed leaves and dirt off two mangled plastic boxes then looked at them more closely. The impact must have blasted the boxes out the windows when the Jeep landed. Nick picked up a skein of yellow nylon rope while she went through a pair of banged up cardboard boxes. A half-dozen smashed granola bars were all she could salvage from a box. She tucked the food in her pack and looked to Nick.

A small tool chest teetered on the lip of the chasm beside a pair of sleeping bags. Crystal-like pieces of window glass glittered on the bags in the scant sunlight. Pulling the chest toward him, Nick opened the tool box and rifled through it. With a frustrated sigh, he slammed it shut and looked at Meredith.

Crap, he's going down there.

CHAPTER THIRTY-TWO

Thursday, May 21, morning

Machiavelli understood progress happened through the sacrifice of soldiers. Steiner held the same belief, and tried to read a little Machiavelli each night. But right now he wished he could pick these two as the first of his men to grease the treads of the enemy's tanks.

"You fuckin' idiots." Steiner spit as he yelled at the two shaggy-haired, pimple-faced recruits. "You did exactly what I didn't want, you fuckin' morons." He back-handed the younger of the boys. "I wanted them stopped, not killed. Now you've stirred those damn cops up like a hornet's nest." The young man swayed from the blow, then straightened, his hand covering a cheekbone.

For Steiner, the pressure was on. He wasn't merely fighting time, now his own men's incompetence jeopardized his mission. Pissed-off cops in the area could endanger it.

For a moment, Steiner considered the process for admission into Black Corps. He'd been wrong when he judged the Lewis brothers worthy to be in his elite fighter unit. Their enthusiasm was due to savagery, not political or religious zealotry. Savagery couldn't be managed. Steiner had believed them when the boys spouted Aryan Brotherhood platitudes at their initiation. But after spending the past months together he saw them for what they were. They like to brawl. The Covenant Family Black Corps became the means to hide their cruelty.

Steiner wanted more from his team. He wanted some intelligence to temper the action. A dash of common sense would be nice, too. The Black Corps was the machine that would control the Covenant Family's journey and fulfill Steiner's plans.

Standing behind the brothers, his bodyguard Barry Lampson's face was like stone. Steiner figured the bodyguard hadn't conveyed the detailed orders to the brothers. Lampson spoke in monosyllables that weren't always clear. It was also possible that Lampson didn't understand Steiner's directions. It didn't matter, the damage was done. Now he'd have to move up his timeline—after he made sure they couldn't warn anyone. He would not fail.

"Did you check to see they were all dead?"

One of the boys began, "Uh, sir, no one could've survived—".

Those fucking Lewis brothers got a woody every time they raised some hell. They didn't think about repercussions. What if one of those damn cops had survived the crash? What if they all survived? They'd be mad as hell. But dead, they wouldn't talk to anyone—at least until the bodies were found. Steiner had to make sure everyone in the car was dead.

What a fucking disaster. "How much damage does your truck have?" He squinted at the older of the two men. "Is it drivable?" He wasn't going to take his Escalade on these rough roads, especially not with the stuff he'd loaded into it.

"Y—yes, sir," Older stuttered.

Steiner jabbed an index finger into the man's chest—hard. "You're gonna go to the wreck and find out if anyone's alive. If they are, take 'em out, right there." Steiner considered scenarios. "Then, go to the base. Any survivors will go back there to nurse their wounds. Healdsburg or Cloverdale are too far to make on foot. That base needs to be disabled anyway. And make sure everyone's dead."

Steiner watched the young men's eyes open as they understood his message. Time to destroy the cops and anything that could be used against the mission.

He snapped his fingers for his bodyguard, Barry Lampson.

CHAPTER THIRTY-THREE

Thursday, May 21, morning

Nick had to know if DeGraf was alive. It was less the idea of leaving a man behind than it wasn't in Nick's character to resign DeGraf to an anonymous, solitary death. Or, what if DeGraf had defied the odds and survived? Guaranteed, he would have major injuries. Could he get the agent out of the demolished Jeep? Could Nick bring him up to the road? Then what? With no way to call for help, he'd have to stabilize DeGraf, then get him to medical attention. Nick would figure it out when he took stock of the situation. Even if Henry One was at his disposal, Nick believed it would soon turn into a recovery mission instead of a rescue.

One thing was for sure—Nick couldn't leave DeGraf. The uncertainty, simply not knowing, didn't work for a detective of Nick's credentials.

His mind raced through the logistics, then he was in motion. Slinging the rope around a knobby tree stump, he tied a bow line knot and wrapped one end behind his waist, the long end trailing down the slope.

"Nick," Meredith put a hand on his arm and began a protest.

Ready to move, he met her searching gaze with disapproval. He looked away as her hand dropped, grateful she didn't push her objection.

"You sure you want to do this, Sergeant?" Cavanaugh's lips pressed together, a study in dread. "Even if you get down in one piece, you might need more help than we can give you to get back."

"Keep your eyes open, Mr. Cavanaugh. In case they return." Nick shook the kinks from the coil. "Watch the rope, will you?" He dropped over the ledge and descended the hillside with the knees-and-elbows motion of a marionette whose strings were pulled by a silent, unforgiving puppeteer.

CHAPTER THIRTY-FOUR

Thursday, May 21, morning

Meredith watched Nick make his way down a route through sparse brush. Studded with outcroppings of granite and tenacious shrubs, the ravine wall was steep enough to make the rope necessary. Falling was the only other way to descend. The chasm narrowed to a rocky creek bed that held a few pools of water. This route put him on the ground ten feet from the wreck.

Meredith watched Nick untie the rope and drop to the creek. He crawled over rocks, past bushes and through the water to the Jeep. Then he crouched at the driver's side of the Jeep for what seemed an eternity. Nick's voice, low and steady, drifted through the speckled rays of sunlight. She wondered if Nick was praying with DeGraf—or for him.

After thirty minutes, Nick started moving around, climbing from one side of the Jeep to the other. Meredith couldn't see what he was doing. He had his raid jacket in one hand and it looked like he stuffed something inside it. Now, it looked like a body. It dawned on her that he was setting the scene for militia who might come looking for survivors. From a distance, it would look like there were at least two corpses. Nick pulled a faded Giants baseball cap from his pocket and placed it where a head would be.

Ten minutes later, Nick tugged on the line for Meredith to pull him up.

The rock shelf halfway up the cliff, where Cav and Meredith stood, marked the bottom of a burn line from years past. Cavanaugh found a second, smaller coil of rope, and looped it around the smooth skin of a scorched tree stump. He shouted down the ravine to Nick. Using the rope and tree stump like a pulley, Cavanaugh and Meredith readied to pull him up.

Nick signaled thumbs up, grabbed the rope, and boosted himself onto a rock. Picking his way across the cliff and rough brush, he made his way upward.

Meredith worked well with Cav. The rancher knew what he was doing, and worked hard dragging the rope upward while Meredith pulled slack and acted as an anchor. It was like directing traffic around an accident scene at a busy intersection with another cop. It needed to be a cooperative effort, but sometimes things didn't flow. Missed cues could lead to uncoordinated chaos. Cav fell quickly into the smooth rhythm of their work. Meredith appreciated that.

Just below the granite lip, Nick swung his body sideways to grab for a hand hold. Rock came apart in his hands. Meredith held her breath as he dangled, swaying and held by the single line. He'd have fallen without the rope.

On his second pass, he found a solid rock. Now, with a foot hold, he stood and extended a hand to Cavanaugh. Meredith doubled down on her grip, putting everything she had into one last yank. She had to pull Nick over the rock precipice and back to the ledge.

Lying on his side, panting with the exertion, Nick rested a moment. His face, a mask of mud, engine grease and anguish, told her the bad news. Her gut clenched. She didn't need details. She knew the look. Nothing else mattered now. Something was going to happen and Nick was going to orchestrate it. Someone would pay. The loss of DeGraf and the attack on their car was a crime Nick couldn't ignore. It wasn't revenge, strictly speaking. It was more that Nick wouldn't let those who perpetrated this assault go unpunished.

The logistics of getting to a radio or finding cell reception to get a team up here were shaky. How long would it take them to call for back up? Could they wait for help? They had the militia man's homicide to investigate. It would fall to second place now as DeGraf's murder took priority. No matter what protocol dictated, Nick would shift gears to find De-Graf's killer. The two murders were linked. They needed to find out how.

A clock started ticking in the back of Meredith's mind. Its dial was fuzzy and the second hand swept wildly. How long did they have?

The militia had something big planned, soon. They were vested in keeping it secret—whatever it was. Hence the attack on the Jeep. She wondered how they knew the team was a danger to their plans. The soldiers took a risk trying to kill the detectives—all they had to do was let them leave. Why hadn't they?

Someone warned them. She recalled seeing Jerry Steiner reaching into his pocket as they drove off, a couple of hours ago.

Steiner. How the hell did he have cell service?

"DeGraf's gone," Nick shook safety glass fragments from a rolled sleeping bag and sat on it.

Questions would wait.

CHAPTER THIRTY-FIVE

Thursday, May 21, morning

The road back to the encampment was smooth enough that the Escalade chewed up the miles. Steiner's mind wandered back to a dark Missouri Road House last spring. His mission and convincing Barry Lampson to join him at the Covenant Family. They had been cellmates. Months before, Steiner had been released from Jefferson City Correctional Center after serving the minimum sentence for assaulting a police officer.

Jerry Steiner's small size made him a target for anyone itching to prove himself. For protection, he'd joined up with the Aryan Brotherhood. They welcomed him. What he lacked in muscle, he made up for in brains. In prison, Steiner honed his natural manipulation skills into masterful strategizing. The Brotherhood leadership recognized his cunning. Under their guidance, Steiner learned logistics—the planning and execution of coordinated incidents. Lampson was a natural to act as his bodyguard, defending him against rival gang attacks.

After serving his four years, Steiner was released. Once on the outside, he ducked below the law enforcement radar, moving from state to state to find a group that suited him. He noticed large populations of disenchanted Americans living off the grid. It didn't take long for him to see opportunities, but first, he needed to be accepted. He joined The Covenant Family, a small compound outside of Mound City, Missouri. They welcomed him—a brother of the same beliefs, a man who'd challenged the government and survived.

Using the skills he'd learned in prison, Steiner worked with the sovereign citizens. It was easy disguising his scheming. During the two years he lived with the Covenant Family, he immersed himself in their belief system. He learned the structure and complexities and used them to manage the members. But particularly those in the Black Corps, the elite squad he'd volunteered to head up. Most of these guys were the cream of the combative crop, fighters who believed in the cause.

After two years, the militant arm of the Covenant Family went from providing security to buying and stockpiling arms, regimented training and exercises, and small, specially-planned incidents. These events were kept from the Family's governing body, the Elders. Steiner knew they would never approve of holding up a gun store. His philosophy was bolder and more aggressive than the Elders would condone. What they didn't know wouldn't hurt them—at least for now.

From Steiner's prison experience, combined with his stay with the Covenant Family, a vision for his future emerged. By joining with other sovereigns, he could forge them into a serious force. He'd heard estimates there were hundreds of thousands of sovereigns in America. By connecting them, he had visions of a massive crime syndicate with him at the wheel. The big money was in guns and armaments. But as in any burgeoning business venture he needed capital.

And Steiner needed Lampson as his enforcer. Steiner had intelligence, guile and enough of a ruthless nature to carry out his plan. But a brutal mountain-of-a-man like Lampson, would make it easier to exert total authority and control. The Black Corps was where the real power lay within the organization. Because of Steiner's stature, it had taken time for the Elders to accept him as the Black Team leader. The path smoothed out when he had his own personal gorilla to encourage cooperation. The Elders soon forgot Jerry Steiner's size.

That afternoon in the Missouri road house, Lampson slurped on his Budweiser while Steiner explained the basics. The Covenant Family was part of a sprawling subculture of "sovereign citizens" in America. They are far-right constitutionalists who believe they, not the existing civil authorities, should decide which laws to obey and which to ignore--including tax regulations.

The belief system Steiner adopted was based on a decades-old conspiracy theory. In the beginning of U.S. history, he said, the founding fathers set up the American government with a legal system the sovereigns refer to as "common law." Steiner preached a new government system, based on "admiralty law, the law of the sea and international commerce," had secretly replaced common law in 1933, when America abandoned the gold standard.

Steiner told of judges around the country who knew all about this hidden government takeover, but denied the sovereigns' assertions out of treasonous loyalty to hidden and malevolent government forces. Under common law, sovereigns would be free men. Under admiralty law, they remain slaves, and secret government forces had a vested interest in keeping them that way.

"We call ourselves 'free men' to distinguish ourselves from the slaves of the federal government." Steiner searched the other man's face to see which way his friend would go.

"That's too deep for me." Lampson slammed his Budweiser on the varnished bar table. "Besides, we're all slaves to something."

"No, we're not. We have a choice of how to live. Here's how it works: Since 1933, the U.S. dollar has been backed not by gold, but by the 'full faith and credit' of the federal government. This means the government has pledged its citizenry as collateral, by selling their future earning capabilities to foreign investors—effectively enslaving all Americans at birth."

"No shit?" Lampson's eyes narrowed. "Slavery, huh? How does it work?"

Steiner allowed himself a small smile. "When a baby is born in the U.S., a birth certificate is issued. The government then uses that certificate to set up a kind of corporate trust in the baby's name, a secret Treasury account, which it funds with an amount ranging from $600,000 to $20 million. By setting up this account, every newborn's rights are split between those held by the flesh-and-blood baby and the ones assigned to his or her corporate shell account."

"Nah. A secret Treasury account?" Lampson swiveled his bald head in denial, his voice a little too loud. "That's just conspiracy theory bullshit."

Steiner leaned toward him. In a tone above a whisper, he said, "You want proof? Look at a birth certificate. Since most certificates use all capital letters to spell out a baby's name, JOHN DOE is the name of the corporate shell straw man, while John Doe is the baby's "real" flesh-and-blood name. As the child grows older, most of his legal documents will utilize capital letters, which means his state-issued driver's license, his marriage license, his car registration, his criminal court records, hell, even his cable TV bill, and correspondence from the IRS will all pertain to his corporate shell identity, not his real, sovereign identity."

Lampson was silent. "I don't get it. How do you get to that secret Treasury account? I want my money."

"We've figured a way to split the straw man from the flesh-and-blood man. It's called 'redemption,' and its process is two steps. Once separated from the corporate shell, the newly freed man is now outside the jurisdiction of all admiralty laws. By filing a series of complex, legal-sounding documents, he can tap into secret his Treasury account for his own purposes." Steiner leaned back on the bar stool, as if his work was done.

"How do you get to the money?" Lampson's eyes were bloodshot.

"Hundreds of sovereign promoters are trying to perfect the process by packaging different combinations of forms and paperwork."

"Trying to? So no one has gotten to their money?"

"Not yet, but—" He grabbed Lampson's huge bicep. Steiner's face shone with the believer's moral certainty. "They're close, man. All it'll take is the right combination of words."

God, was he a great liar. It was his means of getting what he truly wanted—power. Lampson wanted money. Well, he could offer that, too. But he had to at least sound like a sovereign citizen to convince Covenant Family followers. If Lampson wouldn't go for the Family theories, he would for the money.

Lampson hiccupped, then wobbled on the stool. "That could take years. How do you live in the meantime?" Lampson wasn't always as dumb as he looked.

Steiner wasn't interested in promoting a scam. He'd leave it to others in the sovereign culture. Inside the Family, he found his strength lay in organizing and leading these people trapped in a single ideological belief. In the years before finding the Covenant Family, he'd used the guise of a sovereign transient to gain a working knowledge of other group operations. They were all similar but separate and, until now, no one offered a cohesive blanket of power.

"Here's my plan: to unite all these small sovereign groups separated by minimal ideological differences and form one great force. I already have verbal commitments from a half-dozen communities. Of course, I'll have to beef up the Black Corps, like the SS in Nazi Germany. Having a trained, paramilitary force under my control—a crack army—will convince those who need it." He would work them, drilling, shooting, and emphasizing discipline.

Lampson's eyes widened. "Then what? You have a bunch of losers who believe in a fairy tale."

"No, dickhead." Steiner's disgust curled his lips. "These groups all have their own gig to raise money to support themselves. Some of them have gotten pretty damn inventive."

He'd finally caught the other man's interest. Lampson asked, "Like running guns and such?"

Steiner drew the bottle to his lips and didn't answer. Let Lampson believe what he wanted so long as Steiner got what he wanted.

"Now you're talking." Lampson's eyes grew wide with the possibilities. "There's big money in guns."

Steiner's smile was an ugly twist of the lips. "The more groups we have, the more money rolls in."

The prospects were staggering.

CHAPTER THIRTY-SIX

Thursday, May 21, morning

Nick rested for two minutes until his breathing slowed. When he stood, he felt an acute sense of purpose. His mind jumped from question to answer to possibility, then back to new questions. Planning. He felt for his Glock, relieved when his fingers touched the metal. He'd found it on the seat of the Jeep. Out of the corner of his eye, he caught Meredith glancing down at her nine mil.

Cav stood. He put a hand on Nick's arm. "I want to say something."

Nick met his look and the rancher began. "I know you guys—I mean cops—take a lot of crap for brutality and such. But these militia idiots are serious." He looked from Nick to Meredith. "They'll kill you in a hot second."

Nick frowned. "We know that—"

Cav drew up close to Nick's face. "What I'm getting at is, you better be ready to do the same to them—before they do it to you."

Meredith stared at the rancher's stiff posture.

Cav looked at Meredith. "Any of these jokers will take you out. You can't act all sweet like it's a prom date. You tie him up and he will kill you another day. DeGraf was wrong, and the next soldier you come across won't hesitate. This is like war. Kill or be killed."

He was right. The Covenant Family had already killed DeGraf, and now they were searching for the rest of them. "We'll take every circumstance as it comes," Nick said. "We've got to work within rules, laws." Nick met Cavanaugh's gaze, and he conceded. "But you're right. These guys are stone killers. I'll—we'll take your warning seriously."

With a thin-lipped smile, Cav squeezed Meredith's shoulder in the pressure of reassurance. Nick felt a flush of warmth for the old man as he passed to climb up the slope. Nick was sure Cavanaugh's words were aimed at them both, but the rancher had recognized a vulnerability in Meredith few could see. He'd treated her with the respect she deserved.

CHAPTER THIRTY-SEVEN

Thursday, May 21, morning

"I'm thinking we should try to walk out toward the coast," Meredith said, swallowing. She sneaked a look at Nick, gauging his reaction.

"Yeah," Nick sighed. "That's our only viable choice. I don't want to sit here, waiting for Henry One to find us." She thought how it wasn't in Nick's nature to wait when he could be doing something. With a mental smirk, she realized she was the same. Had she learned that from him, or had she always been that way? "Tick tock," he added.

He was right. She felt a flush of dismay over her selfishness. This case hadn't gone like normal: she interviewed victims and witnesses, rounded up alibis, searched for motive, and found the opportunity. Then, with a suspect, make an arrest, interview and charge. This was something different. This was guerrilla warfare—gloves off if you're going to survive. It's what Cav said. The soldiers had something big planned. People would die. They must move. Get to where they could call for help.

Nick's eyes met hers. "Let's find someplace where we can make a call."

They were on the move again.

CHAPTER THIRTY-EIGHT

Thursday, May 21, morning

Nick walked uphill and mulled over his options. First, contact the office for help. He'd hoped for Henry One to return by now. But Ferrua would have called them off. Nick had told his lieutenant they'd get a ride from the DOJ agent this morning. Ferrua would expect they'd show up soon. In any event, he hoped to have communications once he got to the base. He'd searched the Jeep but hadn't seen a radio in DeGraf's possession.

Next, he had to get the three of them to safety, particularly Cavanaugh. He didn't like having a civilian along, but there hadn't been a choice. And he worried about Cavanaugh's health. The old man wheezed sometimes as he climbed. Nick hoped he wouldn't have a heart attack or something. But for now, a safe place would suffice.

Contingencies? The possibility of another attack? Probably not. Those two soldiers wouldn't have left if they thought there had been survivors. An extended stay up here in the hills? Not likely, but they had to wait hours before Ferrua would declare them "missing in action." It would take that long to get back to the base, longer to get to the Sheriff's substation at Lake Sonoma.

Nick started moving up the top end of the cliff. Thankfully it was easier going. They were silent as they hiked between the burned-out tree trunks and the ground worn raw from the dying Jeep.

On the road, Nick scanned the hillsides. He had to call the lieutenant. He felt the phone in his pocket and looked back at his partner. "Mere, you still have your phone?"

Meredith stopped. Beside her, Cavanaugh looked on as she searched her pockets. Nick noticed her neck start reddening. She was getting upset. "No, I was texting Maria before the wreck. I don't remember having it after that."

"Were you able to send the text?" A nagging hunch started deep in his gut.

"I'm not sure." She threw her hands up in frustration. "I don't know if my finger hit the send button before the crash."

He'd have to anticipate it didn't go through.

She looked at him and shook her head.

Nick wondered. "Mr. Cavanaugh, do you have a phone?"

The rancher also shook his head.

Only one phone. He'd better make this work.

CHAPTER THIRTY-NINE

Thursday, May 21, late morning

The chill evaporated, and the morning sun warmed Meredith's back as Nick led them in a steady climb through the tall grass. Cavanaugh followed Nick, and Meredith brought up the rear.

Sorting out her anger over DeGraf's pointless death, Meredith's clenched jaw ached. She massaged her jaw muscles as she hiked along. She thought how agonizing it must have been for DeGraf, dying a lingering death. While Nick didn't elaborate, it was clear the agent had lived some time after the crash. He must have been in torture with the weight of the engine on top of him. At least he wasn't alone.

Nick had been there. Thank God for her partner. Nick.

Nick. Why didn't he tell her about the sergeant's test? She would have been more understanding if he'd told her—and supportive, for God's sake. His lame-ass excuse of jinxing his chances was ridiculous. She was insulted he'd use that on her. When she came down to it, she could ask him. They used to be able to talk things over. Now feelings tangled with purposes resulting in a mess.

That was what she had to do—ask him. Talk it over, like they used to.

As they walked on the road for an hour, she mulled over what words she would use, still watchful and listening for any sign of danger.

Finally, they reached the fenced area where DeGraf had drawn down on them the night before. The gate stood open, in creaking contrast to their first arrival. Standing outside the gate, she remembered closing and locking it. Did Steiner leave it open?

Nick's gaze conveyed the same alarm she felt. Her hand moved to the Beretta as his went for his Glock.

Cavanaugh pulled up, squinting. "That gate was closed when we left."

His deep voice resonated among the three of them.

"I know," Meredith said, her voice low. "I closed it."

"Tire tracks. New ones," Nick whispered, pointing where DeGraf had driven hours earlier.

The road to the base was laced with fresh tire impressions, mounds of dirt carved in sharp relief against the dusty road, edges not yet worn down by the afternoon breeze. The tracks were from a single vehicle with wide tire base—a truck.

The group crested the rise and took in the compound below. Every structure was damaged, some destroyed. Metal siding and splintered wood lay scattered, exposing equipment racks. Shards of window glass glinted in the sun. The towers stood, unsupported by loose guy wires dangling over bent girders that lay in the dirt. Nothing was left untouched.

Following Nick's signals, Meredith crept toward the back of the Quonset hut, her Beretta out. Had to make sure they were alone.

Outside the hut, wide tire impressions like those of the monster truck were etched in the dirt spread all over the compound. The Quonset hut had some exterior panels torn away, and the front door dangled on one hinge. The broken windows gaped like a toothless smile.

"Clear it first, then let's see if they left anything we can use." Nick's feet crunched the broken glass as he entered.

Meredith paused beside the rancher. "Cav, stay outside," she said. "Yell if you hear anyone coming." She followed Nick, scanning the interior as her eyes adjusted to the dim light inside. The pungent smell of wood smoke reached her. That can't be good, she thought.

The destruction in the hut was complete. More than mere vandalism, every corner had been ravaged. To her left, the office was a mess, the desk turned over, and papers scattered. The portable radio base had been smashed by a crumpled metal chair laying on its side. Without much hope, she checked for power.

Nothing. Not even static.

Their check of the interior revealed no one. Holstering her sidearm, she met Nick as he came out of the kitchen. "The radio is trashed."

Nick's jaw flexed. "They took most of the food, too."

"Is your cell working?" She dreaded his answer.

They stood in silence as he powered his phone up. He punched several keys then said, "Is Lieutenant Ferrua there? Don't put me on hold—" A second later to Meredith, "Goddamn it. I called his office hoping it wouldn't go to voicemail. It was Irene in dispatch. She put me on hold." He looked at his screen. "Battery is running low. I'm staying on the phone until someone picks up."

Meredith shrugged at his irritation. While she didn't know Irene, Meredith was sure she wouldn't want her job in dispatch for anything. She'd much rather broil under the spring sunshine while trekking around the tick-infested hills of Sonoma County than sit in a cubicle talking to cranky deputies and panicked civilians.

They weren't getting out of here anytime soon. Her hope for a quick return to civilization was fading. They'd been in tight spots before— worse than this—and gotten out. There was a priority here: figure out what was going on, find a murderer, then leave, hopefully in one piece. Dealing with these clowns was tricky. She hadn't gotten a bead on who or what they were, except they meant business.

Meredith took a deep breath and moved into the wrecked kitchen.

"I got through to state dispatch. I gave them our location and they said they'd relay that and a message to the SO." Nick looked around the room.

The refrigerator was tipped on its side, rivers of unidentifiable liquids streamed out. The cupboards were stripped of everything but a pile of energy bars tossed in a corner.

Meredith grimaced at the irony, and stuffed the food in her backpack. Damn energy bars. Even the bad guys left them behind.

From outside came the sound of boots slapping against packed dirt. "Hey." Cavanaugh skidded to a stop at the front door, his voice shattering the gloom. "Someone's coming."

CHAPTER FORTY

Thursday, May 21, late morning

"On second thought, I'm coming with you assholes to be sure it's done right." Steiner caught the younger brother rolling his eyes under the brim of his ball cap. Pissed at the disrespect, Steiner slugged the kid again, this time in the eye. "You're on a short leash, dickhead."

Younger Lewis stumbled, more from surprise than from the blow. Blinking, he bobbed to attention. "Yes, sir."

"And you, too, stupid."

Older Brother focused on his shoes. "Yes, sir."

"Now let's get this job done." Steiner opened the truck's passenger door. "Get in back," he snapped to Younger Brother. He'd have called the boys by name, but he couldn't remember who was who. Older and Younger would do. The kid started for the pick-up bed.

Steiner didn't try to hide his disgust. "Get your guns, for God's sake." Frankly, he didn't care enough to know their names. "And a half dozen grenades, too."

The Lewis brothers' truck had springs that put Steiner airborne every time they hit a bump. And the road was rough. An old Forest Service road, the packed dirt hadn't been graded in years. At the roadside, the terrain was open, with oaks and pines growing in the folds of the grassy hills. Farther down toward Healdsburg, vineyards lined Dry Creek Road. But up here, the isolation was almost a living being. Some people liked it, but Steiner couldn't figure why anyone would want to live there. It suited his needs for now. It was far enough away to allow him freedom to achieve his mission. His activities were best completed out of general view. It was a royal pain in the ass when he needed something from Santa Rosa, though. Depending on weather, traffic and what he wanted, it could be a half-day trip.

Sketchy communications were one major problem. He'd had to spend some big bucks to buy a satellite phone. It was crucial to stay in touch with his people up in Susanville. His force of thirty men to assist with the assaults on the police buildings had to be kept updated. After all, he would need them to assist the Black Corps when it came time to complete the mission.

Three rough miles later they arrived at the ravine where the Jeep had crashed. Standing on the road, Steiner stared at the wreckage for some time. He studied it; used his binoculars. There, one behind the wheel— DeGraf—and another, the top half of a body visible in a raid jacket with SHERIFF stenciled across the back. Scanning the slope, he knew there was no way to get to the wreck to confirm the agents' deaths. A glance at his watch—eleven o'clock—told him to get his ass moving, check the base out and get back to camp. He'd have to take a calculated risk they were all dead. Risk—he didn't have a good record for taking risks. Shit.

Then, furious at the fuck-ups, he got back into the truck. "Get this heap of shit to the cops' base, now."

Older Lewis drove too damn reckless for Steiner. His knuckles were white on the hand grip above the door. The more he yelled at the kid, the wilder he drove. Turning on two wheels, skidding on gravel and dirt surfaces, four-wheeling over rock-lined washes made Steiner furious by the time they approached their destination. It felt like hours tumbling around inside the ridiculous truck, but it had been a mere thirty minutes when they dropped into the shallow basin that held the remains of DeGraf's base.

The pressure was beginning to eat at Steiner. In under twenty-four hours, he would execute his plan. He was getting heartburn.

First, he and his men would split into small teams and disable the major law enforcement buildings in the county. They'd blow them all to hell at a synchronized time. Then, he would call the Chairman of the Board of Supervisors, and demand two million dollars. If he wasn't paid in twenty-four hours, the Black Corps would release the toxin cryptosporidium into the water supply. The timing had to be impeccable. While the pathogen is wending its way through the Sonoma County population, people would get sick, some would die and there would be no intact law enforcement agency in Sonoma County to preserve order. Civil chaos would ensue.

But it was the power and money he was after. He didn't give a rat's ass about the citizens of the county, nor did he care about what happened to the Family. He'd get his money and leave, setting the stage for the next part of his plot. Time was marching on; he had to get this distraction taken care of. Then he'd get back on schedule.

From the road looking down on the base, he saw the Lewis boys had finally done something right.

Steiner motioned for Older to stop. While the engine throbbed on all eight cylinders, Steiner opened the door and leaned out. He had a view of the entire base. The area was in shambles; it wasn't the tidy camp it had been when he arrived yesterday. Except for the antennae, which would've taken a D8 tractor to take the antennae down.

With a smile, Steiner ducked back into the truck and signaled for Older to move down the road to the base.

CHAPTER FORTY-ONE

Thursday, May 21, late morning

"We gotta find cover," Cavanaugh's voice rasped.

Meredith scooped up her pack, moving as Nick grabbed her hand. From outside came the whine of an engine climbing a grade in low gear. Cavanaugh loped from the hut, a hand clamped onto his hat as he hustled toward a small well-house on the far western side of the base. Nick yanked Meredith in the same direction, putting them out of view from the road. Cav's urgency fed Meredith's own fear of the unknown. Behind the shed, the ground dropped in a weedy, steep six-foot decline.

They ran through the weeds, trying to keep dust down as they sprinted down the slope. Meredith struggled for balance as Nick pulled her faster than she could run. Cavanaugh caught her other arm, and yanked them both into a bramble-covered space at the bottom of the slope. They slammed to the ground. Nick pressed his arm across Meredith's back and her elbow scraped across rough concrete. Concrete?

While trying to look around, she struggled against an arm anchoring her. Where was the hazard? What the hell was Nick doing?

"Get your head down," he snapped, pressing her face back into the concrete. Concrete?

The rhythmic sound of an engine thundered over them. The ground beneath Meredith's body reverberated from the motor's noise. Then, it stopped. In the ominous silence following, she shifted to get up.

Cavanaugh shoved her down again. "Wait," he whispered. "They're still here." There was the soft sound of metal falling into place against metal. They're getting out of the truck.

"Shit," Nick breathed, sliding his entire weight over her.

Get off me, Meredith thought.

A man snapped terse orders, close by. It sounded like Steiner. "Bring these buildings down. I don't want nobody to use them. And shoot anything that moves." Though she expected shooting, the distinct rat-a-tat-tat sound of an AK-47 made Meredith jump. It was a sound she'd never forget. They were shooting into the base, hooting like hillbillies at a county fair. She heard an explosion in the distance—she couldn't tell where. A quick blast—could be a grenade. Then, another. And, moving closer, a third.

When she heard the click, fear spiked throughout her body. A gut-clenching pause, then the explosion. The ground shook as dirt and rocks rained over them. More shooting in the distance. How many were there?

Another blast farther away made Meredith sigh with relief. Nick reached for her arm, scooting himself over her again.

"I can't move, damn it," she thought. Or did she say it? He wouldn't have covered Willis this way. He should be shielding Cavanaugh.

The shooting resumed twice again, for a few minutes each. They'd found another target and emptied a magazine into it.

Amid high school hoots, it like sounded two guys, the big truck motor started up again ten feet above them. They were leaving.

The engine sound faded. Finally, Nick rolled off her. Meredith flexed her cramped muscles, glad to be free. She sat up, rubbing her eyes, and shaking dirt out of her hair. Her ears were filled with the silence created by the sudden absence of loud noise, another type of hissing. This silence-stuff was disconcerting. She preferred noise—traffic, people talking, other signs of life—but not grenades.

"Holy shit," Nick's startled voice rose at something new, "what the hell is this place?"

Meredith followed his gaze. The vertical surface they'd run into was an iron door built into the side of the hill. The portal had been concealed by blackberry bushes. She scraped her shoe against the ground, remembering the concrete rubbing against her elbow.

An old yellow-and-black Civil Defense plaque was posted over the door. It was a walkway into an old fallout shelter.

And the door had been blown wide open.

CHAPTER FORTY-TWO

Thursday, May 21, noon

Steiner knew there were survivors from the wreck. He just knew it. At the collision site, he saw two dead bodies, the one behind the wheel and one laying half out of a window. There should've been more corpses. Some had survived and escaped. These damn cops were like rats scurrying around in the dark, spreading trouble. They had to be exterminated, especially that wet-back sergeant. He'd been suspicious of Steiner since his arrival. A sneaky spic. The girl, too. She'd been quiet, she'd been listening to everything.

DeGraf was a loss, though. Against his instincts, Steiner had grown to like the agent. Steiner had spent the last season encouraging DeGraf's natural racism, hoping to turn him to his cause. Steiner had heard of cops in the Klan. Why not a cop in the Covenant Family? Steiner hadn't the time to cultivate DeGraf into the Family, so he had to go. His recruitment had been fucked-up when of one of the scouts went missing and the subsequent arrival of the investigators. He'd hated to lose DeGraf as a buddy, but he couldn't take a chance now.

The others were of no importance; other than the shit-storm this mess would soon rain down on them. By then, he would be long gone from the Dry Creek area.

CHAPTER FORTY-THREE

Nick didn't bother telling Cavanaugh to stay behind. The man had taken down DeGraf and saved them by alerting them to the return of the marauding militia. He'd earned the right to come with them. Nick would continue to keep an eye out for his safety though—that was his job.

For now, Nick wanted to see what was inside the bunker. He rolled a rock to make a doorstop, wedging the heavy iron door open.

Damp, but surprisingly fresh air greeted them as they stepped inside. Nick flicked on his flashlight. The beam penetrated the darkness of the interior.

It was a large concrete tube of a room, void except for valueless items left behind. On the floor, a metal tool box lay open on its side, a broken clipboard and a wadded-up Lucky Strike cigarette wrapper in U.S. Army green. They looked like they had been left yesterday.

Nick's light stretched to the back of the room and fell on an open cubicle. The hole in the middle of the floor suggested a latrine. To the right, a kitchenette with a sink and counter, but no appliances, lined up under a staircase. Living quarters? The place was a skeleton from the past, filled with the dread of wartime purpose.

Nick wasted no time crossing to the stairs, Meredith and Cavanaugh following. Fighting an eerie feeling that he was stepping back into someone else's past, he forced himself to climb the stairs. With vague urgency, he moved upward toward wisps of light. A door? He hadn't seen anything from outside. He moved slower now. What if someone was up there? No, it was wisps of sunrays.

Four steps from the top, Nick paused. He couldn't shut off the reflex, but he felt silly putting a hand on his Glock. Getting to his gun was the Holy Grail of survival training, and the near ambush had sent his instinct into overdrive. Silly or not, he was ready.

Horizontal embrasures for sniper fire lined the space below the concrete ceiling. Sunlight got through only a few, the rest were covered by brambles. With almost enough light to see, he switched off the flashlight and shoved it in his pocket. He scanned the empty concrete room and let the place breathe its story.

There didn't seem to be much to tell. From the ring-shaped buckles near the largest window, it looked like it had been built for a gun emplacement. Not a big one like the guns at the mouth of the Golden Gate during World War II, but big enough. Despite the decades of disuse, he noticed the circumference bore no evidence of wear. Had this place ever been used? Nick couldn't tell, but the dated debris indicated someone had been here—decades ago.

Maybe the shelter was not used after it was built. Maybe it had been completed at the end of the war. When the Cold War advanced, someone remembered the housing and tacked up a "civil defense" sign? It could've happened.

He walked on. As below, the entire structure was concrete—walls, ceiling, steps. An enormous open window filled the wall. The big gun would have been pointed out there. The ammo storage was near, in a concrete and steel closet. The room presented as a place for a last stand. If they'd had to defend this position, there wouldn't be much hope for rescue. The floor below would accommodate radio personnel and any guards posted here. Only God knew what would happen to them if the place was attacked.

Meredith stood beside Nick while Cavanaugh walked around, his boot heels echoing.

"World War II vintage," Cavanaugh fingered a rusted steel door.

"I've seen batteries at the Presidio in San Francisco and the Marin Headlands." Meredith squinted at the track imprinted in the concrete. "They make sense there. But why twenty miles way the hell inland?"

Cavanaugh thought for a moment. "Maybe to protect the workers at the radio towers." He shrugged.

"Hm," Meredith said. "Protect from whom? Nazis? Communists?"

Cavanaugh muttered, "Pick one."

CHAPTER FORTY-FOUR

Thursday, May 21, early afternoon

There was a deli in Roseland Nick and she liked when they worked patrol. Good pastrami and some guy who came in early and baked fresh sourdough bread. Great bread. Nick always commented on it. There was a sense of peaceful familiarity that came with a place like that, a warm sandwich in a paper bag. Meredith thought about the deli often when she was far from home and hungry.

"Granola bar?" Meredith held up a brightly covered snack for Cav's inspection.

"Sure." Ripping off the wrapper, he studied the food with the enthusiasm of a man inspecting a pile of dog shit. About the size of a small candy bar, the chocolate coating had melted and re-solidified, white bubbles making it unappealing. He crammed the bar in his mouth so he wouldn't have to taste it. "It filled the hole." He used a hand to balance as he settled on the floor against a wall.

Meredith smiled and offered a bar to Nick, who sat on a concrete ledge, his back propped against the wall with knees to his chest. He looked so absorbed in thought he didn't hear her.

She dropped the bar in his lap. Startled, he looked at her with such intensity she wondered if he had been thinking about her. About them.

It surprised her she could even consider establishing a relationship, given the current predicament. Maybe they were doomed to this—always close, but never close enough. Too much time together with the gun out and the safety off. At some point, they had to talk about it.

Maybe she was wrong about him. It wouldn't be the first time. She let the thought pass. For now, there were more pressing matters. She'd better get back to business, before they were all wearing their brains on the outside of their heads.

By the set of his shoulders, Nick was in business mode. His face was a blank mask, meaning she was wrong about him thinking about her. Pushing her feelings aside, she figured it didn't matter anyway. For now, getting out of here was the priority.

Nick stood, stuffing the granola bar in his pocket. "I'm going to see what's below this place."

"I'll go with you—" Meredith began.

He waved her away. "Don't need you. Be back in a few."

And he was gone.

Ignoring her bruised feelings, Meredith sat cross-legged on the floor beside Cav. Clenching the granola bar wrapper with her teeth, she tore it open and took a bite. It tasted like cardboard with a chocolate coating that had separated—from sitting in DeGraf's car on the way up. Yeesh. But Cav was right—it filled the hole.

The concrete emanated a chill. It was a welcome relief from the heat of the day. Cavanaugh and Meredith sat in comfortable silence, exhausted yet keyed up.

When he spoke, his voice was low. It was his story and he'd tell it how he wanted. It was for her alone, but he made her work to hear the words. "I spent three years in Viet Nam, U.S. Marine Corps. Left Khe Sanh in June of 1968."

Her voice was almost a whisper. "Wasn't it a big battle? Like, the Tet Offensive?"

"Big, yes, but I was miles from the places where the Tet was being fought. General Westmoreland lost his job because he bolstered up the defenses there. But a lot of politicians in Washington thought Khe Sanh was just a diversion from the Tet." He rubbed his eyes. "Our side lost 155 men, the Viet Cong, over five thousand in 77 days."

Meredith blew out a breath. "That's a lot of death."

"'Crack the sky, shake the earth.'" In his periphery, Cavanaugh saw her brows draw together with confusion. "That was the message to the People's Army of Viet Nam. To the Communists, there was only one Viet

Nam. The South was considered a renegade state. The Army was told they were going into the greatest battle in the history of their country."

Cavanaugh turned to her, watching her face. The detective's eyes widened as she waited for him to continue.

His mind was a world away while his sinewy fingers shredded the granola bar wrapper. "My squad was on a plane headed for Hue City. Got re-routed to Khe Sanh in the air. They were under mortar attack. The plane didn't even stop. We had to bail out on the landing strip. I was in a re-con group, and we were ordered forward to protect the outposts in the hills from bombardment from the NVA mortars."

His lips curled into a smile. "It was funny—the hills were so serene. The trees in the fog reminded me of home. But you turn around, and you're in a combat zone." His smile faded. Anyway, we fought all night, shooting at anything that moved, screamed or yelled. The grenades went off so close, they blew dirt and blood all over us. Then, when Charlie made it to our trenches, it was hand-to-hand." He dropped the last corner of the wrapper. "It's a different thing—fighting up close with your enemy. Different than shooting, where you see muzzle blasts. In the trench, they were so close I could smell the stink of their fear just before I killed them."

He glanced at Meredith. Sweat beaded on her upper lip. It was as he thought: she'd been there.

"It's personal, then. Doesn't matter if he's the enemy or not." After a few moments, he said, "It takes away a little piece of your humanity, I guess. I'm no psychologist or philosopher, but I know you're never the same afterward."

Meredith's voice was small. "How did you function—after?"

"When I came back to the world, everything was different. Anti-war protests in the streets," he sighed. "The military was a dirty word. People were either hawks or doves, and no one admitted to being a soldier. I was lucky. I had a good woman who loved me and a life we'd built together. She let me work out my problems, but kept on loving me—no matter what crap I dished out."

"Does it ever come back to you? I mean, the fear?"

"I can't say I was afraid for myself." He paused as he put words to things that had bothered him for decades. "I had to kill them before they killed me. Simple. Besides, I fought for my buddies, not my country. My only fear was that I'd let my pals down."

The silence hung between them. He wondered if her mind was following where he led. "Thing is—I did what needed doing." Her eyes caught his and held them as he continued. "It was war. People kill each other. When it was done, I came home and resumed my life."

"But you said you're different after you kill a person."

His head bobbed. "It's true. I couldn't change my history, any more than if I'd had an arm amputated. I learned to live with it."

"An amputation is visible."

"True. Easier to 'hide' what I did." He sighed. "If you have a physical disability, people feel like they need to help you, make excuses for you. Doesn't matter whether it's from guilt or helpfulness. It made me question my morality. It got in the way of healing. I couldn't let that happen." He shrugged. "If they don't know my history, I don't tell them."

"Healing." She echoed the word.

"Yeah." Cavanaugh pulled off his Stetson and rested his head against the cool concrete wall. He was growing weary of talking, but needed to finish his thought. She'd understand. "Call it whatever you want—getting over it, moving on, healing, whatever. Reliving it means staying there. That's not good."

After a minute, Meredith put her hand on his arm. "You said your wife helped."

"It was easier for me than for her. She had to put up with my temper, my drinking, and my bad dreams." A glance at her told him she'd been there, too. "Because of her, the drinking didn't get a hold of me. She made me take part in my kids' lives. She wouldn't let me feel sorry for myself. And there was the ranch. Nothing would get done if I didn't get out and do it. I had mouths to feed. Shirley did all the work while I was overseas. She had a little help from a Mexican neighbor fella, but she fed the cattle and took care of our boys." A grin took hold of a corner of his mouth. "Like I said, it was harder on her than me."

Two heartbeats later, she said, "I killed two men."

He knew they'd been in the same place. This darkness of doubt was made worse by ignoring it or giving in to it. He waited for her next question.

"How do you 'move on'?"

"Be tougher, meaner than it is—"

The plea in her eyes told him she hadn't bought into his tough guy bullshit. He knew better, but it was hard to turn it off.

"Right." Raymond Cavanaugh exhaled with the relief of telling the truth after all these years and knowing his experience might help this young woman. She was one of the rare individuals who'd found that honest place in him. "Everybody's different. For me, the answer was to trust myself. I knew what I did was a necessary evil, one I couldn't avoid. It didn't make me a bad person. I did what I had to, to get out alive." He let his words sink in. They helped him, too, as he said them. "Make the experience part of who you, are but don't let it push you around."

CHAPTER FORTY-FIVE

Thursday, May 21, early afternoon

When Nick returned, Cavanaugh and Meredith were both resting against a wall. Quashing a sudden jerk inside his chest, he saw the ease with which they sat together. Why couldn't she be that comfortable with him anymore, damn it? They used to be able to confide in each other. Nick was sure she'd been talking to him. Funny, because she was so guarded about what she said to strangers.

Not that Cavanaugh was a stranger, anymore. He'd taken care of himself and saved them from—what? Being killed? Being taken hostage? Some kind of trouble, for sure.

In a sudden insight, he saw what Meredith liked about the old rancher. He was tough, and while he didn't tell them what to do, he knew what needed to be done. He lived and breathed these hills—but wouldn't give advice until asked. Nick appreciated people who didn't talk too much.

"Mr. Cavanaugh? Mere, nothing down there that will help us. Let's get moving. We'll head west."

Outside, they walked through the debris. Each area around the blasts was defined by small craters. The Quonset hut stood like a shapeless hulk, a portion of its walls peeled like a sardine can. Metal sheathing crumpled at the surrounding sheds, with cinder block walls shattered and wood framing splintered. The structures were damaged beyond repair.

Nick sighed. "Unbelievable." He used a stick to turn over a chunk of smoldering 2' by 4'. "It's a good thing you heard them coming, Mr. Cavanaugh."

"Easy. I heard a truck coming. Figured it meant trouble. The grenades were a surprise, though."

"Glad you got back here to warn us," Meredith said. "If you hadn't, we could've been in big trouble."

Cavanaugh snuffled a sound that might have been a chuckle. "Instinct." He toed aside a splintered two by four. It slid off a cinder block with a crash.

Meredith walked past him and bent to retrieve Nick's ball cap. "Here." Smoke wafting from the bill, she handed the hat to Nick. "You're gonna need this."

He rubbed the top of his head where the sunburn was starting. "Thanks." Nick squinted at the scene. "I'm going to take some pictures. Use my camera."

Cavanaugh's hand wrapped around the crown of his Stetson, settling it on his head. "I'll come with you."

The two men set off for the short walk to the opposite end of the base. Meredith trailed behind.

The creases at the old man's eyes hinted Cavanaugh had some experience with the devastation, and a lot more. "You see this kind of thing before, Mr. Cavanaugh?" Nick asked.

"Not here, no. Saw enough to know trouble when I hear it."

"Viet Nam?" Nick suggested.

Cavanaugh nodded.

They walked in silence to the epicenter of the nearest blast—rocks blasted into gravel. Tendrils of smoke curled from the wreckage of what had been a shed. Twisted panels of metal curled from the intense heat, peeled like a banana. Surrounding it, the burned earth created an eerie moonscape-like scene. Singed wood and other debris had fallen twenty feet from each of the dozen explosions. The acrid smell of material consumed by fire was thick in the air.

The destruction belied the stillness of the afternoon. It was as if the very particles of air were filled with the memory of the explosions. The sudden, violent vacuum was gone. And now, after the fact, shattered molecules stumbled back into the space.

"There." Cavanaugh pointed to a crater. He used his whole hand to paint a picture of the grenades' damage. "The blast sent fragments out this way." The pattern of the explosions flattened the area for twenty-feet rendering the base useless. Metal shards and chunks of wood framing had blown in all directions igniting a dozen small grass fires. "These spot fires are going to be a problem if they spread." He kicked dirt on the nearest patch—a foot square—and knocked it down. He moved to another and did the same. "I'm a volunteer firefighter up here." A third blaze glided along the compound's lip burning dry oat grass and scrub. Cavanaugh stared after it.

"What kind of person does this?" Nick wondered aloud. Why do they do it? And why are they trying to kill us?

"The answers are all around you." Cavanaugh looked around. "This was the militia's doing. No one up here to snoop around. None of my neighbors has a reason or the time for this. They're all too busy making a living."

Nick stopped, moving a ragged panel of corrugated metal out of their path.

"These are brutal people who enjoy hurting others—I've seen their kind before." Cavanaugh squinted into the sun. "People who reshape laws to suit their needs. As for their targets—we are on the list. Doesn't matter why."

"Good point. But I'd still like to know." Nick couldn't wrap his mind around this one. "They must think we know something that will expose their mission. Did we get in their way? And what are they planning?"

"Whatever it is, it's bad." Cavanaugh seated his hat square on his head and shrugged. "Could have something to do with the race. They don't much like Mexicans these days. But they pretty much hate everybody else. Truth is, I guess, they have to be stopped."

Cavanaugh was right. These guys had to be stopped.

Nick squatted to take a few pictures with his phone of the holes left behind from the grenades. He'd take another for perspective of the whole scene before they left. But he had to save the phone battery for the call he'd make—soon.

He straightened, feeling the weight of his job and a strain in his lower back. Faint wisps of smoke drifted in from the base boundary. "Let's get moving," he said to Meredith. "We need to get some help—fast."

Cavanaugh put a hand on Nick's arm. "You realize that they're playing for keeps?" The rancher's gaze penetrated his resistance.

"Yeah." Nick's irritation rose. "What's your point?" He was telling them how to do their job. It didn't seem like part of Cavanaugh's aloof manner. *Maybe you better listen.*

Cavanaugh pulled Nick around face to face. "It means kill them dead before they kill you."

Nick knew he was right. While he had to play by the rules, the militia didn't—and wouldn't to achieve their goals. Cavanaugh was telling him bluntly that they had to match the militia's aggression. The rancher must have taken Nick's silence for hesitation over using lethal force.

"These guys will take you out without a thought. Like you were a fly buzzing around a pile of shit." Cavanaugh released his hand, straightening. "You can't arrest them, detain them or tie them up until help comes. There's too many of them close by and only the two of you. You kill them first before they make a corpse out of you."

The rancher's lips pressed together signaling the end of his speech. He pulled off his Stetson, wiped his brow with the crook of his arm. Then replacing the hat, he stomped through the field of debris.

Nick was silent. Cavanaugh had said it all.

CHAPTER FORTY-SIX

Thursday, May 21, early afternoon

Meredith watched Cav shift his battered Stetson after wiping the sweat off his forehead. He was right. She knew what kind of force they must use to win over the militia. The possibility of getting into a fight with them haunted her like a vulture circling over a road kill.

Hiking from the base, Nick led them up a narrow game trail to the summit of the highest hill where he'd make the call. Cav followed, then Meredith. It was a steady but gradual climb in late spring sunshine and she figured it to be around three in the afternoon. She could only estimate because she used her cell phone for telling time. She reached into her pocket, instantly missing her phone. But she found a hair band and pulled her thick auburn mane up into a ponytail. Her hairline was drenched with perspiration.

After a while, Cav's stride slowed, then he stumbled and righted himself. He paused, his breath coming in gasps.

"I could use a breather," Meredith called to Nick. Pointing to a granite boulder, she steered Cav to its shade. "We've been walking uphill for over an hour." The rancher sat and she rooted around in her pack to pull out a fist full of granola bars. "Anyone hungry?"

They ate, leaning their backs against the shaded rock. Cavanaugh pulled off his Stetson and cradled it in his lap. Meredith passed around her water bottle.

Before they could settle in, Nick rose. "We gotta get moving."

Meredith groaned, then rose. She held out her hand to Cav. After a brief hesitation, he took it.

As she pulled him up, he mumbled, "I hate slowing you folks down."

A corner of Nick's mouth turned up in a half-smile. "You're doing fine,

Mr. Cavanaugh."

The rancher wiped the back of his neck with a red bandana, then slipped on his hat. "Maybe I should wait here for you."

Nick's smile evaporated. "We stay together. That's non-negotiable."

"Alright," Cavanaugh's wavy hair dangled in his eyes, obscuring them. She got the feeling he was studying Nick. Then, he replaced his hat, dipping the brim low almost obscuring his eyes. "No man left behind, eh?"

Their gazes locked. Nick had seen the surreptitious study, too. "Something like that," Nick answered.

The two men set out, side by side. Meredith listened to them talk. "You've got my respect, Detective. It would've been easy to leave me here." A gnarly hand swept the surroundings. "It's not like I don't know this country. Hell, this is probably my land."

"It's not the countryside that's dangerous, Mr. Cavanaugh."

"I realize that, sergeant." The rancher squinted at Nick. "But I'm not without resources."

Nick slowed, surprised at Cavanaugh's response. Cavanaugh stopped, put a boot heel on a rock and pulled up a pant leg. Inside the shank of the rancher's work boot revealed an ankle holster with a snub-nosed .38 caliber revolver.

Meredith couldn't help smiling. She shouldn't have been surprised. She liked the old man's quiet strength. No way would she leave him behind, even if they had a choice. Just because he was old didn't mean he wasn't capable. He'd proven himself several times over. She loved seeing the amazement in Nick's eyes.

Finally, Nick laughed, then eyed the hill. "Ready?"

In that moment, something happened that Meredith couldn't put her finger on. It was like Nick acknowledged Cavanaugh had earned his position within the trio. The fact that Cav—a civilian—had alerted them to the coming base attack was huge. Truthfully, she'd known he could hold his own after they hid in the grotto.

The two men walked side by side with an easy camaraderie. As she set off behind them, Meredith thought she smelled smoke. She turned to look.

A mile away, two hills over where the antennae stood, fire licked up one of the digger pines surrounding the radio base. It exploded into flames.

CHAPTER FORTY-SEVEN

Thursday, May 21, early afternoon

Jerry Steiner sat at a kitchen table inside a dilapidated trailer at the hunting camp he and his men had taken over. He never got used to the quiet. He couldn't explain it, but he needed noise, activity and energy around him. The stillness of this place disoriented him. But this was the best place for them to organize, train and prepare for their mission. Because it was so remote, the site enabled them to do what they needed without prying eyes of neighbors or cops. Of course, the very fact that it was remote also brought its own set of problems. Getting up and down the hill to Highway 101 without being spotted could only be done during the night. Although there'd been one pain-in-the-ass patrol deputy who sat at the Warm Springs Bridge watching for anything on the road that moved. It hadn't taken too long to figure out his schedule and take steps to avoid him.

No one else moved after dark in Dry Creek. Winery tourists visited the valley floor's vineyards on paved but narrow country lanes during the day. The roads twisted around low hills graduating into Dry Creek uplands and Lake Sonoma. After sunset, the way was hazardous because of the windy route, the lack of lighting as well as the abundant wildlife crossings.

Tonight, his men would make the trek down the hills and south to Highway 101. The convoy of a dozen vehicles would not be noticed.

Steiner smiled when he considered the effects of his plans. If the Supervisors didn't meet his demand by tomorrow noon, he'd turn loose his avenging "angels" on Sonoma County. By then the cops would be crushed and unable to respond to disturbances from an irate public clamoring for solutions. The breakdown of Sonoma County would be catastrophic.

But now, Steiner awaited the report from the squad he'd assigned to patrol the roads around their compound. As crudely as it had been done, the Lewis brothers had taken care of the narc and his pals, the deputies.

At least he didn't have to worry about them. While he didn't see corpses, nothing could have lived through their attack.

All his preparations were set. The plan would be in motion within hours. He glanced at his watch—less than four hours to be precise. He would be at the head of the caravan that would travel to highway 101. Assigned vehicles loaded with ammonium nitrate and gas cans filled with fuel oil, commonly called ANFO, along with their detonators, were to peel off to their destinations. Targets were the five major police agencies in the county: California Highway Patrol office in Rohnert Park, Sonoma County Sheriff's Office, and Santa Rosa PD in Santa Rosa, Rohnert Park Department of Public Safety and Petaluma Police Department.

In a stroke of genius, Steiner volunteered to help with traffic control around the Tour of California Bicycle Race. The route took cyclists right past the Santa Rosa Police Department—Sonoma Avenue and Brookwood. With a smile, he imagined the chaos as a truck labeled "SRPD" parked in the front lot exploded while fifty to one hundred of the world's best cyclists pedal by. Televised, no less.

Assaults on the departments would be coordinated in a chilling stroke of devastation. With vehicles loaded with explosives and painted like department trucks, there would be no difficulty getting them in or near police facilities.

Steiner's lieutenant, George Franks had assigned strategic positions to his teams from Susanville. They'd be in place to help make sure vehicles loaded with the ammonium nitrate were parked for optimum damage.

Steiner's Escalade would follow the Lewis brothers' truck which carried the cryptosporidium pathogen. They would be loosened at the Redwood Water Agency's Collector Wells. Before the caravan hit Highway 101 in Santa Rosa, Steiner and the Lewis' would turn off to their destination at Rolling Hills Estates.

Steiner sent Franks to make sure the Lewis brothers didn't screw this up. He knew an operation of this magnitude would cost the lives of some of his men. Though the Lewis's mission was the simplest piece of the plan, it was critical. Steiner had no qualms about releasing the toxin if not paid on time. When he got the money, he could always stop the discharge of the crypto—or not. With Franks to keep an eye on them, the task would go as planned. The microorganisms could reach all half million Sonoma County residents in less than two hours. But it must be contained until he gave Franks the word. After Steiner received the money, the brothers were expendable.

Settling back in the chair, Jerry Steiner sighed and closed his eyes. He recalled a day years past, he thought about his father. If he could only see him now.

His daddy squatted in front of him, his pores stinking of last night's beer. "You listen to your Daddy." His father squeezed his chin, holding it firmly inches from his own. "Pay attention, now. Don't be a loser, boy. When you do something, do it big—so it means something."

What was he talking about? Maybe Ronnie Potts? That stupid kid had made his life miserable for months, pushing him around, taking his lunch bags, and yesterday, giving him a black eye. Ronnie Potts was the biggest kid in the fifth grade. That dickface had humiliated Jerry for the last time. He couldn't hide the beating from his Daddy now. The bruised eye socket told the tale. Someone was thumping on him at school.

He looked at his Daddy's bloodshot eyes. He knew.

"Daddy, I can explain—"

Jerry's father gripped his Tee-shirt and slapped the side of his head. "No excuses, kid. No excuses. Make him pay and make him remember it."

Yes, Daddy would be proud.

CHAPTER FORTY-EIGHT

Thursday, May 21, early afternoon

Pacing himself to save energy, Nick settled into an ambling stride next to Cavanaugh. The slope was a sea of green and golden oat grass, transitioning between sparse growth and maturity after the four-year drought. A light breeze blew across the hill, cool enough to suggest it came from the ocean. The going was easy enough for Cavanaugh.

Thirty minutes later, after an uneventful climb up a narrow ravine, they reached the summit. Set into the hilltop was a granite boulder large enough to shelter them from the wind. With his hand clamped on his Stetson, Cavanaugh folded his legs and dropped to his butt, leaning against the rock. Meredith rested but stayed on her feet, watching.

Nick pulled out his phone. Three bars. He punched in the number for the dispatch business line.

"Sonoma County Sheriff's Office."

"This is Sergeant Nick Reyes from VCI." Twenty people always on duty in dispatch and he never talked to the same one twice.

"Sergeant Reyes!" The excitement in her voice took him by surprise. "Lieutenant Ferrua has been looking for you. Hold on and I'll transfer you to his cell."

"Wait, wait!" Nick shouted, to be heard over the wind.

An embarrassed voice replied, "Yes, sir?"

"There's a fire in the Dry Creek hills. We're off Rockpile Road. I don't know the mile marker but our units are parked on the shoulder of the road. It's the access point for the homicide up here."

Tap, tap, tap. "Okay, I see the incident. Using that landmark, where are you?"

It took a few moments to narrow down their location but soon, the dispatcher had enough info to send Cal Fire and the local volunteers. "Now, you can transfer me to Lieutenant Ferrua."

Clicks and pauses, then Nick heard Gil Ferrua's blustery voice. "Jesus Christ, Reyes. Where the hell are you?"

"The middle of nowhere, Lieutenant."

"Stop joking around, Reyes. We've got to get you outta there." Ferrua's voice rose. Nick pictured a warm summer morning in San Quintin, Baja Mexico, while visiting his mother's family when he was a kid. Auntie had chopped the head off a chicken and its headless body skittered around the barnyard until it dropped, spent. Auntie's sly smile made Nick believe she'd done it to shock the city boy. Now he knew it was a post-mortem muscle spasm.

The lieutenant's conversation ran around in much the same way. "You can ping my cell," Nick said. "I've had it off to save the battery. But listen—"

"We've got a situation here and I need all hands. That means you and Ryan, ASAP."

"Gil, listen to me."

"I don't care where you are in your homicide investigation. I want—"

His boss' hysteria was getting in the way. "Lieutenant, stop and listen." Nick paused for Ferrua's shocked attention. "There's a militia up here, The Covenant Family—they're domestic terrorists. They've got something planned—something big and it's going to happen soon."

Even with the wind gusting around him, Nick heard Ferrua's deflated sigh. The words domestic terrorists got his attention. "For Christ's sake. What kind of something?"

"I don't know. But they're serious enough that they came after us when the DOJ Agent was driving down the hill. Gil," he cleared his throat. "They killed the DOJ guy."

"What? Why didn't you—" the Lieutenant stopped. His voice deepened. "What happened?"

"We were in the agent's Jeep headed back to Santa Rosa. We weren't a mile from the radio towers when a truck slammed us off the road and down a cliff. He came at us deliberately and with obvious intent, more than once."

"What happened to the agent—what's his name?"

"DeGraffenreid." Nick tried to find the exact words. "Ryan, the RP and I got out before the Jeep went to the bottom. DeGraf was pinned behind the wheel." Nick's throat thickened with emotion. He'd seen murder many times before, he wasn't used to being there when it happened.

"Are you sure he's—"

"I'm sure, Gil. He's dead."

"Fuck." Gil Ferrua blew a low whistle. "Are they living up there? What the hell are they doing in the middle of nowhere?" Without giving Nick a moment to answer, Ferrua asked yet another question. "Do you know where they are encamped?"

Nick wasn't surprised at the lieutenant's question. "They must be within walking distance," he said, remembering the troop that trudged past them. "I know where you're going with this but we have a civilian with us. Remember, the rancher who reported the homicide?"

"Christ, you never make it easy, do you, Nick? Can you stash the RP somewhere safe and reconnoiter? See if you can find out what's going on."

"Listen, Gil." Nick felt the hair on his neck stand up. "You better fuckin' listen to me."

"Wha—?"

"These guys are stone killers. And we're two deputies up here out-manned, out-gunned, on foot and no dependable communication. We have to get out of here."

"With no wheels, the fastest way out is by air. Henry One is still tied up with the rescue. Highway Patrol in Napa cleared that call but their chopper is down with a mechanical problem. I'll call them to send it as soon as it can fly. Depending on repairs, it may take a few hours, though. Dispatch can ping your phone for your location so be sure it's on by say, seven p.m.""

Nick got the feeling Ferrua picked the time out of his ass.

Sounding frustrated, the Lieutenant huffed into the phone. "What can you tell me now about them besides what I've already heard? How many are there? What kind of firepower do they have, vehicles, supplies and so on?"

"I've seen a minimum of a dozen guys up here. They drill and practice with their rifles. They all carried different side arms, looks like they pack their own. Rifles were AK-47's and AR-15's. Bet they're all modified to be fully automatic." Nick sighed, worrying about the battery life on his phone—among other things. He'd left the flashlight behind.

"Which means they're illegal. I could call ATF."

Sometimes people weren't promoted because they are smart. "Fuck, Gil." Nick had a hard time not shouting at the absurdity of this conversation. "There's only one reason for so many guys to move in formation, wear cammies, and carry assault rifles."

"Yeah," Ferrua sighed into the phone. "Stay away enough to protect yourselves and the civilian, but keep your ears and eyes open. Maybe snoop around, you have a few hours."

"Hours? You're not getting this: we need to get out now." Nick's voice rose in the long-suppressed shout. The lieutenant didn't have a clue of the relative distances by foot in the Dry Creek area. Given their limited time, four hours, how the hell were they supposed to find the militia compound, then make it to a safe place where a helicopter could pick them up? He finally decided they were on their own until the Highway Patrol helo got there.

"Be someplace where the chopper can land at 7 p.m." Ferrua added, "And Nick—watch your ass." The call ended.

"Wait." Unbelievable. After shutting the phone off, Nick's fingers wrapped around it like it was a baseball. He wound up for a furious pitch to get Ferrua as far away as possible but stopped himself just short of throwing it. Anger wouldn't help the situation. Fuck.

He shoved his rage out of his mind then inspected his phone. Only a third of the charge remained in Nick's phone. He powered it down so he could use it at 7 p.m. He'd take Ferrua to task when he got back to the Main. The lieutenant had left the three of them in peril for too long. Nick shook his head, wondering what Ferrua had been thinking. At the office, when he made suggestions, Ferrua followed through. Nick wished he'd told his boss to call 'mutual aid' and get help from another agency. The nearest airship was CHP Sacramento, not much farther than Napa, about sixty miles. Ferrua often liked Nick's ideas—for obvious reasons.

He punched in Ferrua's number again. The call dropped.

Meredith tapped Nick's shoulder. "Hey, look." She pointed behind him.

Clouds of white smoke billowed from where they'd come. A mile away the fire lapped at a pine tree, and catching. The smoke went dark as the tree burned.

CHAPTER FORTY-NINE

Thursday, May 21, mid-afternoon

"Smoke turns black from the resin in a pine tree," Cavanaugh said, watching a digger pine burn. "The tree heats to the point that it gives off a flammable vapor before it can burn."

Nick saw raw intelligence behind the rancher's eyes. There's more to this guy than he lets on.

Cavanaugh continued, "The wood has to be heated to the ignition temperature which occurs when the material changes to a gas. The grass fire ignites the gas, and it blows."

Nick had to reach back to high school chemistry, to recall this same lesson. Then, he thought of something else. "The grenade blasts started small fires around the whole area. Maybe that was the fire's origin. Will it get much bigger? Will the fire reach us on top of that hill?"

Cavanaugh shrugged. "Depends on a lot of factors—the wind, the fuel load. But yes, it could get here." He eyed the boulder above. "We better hope the helicopter can find us."

"We have an optimistic date with CHP at seven p.m." He glanced at his watch then looked at Meredith. "Ferrua wants us to find the militia's camp before we leave."

"We should've expected that," Meredith sighed. "Let me guess—he wants Cav stashed someplace safe."

"I figured I'd let the man decide." Nick met Cavanaugh's gaze. The old guy had a little trouble keeping up but had handled himself fine. "Mr. Cavanaugh, my lieutenant wants you to hide someplace out of danger. I'm not sure that exists up here today. What d'you say?"

Cavanaugh yanked off his Stetson and glanced down the canyon at the radio base. "I think I'm safest with you two."

Satisfied, Nick pointed toward a stretch of dirt road tucked into the hillside below them. "Should be easy enough to track all those boot prints back to their camp. We need to watch our time closely if the helo's going to pick us up at seven."

They started down the hill.

Their pace was steady and Cavanaugh managed with no trouble. Even with a wildland fire in the mix, they made progress. Downhill was easy. When they got to the road, the tracks were clear. Leaving such an obvious sign, the militia must have thought there was no danger of discovery. They'd believed the detectives died.

The wind picked up, a zephyr at first that refreshed them from the heat. As the day lengthened, the breeze turned gusty. The fire behind them was building, but Cavanaugh kept an eye on it and said they needed to keep moving.

Nick hoped the man knew what he was talking about.

CHAPTER FIFTY

Thursday, May 21, mid-afternoon

Meredith pulled her ball cap lower over her eyes, trying to escape the glare from the relentless sun. Her sunglasses were stowed in her day pack and she didn't want to stop to fish them out. The wind had died down. They followed the tracks for thirty minutes stopping in a tree-shaded ravine. The route twisted around a hillock and disappeared. She studied the terrain. Green oat grass bleaching to gold in the sun, game trails criss-crossing the hills, and oak trees in the shallow arroyos that sliced through the ridges. No concealment except the oaks.

"I thought of something," Cavanaugh said. He sat on a low branch, took off his Stetson, and ran his fingers through his longish gray hair. "There was a family who built a hunting camp up here in the late forties. They gave it up about ten years ago. I heard there's buildings and such but they're bound to be dilapidated by now. It don't take too long for nature to reclaim itself up here." He slipped on his hat. "My neighbor mentioned it to me a few days back. I'd bet money that's where these goons have taken over. Squatters come and go up here. Like paradise in the summer but it's harder living than it looks." His blue eyes held Meredith's attention. "This road goes right past it. Been years since I was up there but it shouldn't take more than an hour if you stay on this road."

"What if we walked over these hills?" Meredith nodded toward the peaks to the west of them. "Would it be quicker?"

Nick frowned as Cavanaugh replied. "As the crow flies, yes. It would be much shorter."

"Nick? What do you think?"

"It looks like pretty rough terrain. I'm not sure we can make it." Nick sounded like he hadn't wanted to say it.

Cavanaugh sighed. "You two go and I'll stay here."

Meredith's protest chimed with Nick's. "No, we stay together."

Cavanaugh checked his watch. "You two going overland would be much faster. We don't have much time. Besides, I've got my pea-shooter." He motioned to his ankle holster. "If I have to, I can duck behind the rocks. I'm pretty good at surviving—military taught me well."

Meredith understood his logic. In spite of the decision he'd made a few hours ago, this just made sense. "Why don't we scout out this place and get back here quick?"

"All right," Nick sighed. "Let's get this over with. I want to join up so we can leave together."

CHAPTER FIFTY-ONE

Thursday, May 21, mid-afternoon

Meredith set out at a slow jog uphill, gangly stalks of oat grass slapping against her pants with Nick two paces behind. Cavanaugh's directions shortened the trip above the gravel road. By snaking around hills and ducking into tree-covered ravines, they covered the distance in less than thirty minutes. A gusty wind came up again, but the steady climb drenched Meredith in sweat. They'd climbed the last half mile of a gradually rising plateau, using the cover of trees and approached what should have been a derelict hunting camp .

Near the crest of the hill, Meredith caught her first glimpse of the settlement Cav had described. Set in an oblong valley of several acres, the structures had been built on the perimeter of a large flat field. Along the sides, caved-in roof-lines of the two long horse barns mirrored the shell of a tiny house slumping sideways. The dirt and gravel road curled ten feet from a 1950's-vintage house trailer. From there, it worked its way beyond, maybe all the way to the Pacific Ocean thirty miles away. Opposite the barns sat a new three-sided equipment shed. There was movement near the barns but Meredith needed a better vantage point to see what was going on.

Rather than risk exposure, they skirted the slope, dropping down and picking their way through a narrow creek bed. At the stream's beginnings, they crouched on a shelf. In years past, part of the slope had eroded from the relentless pressure of the heavy seasonal rains. The rocky ravine was deep enough to conceal them. Between here and the camp lay a meadow bordered on three sides with orderly rows of generations-old eucalyptus. Foreign to the terrain, the trees were evidence of man's alteration of nature. They were stiff old codgers that stood out among the gently rounded valley oak and shapely laurels. Eucalyptus was an effective wind break as their planter had surely intended. But a shallow root system made them vulnerable to high winds and their oily trunk was unusable for lumber.

To their right rose a rock outcropping, shaped like a shoulder. Meredith thought it the perfect placement for a lookout. She'd check to see if there was someone on watch.

She tapped Nick's shoulder, pointing to the rock. A thumb to her chest, then palm sideways, she signed she'd be moving up there.

Nick stayed put, watching her back. Going up the cut, struggling against inertia to stay quiet, she found the base of the rock. A narrow path lay before her, beaten by recent boot traffic. She glanced at the twenty-foot escarpment—plenty of hand and foot holds. She decided to climb it instead of walking the path.

Ten feet to the right of the path, she reached up into the rock.

A second of panic set in as she remembered some good-ole boy stories she'd heard at the Duncan Mills Rodeo about hunters and fishermen climbing rocks and reaching into a coiled rattlesnake. Climbing like she was. She always figured they were merely telling stories but they worked on her that moment. She took a deep breath, swallowed and her fingers curled around the knobby hand hold.

She caught a wisp of cigarette smoke. Someone was nearby. Pulling herself upward, her shoe bounced against the rock. She paused, balancing on a shallow lip, praying no one heard her foot hitting granite.

When no response came from above, she lifted a knee and climbed up. On the rock, she paralleled the path and climbed until she spotted the sentry, twenty feet away. A teen, curly red-hair blowing in the breeze, sat cross-legged in position to overlook the plateau and part of the road. He puffed on a cigarette while an empty paper plate beside him held the remnants of a meal.

With an AR-15 strapped on his shoulder, the teen was a menace she couldn't ignore.

She squinted into the sun then ducked behind a coyote brush for the moment getting a sense of what was going on, nearby and in the distance. She focused on the activity beyond the eucalyptus. Men moved purposefully from one building to another. She saw another structure—the house trailer on the south had a sagging lean-to attached. Between the trailer and the equipment shed, the field was vacant. Likely, it had once been used for grazing but the ground had been packed down. Plenty of foot traffic.

Of the dozen figures Meredith saw, most were moving toward the shed. From her angle, she couldn't see what was attracting them. If she could move, she might be able to see what they were doing. Maybe get a clue to their intention.

She held her position, considering what she observed. Ferrua had been clear—try to find out where the threat was based. They'd done that. She could leave now and tell the lieutenant exactly where these vigilantes were. But she couldn't tell him what the actual risk was.

They had another two hours until they could meet the helo. It would take them an hour to get to the helo rendezvous point. They had time to check this out. She and Nick could ease down to the encampment and listen at the shed. The con arguments were the possibility of other sentries and the clock.

The more she thought it over, the more she wanted the militia's plans. If she and Nick missed the helicopter pick-up, they'd be in big trouble. She weighed the issues. Meet the helicopter versus get substantive intel that could help combat the danger. Why were these renegades here, in this remote part of the county? If she got the info, would it be possible to relay it to the department? Did the Sheriff's office have any previous info on a possible incident? Did the Gang Unit know the militia was here?

This couldn't be her decision alone.

Backing toward the escarpment, moving to climb back down, she stepped on a dry twig, snapping it in half. She froze. The sound was like a shot in the silence of the afternoon.

The sentry with the wild hair, Curly Red, whipped his head around, pivoting on a hip then up to his knee, the AR pointed toward the noise. His cigarette dropped to the ground as his gaze settled on Meredith. Stiffening, he said, "Who the hell are you?"

Meredith was caught. She watched Curly Red's eyes widen as he took in the holstered gun on her waist. He walked toward her, three paces—within five feet—then stopped. With his off arm out, it looked like he was reaching for her Beretta. Then his arm dropped and with both hands on the AR, he straightened. "Drop the gun."

She stood to her full height, taking a moment to assess his risk. He wasn't a pro, not with reactions like that. "I'm not going to drop anything, kid. This is a seven-hundred-dollar gun. I'm not going to let the rock gouge it up."

He made a little puffing noise with his mouth. "Okay, then put it down. Careful-like." He pointed downward with his rifle.

Meredith pulled the Beretta out with her right hand, her left visible in front. She bent, wobbled and as the gun hovered above the ground, she grasped a handful of dirt and flung it at Curly Red's face.

The boy winced and shook his head but tightened his grip on the rifle. Meredith kicked it out of his hands. The rifle clattered against the stones out of reach as he stumbled backwards. He skidded against the loose rock, lost his footing and pitched over and down the cliff.

A dull thud, a sound like an egg cracking open.

She knew before she looked over the edge. Twenty feet below, Curly Red's head wound bled onto the gray granite. His eyes staring up at her in a blank accusation. Meredith dropped to her knees, her lungs pushing the air out of her body.

Another death. She'd been spotted and had to respond. Though she hadn't pulled the trigger, he was dead because of her. Crap.

After a moment, she pulled herself together. She had to get back to Nick.

She headed down the rock and to the creek to where Nick waited. Dropping to a rock beside him, he asked. "Did you see anything?"

"Yeah, but I'd have to get closer and there's no cover here. They had at least one sentry which makes me think they have more. They'd make us in a heartbeat."

"Had?"

"He fell off a cliff. He looks dead."

After she filled him in on the encampment, he searched her eyes. "Are you okay?"

With a weak smile, she mumbled an affirmative.

"You want to go for it, don't you?"

She chewed her lip, then said, "We're not only fighting the clock to get picked up. That's crucial, because we have to get the civilian to safety. But, it's a tough choice—these douche bags could be putting their plan in motion any time now. Wouldn't the lieutenant need to know to make an effective stop? The more intel he has, the better he can plan."

Nick sighed. "We got their location, but—" Glancing at his watch, he said, "We've got thirty minutes. A quick look around, then, we get Cavanaugh and meet the helo."

CHAPTER FIFTY-TWO

Thursday, May 21, mid-afternoon

Back at Curly Red's look-out, Nick picked up the AR-15. He glanced over the cliff at the corpse—he was definitely dead.

He wondered how much more Meredith could handle. No, she was a pro. She wouldn't let anything get in the way of her doing her job.

"Okay, what do we have here? Let's list our facts." Nick looked at her to begin.

She took a deep breath. "First, a homicide, a card-carrying member of the Covenant Family. On the body, we find a map of downtown Santa Rosa."

Nick nodded. "The map has the same routes marked as Jerry Steiner's map that we saw the next day."

"Yeah, and he started out denying that he had it until DeGraf called him on it."

"Right." He watched her. "And the soldiers who walked by us said something about preparations for a mission. Somewhere around downtown Santa Rosa, if the map is right."

"And they're serious enough that they aren't afraid to kill cops," she added.

Nick gave her a solemn nod.

"I haven't made sense of it, yet. At any rate, we need to keep our eyes open." She waited for his acknowledgement. "Right now, the most activity is at the three-sided shed. I don't know if they're having a meeting, training, making a bomb, or what. But we need to find out."

He agreed. The soldier who beat Ramey said their mission was tomorrow and it would take time to get the help needed to stop them. But, Nick had to know the time frame and the nature of the incident before they could make a plan. "Okay, recon only, then we'll decide what we're going to do. Let's split up to cover more ground. You take the north end of the shed. I'll take the south." Studying his watch, he said. "Look things over then meet up at the trailer in thirty minutes. We'll leave together." He checked the magazine in Curly Red's rifle.

She took a step, paused, then reached out. "Be careful," she whispered.

She peeled off to his right and was gone before his words came out. "You, too."

***

A puke green '64 GMC step-side pick-up lumbered from one of the barns, past the house trailer. In the pick-up bed, a pair of fatigue-clad young men balanced atop a half-dozen hay bales. Farther down-field, a notch cut from the brush had been made into an outdoor shooting range. Nick counted. Eight men carrying assault rifles heading to a plywood shooting stand.

With gears grinding, the truck slogged past the platform. Using hay hooks, the men in back pushed off bales to place under hand-drawn signs nailed to the trees at 100, 200 and 300 yard increments.

The field in the middle of the encampment reminded Nick of a rough military parade ground. He had to make it across to the three-sided shed before target practice began. The shooting would drown out any chance to hear the militia's plans. In a crouch, he scrambled across the distance. He reached the grayed shed siding and leaned against it. Steadying his breathing, he tried to subdue the adrenaline rushing through his veins. Focus, listen, and filter out superfluous words.

Inside, a man was talking, big talk, slap-you-on-the-back motivation talk. Young men, voices insistently deepened to convey their maturity, shouted "ooh-rahs," with conviction. A peek through weathered slats revealed the speaker. A man with a stringy ponytail, rounded shoulders in a black leather motorcycle jacket stood before the crowd. A rough tattoo of a shamrock on his right temple made Nick's gut clench. Aryan Brotherhood. Other Norse and Germanic runes inkings tracked down his neck, an arrow signifying a warrior, the most recognizable. This was a seriously bad dude, a killer. Bristling with Aryan charisma, he spoke standing in the midst of a dozen teen-aged boys, almost men. "You are our legacy. It will be you and your sons who will be the Black Corps to insure our freedoms. You are the ones—"

Black Corps? Must be the militant arm of the cult. Nick moved on, hoping to find someone else who would cue him to the group's mission. He saw the flash of navy blue in the same position as him at the wall twenty feet away. Meredith. She'd do her job. If anything important happened at the other end, she'd hear it. A glance at his watch—twenty-five minutes left. Enough time to get to the trailer using the eucalyptus tree windbreak for concealment. Maybe a look inside the barns.

If I was in charge, I'd be someplace more comfortable than a shed. Like a trailer.

He pushed through the dense tree row, squatted behind a trunk and tried to gauge the timing for a twenty-yard sprint to the lean-to. He said a quick prayer that none of the soldiers would see him. Once in position, there would be enough room for him to see into the trailer. The lean-to looked like an afterthought someone added onto the back end of the trailer. Made of scrap lumber and corrugated metal, it stored odd machine parts, tires and boxes bulging with god-knows-what.

He went for it.

He scanned the setting while darting across the field. The sun moved behind a peak and cast a shadow over the run-down thirty-foot trailer. At either end, side doors held peeling, faded decals, the insignia of the California Division of Highways faintly visible. It had started out institutional green, a somewhat mobile office for the State of California Department of Transportation, Division of Highways. The trailer's paint had disintegrated to powder, stuck in place by lichen and lack of use. Sun-rotted tires and axles were propped on cinder blocks. The trailer's tongue balanced on an engine block so rusted it looked like it had been abandoned for decades. This thing had been dragged up here over rutted dirt roads.

Heavy boots thumped inside. More than one person. On the far side of the trailer, a generator powered on. Lights inside glowed through the jalousie windows. Nick shifted position, stretching to see inside. Three men. He ducked out of view.

Nick looked across the yard to catch Meredith's attention. He raised his arm to signal her. Two minutes later, she crouched beside him.

Holding up three fingers, he pointed the index toward the trailer. Stooping to stay below view, they darted diagonally across the six feet to the trailer. Taking opposite sides of the window, they squatted to listen. Two men standing; a small wiry guy who was a mere silhouette with his back to the window blocked the view of someone sitting at the dinette. A bald giant of a man stood close by, hand resting near his hip on the butt of a gun. From behind, the big man's shoulders were in "set" posture, ready for trouble. An enforcer?

"We're on for tomorrow afternoon." A familiar voice boomed through the screen. "No one's going to notice you, James. You'll be in a clerk's uniform. You'll be invisible. No one will know you don't belong there." It was Steiner.

"But—" Another voice, lower in volume, sounding tentative.

"What's the matter, James?" The bald man spoke up. His voice was a growl. "You scared?"

"No…uh, yes." James cleared his throat. "I guess, I'm a little nervous about it."

Steiner said, "You can always stand down." Disapproval oozed in every word. It was clear "standing down," meant he'd never get up.

"Uh, no. I'll do whatever you say. But I don't want to trigger an alarm or anything."

Steiner resumed his outline of the plan. "You'll park the truck up front, set the timer, lock the truck, and then leave on foot." His voice dropped an octave and Nick couldn't hear the words. He and Meredith strained to hear.

Steiner. Nick marveled at the guy's nerve—infiltrating a Department of Justice drug task force. The intelligence info he could've obtained was mind-boggling, particularly in DeGraf's company. What a fool the agent had been.

Then James blew a low whistle. "All this depends on me?"

"Yes," said number one. "Along with other variables. But your job is to park outside the police station, activate the timer like we showed you, then move on to the next one."

Boot heels snapping together jolted Nick. Across the width of the window, he saw the whites of Mere's eyes as the three men inside shouted, "For liberty."

Set the timer? Shit. A bomb. Police department buildings? Which ones? Shit.

CHAPTER FIFTY-THREE

Thursday, May 21, late afternoon

Nick nodded to the lean-to and Meredith followed. She looked at Nick, wondering how he figured it. The lines under his eyes stretched as he squinted against the lamplight. She could almost see his mind working. Taking in, sorting, rejecting, and accepting. "What do you think?"

"We need to know exactly where. Let's move around to—" Nick stopped.

Voices. Men's voices.

Coming from their right. More men than—

"Get behind the hay." Nick whispered. Meredith was on the move before he finished the sentence.

She crouched behind the baled hay as four men approached. In a loose formation, the group trudged on, sullen and silent. These guys were so serious. There wasn't a shred of camaraderie, no joking, nothing. This odd assembly made her wonder. Dressed in jeans, denim or camo T-shirts and varying types of hats, they looked any passing guy on the street. Plenty of tattoos, too. Most of it looked like jail house art. The men were within a decade of their thirties, maybe some in their late teens, and white—no people of color. There was an energy in their step; the inertia of a shared purpose. The common denominator became clear in her mind.

As if by silent command, the men stopped at the steps of the trailer. Late afternoon shadows made it difficult to see. Something heavy got dumped to the dirt, tossed by the guy in the black leather jacket. The rest of the men encircled it. The young men from the shed joined the crowd, making it impossible to see what was going on.

Nick said, "This is our chance to get out of here."

After a crisp nod, she turned to head out.

A blast of rapid fire single shots echoed through the meadow. Meredith hit the deck, with Nick following, an arm flung over her back. The duration and intensity of the reports made Meredith think they were shooting as a team. Maybe target practice. Raising her head, she scanned the shadows across the meadow.

Another series of blasts. She was close enough to wish for ear protection. Rolling to her side, Meredith gave a reassuring half-smile to Nick and rose to a crouch. Watching her surroundings, she moved out.

The clamor continued for five minutes while Meredith got to the trees and crept through. Finally, out of range, she stood and turned toward the noise. In an acre-wide clearing, four men lined up at a weathered gray shooting platform. Targets sat in the dappled shade at the far end. Each shooter had a man waiting their turn behind him. Two more stood down-range, near trees for cover, changing targets.

Nick touched Meredith's shoulder then nodded. Then, they circled the camp, finding the trampled path they used to get in, and left.

Ducking into the ravine, five minutes later, it was safe enough to talk.

"So, what do you think? I counted twenty-six guys; ten shooting, another five in the shed, three in the trailer and eight outside." Nick's voice was low. "The Covenant Family? These guys seem more militant than I read about. Maybe they're Neo-Nazis."

"I didn't see any swastikas," Meredith answered. "Vigilantes?"

Nick shrugged and began listing the possibilities. "Minutemen, like they have in Arizona at the border. Oath Keepers, made up of mostly retired conspiracy-minded military? No, too many prison tats. Then there's the White Supremacists, Aryan Nation."

"They're all violent extremists." Meredith shook her head. Their label didn't matter at the moment. Their commodity was hatred. To whom it was directed was the only variable.

"Whoever they are, they've planned to bomb at least two law enforcement buildings. Their firepower is beyond what we can fight." Nick pressed his lips together. "I wish we knew where they are going to park the truck."

"Yeah, which truck? It couldn't be the old puke-colored wreck they used to haul hay, could it? Even downhill, that old heap wouldn't make it." Meredith suddenly wanted to go back and check the barns. There would be room inside for a truck.

"That one?" Nick pointed to the old GMC in the distance chugging back to the shed, a plume of white smoke spewing from the tailpipe. Nick's eyes widened. "Couldn't be. I'm going up there to call Ferrua. You want to get a look in the barns?" He shook his head at her affirmative nod. "Do it, pick up Cavanaugh, then meet me up top."

"Sure."

"Don't screw around. Make it quick."

She sighed at his needless warning, then sprinted off.

CHAPTER FIFTY-FOUR

Thursday, May 21, late afternoon

From in the cover of the eucalyptus, Meredith backtracked to the shed. She'd seen enough activity to make her suspicious. She wanted to know what was going on. After crossing the narrow alley between the trees and the structure, she flattened herself against the gray wood boards. Inside there was movement, men talking, clanging of metal against metal.

Board by board, Meredith crept along the wall until she found a gap wide enough to see inside. A pair of men working on the front end of a truck—the engine and the smashed-up grill. No, not just a truck. It was the monster truck that had forced the Jeep off the road and killed De-Graf. It sat tamely between the grease-streaked men working to straighten the winch and bumper. It didn't look so evil now. In fact, it looked ridiculous, like a Hot Wheels toy with its excessive metal. Look-alike brothers—one older than the other—labored at the front. Three men at the far end cussed while using a drum hoist to load fifty-five gallon drums into the truck bed.

Beyond the shed, a dozen cars and pick-ups were parked in the field.

Damn, she wished she had the SWAT team with her right now. But she had to leave that alone for the moment. There were more pressing matters than payback.

Meredith circled to the north, beyond the shed. The trees ended where a small creek cut from the slope above and drew a natural border on this side of the property. The hill acted like a windbreak.

A few hundred yards away, the gunfire stopped. The group at the trailer had grown to include the shooters. Whatever the cause, the distraction was enough for her to make a quick pass to the barns.

The closest barn was a shamble, the roof caved in across half its width. The dry weather had shrunk the wood siding enough that she could peek inside. The dilapidated side was filled with trash, the detritus of humans living without modern conveniences. Food cans, plastic wrappings and the like were piled against the wall diagonal from her. Roof shingles slanted to the beaten dirt floor on the other side.

Trotting to the nearest corner, she squinted through the boards. Storage. Industrial-sized metal containers, butane fuel, propane tanks, blankets and wooden and canvas military surplus-type cots filled the space. Four sealed fifty-five gallon drums near the door held a hand-written warning, "poison."

Crap, she thought. What would they use this for?

She listened to the men's voices in the distance. They were calling for something, she couldn't hear what, but she hoped it would keep them busy so she could get to the next barn. Was it the voice she'd heard preaching in the shed?

She raced across the twenty-foot expanse to the next barn, crouching in a low profile. No one saw her. Again, she peered between the grayed wood slats into the darkness. No movement inside.

More trucks—box van style—but the one closest to her caught her attention. A Sonoma County Sheriff's Evidence truck. In a moment of disbelief, she thought, this couldn't be.

She'd never seen an SCSO truck like this. Although the box shape was the same as the department's command vehicle, this one wasn't as big. It was more like one used by a smaller agency. From her view, the emblem looked like a Sonoma County S.O. door decal. But looking closer, the colors weren't the same; a three-foot green stripe along the bottom was the agency color, but the truck she knew was white. And on this truck, the printing, "Sonoma County Sheriff's Office" was rough, free-handed. She'd have to get up close and study it to be sure. She doubted it would pass the scrutiny of an S.O. employee who looked at it closely. But she couldn't take the time; she'd seen enough.

This was the truck Steiner was talking about. Behind it was a retired police car with Santa Rosa Police stenciled on the door. A pretty good version of a California Highway Patrol unit was parked next to it. Two more were vehicles near the far wall. By color and signage, a compact SUV from Petaluma Police and a small pick-up from Rohnert Park Department of Public Safety. From the distance, they looked like the real deal.

With these markings, these vehicles could go just about anywhere without being challenged.

Crap. This meant the Covenant Family mission either targeted most of Sonoma County law enforcement or were setting them up. She had to get to the hilltop ASAP so Nick could tell Ferrua on his call-in.

Meredith was on the move. The men's voices sounded distant, meaning they were occupied. She was clear for a sprint alongside the back of the compound. She made it to the trees and glanced back at the crowd.

Heads above the others, Steiner's huge colleague stood outside the trailer. Standing beside him, Steiner and the ponytail guy watched as the man held a sagging figure up by his arm. Seeing the familiar red plaid shirt, Meredith's breath caught.

Cavanaugh.

CHAPTER FIFTY-FIVE

Thursday, May 21, late afternoon

Outside the trailer, Cavanaugh's jaw set in intractable position of refusal, even in Lampson's powerful grip. Soldiers drifted toward them, watching. Steiner had seen this expression before in old men—they were founders of the only real family he'd ever known, the Covenant Family. Some of the old men had lost their nerve for the fight and argued with him as he ascended the ranks. Others, like Cavanaugh, couldn't be cowed so they had to be dealt with. The higher in rank he rose, the weaker the opposition grew. Natural attrition wasn't the only way the seniors died off; some had help. Steiner smiled to himself as he considered how he'd used God to put forth his plans. He couldn't deny that he loved the power in his hands. In God's name, he'd changed priorities and driven his people until they bent to his will. These fools believed him when he said he had a mandate from God. Now as a leader of the Covenant Family, he assumed command of the Black Corps, so he could move forward with his plan. So far, it had worked—using the cult as a work force to accomplish his plans was so much more practical than hiring the work out. Besides, it was less likely for word to get out to the wrong people when his workers "believed in the cause." He would take the money, then loose the crypto, anyway. Because he could.

The old men like this rancher fella never could see the bigger picture. The more passive Christian Identity sects thought doomsday was imminent and the government would collapse on its own. But his Covenant Family believed they would survive by setting themselves above the rest of America, as benevolent protectors. At least that was how it would appear. Steiner believed the plan needed a little help—like he'd had to 'help' the founders. Those old fools couldn't abide pro-action. They wanted to react solely if provoked, not be on the vanguard of change. Their day was history.

Steiner had nudged the Family into a dark descent. Soon, they had embraced the notion that the purpose of the federal government was for world domination and the elimination of Christian thought. Steiner focused their hate against Jews, blacks, homosexuals and other groups. Better to have a concrete target than a vague concept.

Steiner took a deep breath. Stale air dampened by the sweat of the men inside, but he loved the smell. It meant work and work meant progress. In his world, progress would move him to the seat of power. It had been a stroke of genius, really. He'd found the Covenant Family Church as a young man. The history of the sect was rife with false starts, bloody and unsuccessful endings, as well as leadership failures. Steiner looked upon the leaders with disdain as they squandered their true power. After he assumed the helm, he had refined the principles by which his Family lived. They began as pacifists, evolved into survivalists then on to para-militarist. Steiner selected the best men to serve as enforcers and terrorists on his elite Black Corps. It was these men and a handful of logistics officers who were with him here.

Women and children in camp served to weaken his men. Accordingly, he kept the men's families in a safe rural compound in Susanville, isolated much like the Dry Creek compound. While the men were on a mission—no women. No more polygamy, incest, or rape to dilute the soldiers' energy and resolve. There would be time for that after their work was done. Exciting to think about, but no time to indulge now. They had work to do.

Steiner glared at Cavanaugh, a stare he'd perfected at first in a mirror, then on people. Yes, his eyes held a magnetic quality and, using tools like this, he excelled in making people give in to him. It seldom failed.

But Cavanaugh wasn't having any of it. His mouth was a grim slash, his eyes staring straight ahead.

No worries. That's what Lampson was here for. "Find out what he knows."

CHAPTER FIFTY-SIX

Thursday, May 21, late afternoon

Nick had left the dirt road, turning uphill to the peak where he could make a phone call. The afternoon sun warmed the back of his neck. He stopped to wipe the sweat from his eyes. He couldn't escape the nagging feeling something was left undone. Shaking his head, he tried to focus. Everything was "undone." The urgency to call Ferrua was being nudged aside by something else. Meredith? No, he trusted her. She could take care of herself. She's aware of the stakes if she's discovered. She's skilled at sneaking and peeking, too. No, not Meredith.

Cavanaugh? Oh, yes, that was it—Cavanaugh. No matter what release the rancher had given, Nick was concerned about leaving him alone. His first duty was to protect the civilian. But it had gotten complicated—fast. A spike of anger stabbed at him when he thought about the militia causing all this grief. What was their mission? What part had the homicide victim played—if any—in the overall scheme? He knew he'd find the answer to these questions as time went on. But these guys were serious killers who would do anything to put forward their plans.

Suddenly, Nick knew he had to get to Cavanaugh. The old man had reminded him on numerous occasions that he could take care of himself. Now, Nick wasn't so sure. He couldn't put his finger on why, but he couldn't shake the feeling. A quick look at his watch—five thirty p.m. If he hurried, the detour to pick up Cavanaugh wouldn't take over thirty minutes. Maybe they could still make the seven P.M. rendezvous with the helicopter.

Nick turned downhill and trotted along the trail. Another few minutes and he'd be at the ravine where Cavanaugh was hiding.

Even on the move, Nick's anxiety built. His mind raced through all the things that could happen to the rancher, heart attack, a fall, snakebite, being discovered by the militia. What had he been thinking? Stumbling into a crack in the dirt, he admonished himself. Pay attention so you can get Cavanaugh to safety.

A minute later, he was at the ravine's edge. Nick looked under the low tree branches, seeing nothing but leaves, grass and boulders. Then, he called out in a low voice, expecting the rancher to pop up from behind a rock.

No answer. Scanning the area, he saw oat grass swaying and oak leaves rattling in the afternoon breeze. The shaded ravine held enough light to see—no Cavanaugh.

Nick dropped down the ravine's slope, landing on the damp gravel of the stream bed. A glance uphill, then down. Nothing.

A gust of wind rustled the oak leaves. Glancing up, movement caught his eye. Twenty feet away, a white Stetson cartwheeled into a wild blackberry thicket.

CHAPTER FIFTY-SEVEN

Thursday, May 21, late afternoon

On a hay bale outside the trailer, Jerry Steiner took in his men's stares. The number had grown to over a dozen. They stood watching their leader with the prisoner. Steiner liked to put on little shows like this for his troops. The scenes inspired confidence—and fear—in his abilities. He couldn't afford to lose any soldiers.

Steiner glared at Cavanaugh, but the old rancher didn't cower. Maybe he didn't know how impossible his situation was. He sat there, staring ahead.

Steiner knew he wasn't an imposing figure. This was why he used Lampson for interrogations. Lampson spent hours every day on a weight bench, pressing, squatting and sweating. Steiner had long suspected steroid use. The man's volatile temper and acne scars were enough evidence for him. Steiner made Lampson's short fuse work for his cause.

Lampson would force information out of the old man. He'd get answers: had he seen their scout, Easley? Who else survived the crash? Where were the rest of them? Did they get word out for help? Did they know what was going on up here?

Steiner had depended on bad law enforcement communications at the radio base, then the sheriff's own bureaucracy to stymie a warning. He couldn't count on that now and he still had eight hours he needed to keep his plans protected.

He might have to move up his timetable, to be on the safe side.

CHAPTER FIFTY-EIGHT

Thursday, May 21, late afternoon

Meredith stood, brushing aside eucalyptus leaves to see what was going on. There, outside the trailer—Cavanaugh.

What the hell happened? How did these morons catch him? Never mind now. Have to get him out of there.

She needed Nick.

There wasn't time for her to get him, return and rescue Cav. She was on her own. First, she had to see where they put him. The trailer, most likely.

Although she couldn't hear the words, it was obvious by the loud voices that Steiner was using Cavanaugh to illustrate a point. The rancher stood tall, blossoms of dust on his jeans and hair falling into his eyes. Besides being roughed up and humiliated, he looked okay. No blood—other than the dried patch on his shoulder. Thankfully, the big guy held him up by the opposite arm.

While Ponytail shouted their propaganda, Meredith noticed Cav kept his hair in his eyes while his head moved sideways slowly. He was scanning the eucalyptus tree line. She felt a surge of respect and admiration for the rancher. No matter how he got caught, he kept calm, and didn't quit. Now, she guessed he was looking for Nick or her while searching for an escape route. He was getting ready for his opportunity.

Ponytail and the big guy followed Steiner inside the trailer, dragging Cavanaugh in with him. They'd want to find out how the rancher got here, and who else was with him. They might figure he'd been in the Jeep, and had witnessed DeGraffenreid's murder.

Meredith's chances of getting to the trailer the way she and Nick had come earlier were slim. She had to see what was going on, anyway. She wove her way through the trees to the base of the slope. Near the outbuildings, then dashed from the trees to the cover of the shed and to the back of the trailer. Creeping up to the lichen-encrusted metal, she cringed at the sound of a fist hitting flesh. She knew it well from her patrol days. They were beating Cavanaugh.

It was hard to see through the window, filthy from moss and grime on the glass. There were four straight-backed chairs and a battered wooden table in the front. A lone light bulb, mounted on a shadeless lamp, sat on a table. It put the remainder of the interior in the shadows. Meredith got the impression of sparse office space at her end. Three men inside, not counting Cavanaugh, who was tied to a chair. All three had nasty-looking Ka-Bar combat knives sheathed on belts along with semi-auto pistols of varying caliber.

These were scary guys and Steiner called the shots. Meredith pegged the third man as Steiner's enforcer and bodyguard. Easy to tell with well-inked bulging muscles. Dressed in jeans and an olive drab wife-beater, it was this man who leaned over Cavanaugh. She noted the acne on his back and the way the veins in his neck pulsed. A juicer.

The bodyguard's words were lost, but Cavanaugh shook his head in steadfast refusal. A slap, this time, open-handed.

Cavanaugh's head bounced from the impact, then his chin dropped to his chest. The bodyguard's voice rose as Steiner and Ponytail walked away from their prisoner. They were inches from where, on the other side of the wall, Meredith had dropped to a crouch, listening.

"...did he come from?" Steiner snapped.

"Look at him, Jerry. He's a rancher, a farmer. He must live in these hills," Ponytail answered.

Steiner demanded, "What are the chances he'd stumble across us way the hell up here?"

"Who knows?" Ponytail shrugged his thin shoulders. "The most important question is what does he know about our plans?"

"Yeah," Steiner rubbed his chin and glanced at Cavanaugh. "And if there are any more from where he came from."

"He said he was alone."

Steiner's rounded jaw set. "Well, Franks, he would say that, wouldn't he? He ain't gonna give up his pals."

Franks was Ponytail's name. "He'll have to be eliminated."

Meredith's heart pounded so loud she thought the two inside could hear it.

"But first, but you have to find out what he knows about the crypto and the rest." Thank God. There was time—not much, though. Crypto? What was "the rest?"

Franks must have given him a questioning look.

Meredith lifted her gaze to inside the trailer.

"If he's told the neighborhood watch captain, we'll have to make adjustments." Steiner eyed the other man: a challenge to his authority? "It'll be done soon—we move at four A.M. tomorrow. I want everyone to be in place for a three P.M. start."

Franks straightened with surprise. He recovered soon enough. "You done with him for now?"

Steiner nodded. "I'm done. Let Lampson do his work—see if he can get any information of value in the next hour or so. We have other things to do. When it's time, we'll need everyone in the field. I want to be there when you give out the MAC-10s. We don't have enough to arm everyone. You'll have to manage the griping and keep morale up."

Meredith dropped to her haunches again and blew out a breath to push back the anguish she felt for Cav.

What was her next move? To get to the guard, she'd have to get into the trailer. She was no match for him hand-to-hand given his size—especially with that damn Ka-Bar on his hip. He'd use it, too. She couldn't just shoot him—that would alert everyone in the camp. She couldn't do it alone.

She needed help. She needed Nick. That was her next move, time-crunch or not. She had to get her partner to free Cav.

CHAPTER FIFTY-NINE

Thursday, May 21, early evening

Tied up in the trailer, Cav had time to recall his mistake.

Waiting for the detectives, he'd sat on a rock in the open, catching the last rays of the sun. He was damn tired, and he took his rest when he could. After the deadly car assault, they'd been on the move for the entire day, searching for a phone signal and trying to get off the hill. He'd sat back letting the warmth from the rock and the fading sun settle into his bones. Rubbing his eyes, he felt every year of his age. Sixty-seven wasn't as old as it used to be. His parents had worked themselves into an early grave, hammering out the family land holdings and cattle business. Neither lived to see his age.

He attributed his longevity to his wife, Shirley. After his return from overseas she'd kept him anchored to the land and focused on their family—and therefore, sane. A steady and stoic presence in his life, she'd devoted some of her precious time to growing her own vegetables and fruit. The daily physical exertion of working the ranch, along with nutritious food, ensured the family's robust health. Until Shirley got cancer. Since her death, he'd admitted he'd begun to feel his years, with arthritis in his spine gripping his mobility tighter every day. He had a bad shoulder: bursitis, or maybe a rotator cuff injury. He hadn't bothered to see a doctor, nor would he.

God, he hoped Jake or Manuel fed the stock and checked the water pumps. He'd needed to get the back gate fixed to the upper pasture, too. It pissed him off that he wasn't there to do his own work. He was sure one of the boys would take care of the feeding, wouldn't they?

Stop feeling sorry for yourself, Cav thought. Making a determined change in the train of his thoughts, he thought about Meredith and her sergeant, Nick. Cav was sure once he came to his senses, Nick Reyes would be a happy man. He'd have his hands full with Meredith Ryan, no doubt about it. But they were a custom fit, like the smooth leather of a broken in saddle. Comfortable, efficient but letting you know it's there by squeaking now and then.

She was easy on the eyes in a wholesome way, with a sharp and discerning mind. When comfortable with those around her, a quick smile came to her face. When she wasn't comfortable, she was direct, almost brutal. He appreciated that in a woman.

Cavanaugh smiled. She was a pistol, that one. He thought Nick would value that, too. The sergeant listened to what Meredith had to say, even while pretending not to.

Cav found himself caring a lot about them both. He liked Nick and respected the way he worked, a warrior mindset balanced with real-world conflicts. Cavanaugh felt as safe with both of these deputies as he had with his SERE-trained team. He marveled at the immensity of the thought.

He'd let his mind wander too far from the present while waiting at the ravine. Something scuffed against the rocky dirt behind a tree. Then a shadow crossed his vision and pain exploded in his head. His last thought was what a fool he'd been to let his guard down.

Now, he was in their camp tied up. Cav's holster rubbed against his ankle. The stupid goon who searched him did a piss-poor job. But having his shooter wasn't an advantage at the moment. He couldn't get to it. Maybe he'd get a chance before they beat him senseless. Now he was tied up here, waiting for a beating, at best.

CHAPTER SIXTY

Thursday, May 21, early evening

Nick clambered up the short rocky slope and stepped into a meadow. On one side, it flattened to the road, the other side led to a gradual upslope. Blackberry thickets crowded in between. The Stetson was caught in the brambles, a glaring sign of Nick's failure to keep the rancher safe. Nick plunged into the bushes, ignoring the thorns tearing at his skin, and considering the first step to getting Cavanaugh back.

He straightened, breathing in the warm air. The breeze had abated. Gentle noises, a hawk's wing-beat overhead, crickets in the grass, were enough to lull one into a sense of contentment. But he knew better.

His grip on the Stetson tightened as he thought over what had to be done. With the wind calmed, smoke—a mile away—hung in the air.

The sound of an engine cut through the silence. From the west, a cloud of dust approached led by a car coming with absolutely no stealth.

A decades-old Chevrolet van crept along the road. Coming out from the brambles, Nick watched. He could run faster than this vehicle was moving. But he didn't need to, someone inside saw him. The tires scrabbled to a stop twenty feet from him. He counted four heads inside. De-Graf's team of DOJ agents.

Nick put the AR on the ground and walked out to the road, holding the Stetson in one hand, the other gripping his identification and badge at his chest.

Both front doors swung open and men stepped out. The passenger was a tanned blond man, carrying twenty extra pounds around his middle. He moved stiffly, eying Nick while keeping his hand on the holster at his belt. From the driver's side, a hook-nosed Greek with a deeply receding hairline jumped out. His hand was also on his holster.

The driver spoke, his voice deep. "Help you, sir?"

Nick was careful to keep his hands visible and away from his body as he approached the van. "I'm armed. I'm a sheriff's deputy, Sonoma County."

Two more men piled out the passenger side, waiting in the same posture as the driver, all with guns at the ready.

"Okay, deputy. Turn around. Put your hands on the back of your head."

Nick dropped the Stetson. It bounced off the crown and rolled.

A man was on him, searching his body, keeping a controlled hold on Nick's hands. Someone took his Glock from the holster and took his ID from his hand.

Nick hated that he couldn't see what they were doing, but it had to be done. If these guys were who he thought they were, he needed them.

"Awright, relax." The blond guy seemed to be in charge.

Turning to face them, Nick took his Glock from the dark guy. As he shoved it into his holster he noted all the other guns were being holstered. He hung the badge around his neck then leaned over to dust off his pants, listening as the others circled him.

"Okay, Sergeant Reyes, Sonoma County Sheriff, we know who you are," drawled the driver.

Nick cut across him. "—and your ID?"

The passenger ducked as the driver shoved his identification card and badge at Nick.

Nick read, "California Department of Justice, Bureau of Narcotic Enforcement, Supervisory Special Agent Stephen Germain." He handed it back. DeGraf's team.

Germain's big arms folded across his chest. "What are you doing up here?"

"My partner and I were up here on a homicide investigation." Nick waited while this sunk in. "We ran into some trouble."

One of the passengers, a pale guy with glasses, asked, "Where's your partner?" They all glanced around.

"I'll get to that in a minute." Nick wasn't crazy about breaking the news about their lieutenant. "I take it you guys are narcs from Nor Cal MET."

"Yeah." Nick understood the suspicion in the driver's eyes.

The passenger scowled as he extended his hand. "Germain."

The dark man stretched to Nick for a handshake. "Al Caranica." Caranica flung a thumb over his shoulder. "Lucky Tedesco and Roy Hughes."

Hughes took Nick's hand in a solid grip. "Glad to meet you."

Germain glanced around. "What're you doing out here in the middle of nowhere with no car, no partner?"

Nick kicked at the dirt. "Good question. My partner's up doing some recon on a group of militia-types. They attacked—let me back up a minute."

Lucky Tedesco, a swarthy Italian with kinky hair, pushed past Germain. Inches from Nick's face, he shouted, "They attacked what? What the hell's going on around here?"

Germain pulled roughly at Tedesco's arm, shoving the man back. "Let me handle this, Lucky. Chill."

Tedesco glared at Nick while he stepped behind the sergeant. Germain's attention pinpointed on Nick. "Lucky's a little on edge." Germain shrugged, but Nick saw it as a hack to put him at ease. They were all tense. "We get here to meet up with our lieutenant, and he's nowhere around. The base where we were going to stay is burned out and a fuckin' forest fire is building all around us." His smile didn't reach his eyes. Again, Nick saw the tension and suspicion boiling beneath his shrug. "Then, you show up, on foot and alone. What would you think?"

"Okay." Nick put his hands up in a surrender. "There's no easy way to tell you. Your lieutenant is dead."

To a man, they were expressionless, but Nick saw Caranica's hands curl into fists. A voice filled with shock, someone in back said, "Fuck."

"What happened?" Germain choked.

"Like I told you, my partner and I were on a murder investigation up here. We had the RP and got caught on the wrong side of a landslide. We were hiking out to the west when we stumbled onto DeGraf. He offered to drive us back to Santa Rosa first thing in the morning. Just after dawn, the militia-types ran us off the road and down a cliff." Nick swallowed. "DeGraf didn't make it."

They had questions; all asked at the same time. Germain took control. "Wait a minute." He looked from his men to Nick. "What happened?"

Nick told the story like it was a police report—in language these men would understand.

"How can you be sure he's dead?" Tedesco blurted. "Was he alive when the car fell the second time?"

Nick shook his head. "The engine crushed him. He's gone. He wasn't breathing, no pulse and his eyes were fixed. No vital signs." He paused. "I was with him when he died." The image of DeGraf's crushed and broken body sprung into his mind; the trickle of blood at the side of his mouth. The look in his eye said he accepted his fate. "Hail Mary, full of Grace," the first few words of a prayer Nick finished for him— "pray for us sinners now and at the hour of our death."

"Fuck me," Tedesco hissed.

Germain's voice rose. "Where are these assholes? Is that where your partner is now, doing recon?"

Nick nodded. "Their camp is a few minutes over that hill. It's a hike but it doesn't take long. But there's more."

"More?" Germain snapped.

"The group is planning a mission tomorrow that sounds bad. Two or more police stations are targeted with bombs. We've got no radio comms and sketchy cell service up here so we don't know which ones yet. I was on my way up there to call my office for help." He looked at the hill to his left. "But, the militia snatched our RP, who was with us. I want to get him back, but two against thirty isn't good odds."

"But six against thirty might even it out," Tedesco snarled.

Nick held his response. Because one guy volunteered his team didn't mean the sergeant would go for it.

Germain turned, and after receiving a nod from Hughes and Caranica, faced Nick. "Do you have a plan?"

It so happened that he did. "You guys have flashlights?"

CHAPTER SIXTY-ONE

Thursday, May 21, early evening

Meredith was thirsty as hell. Keeping up this pace without water would soon be a problem. As thirsty as she was, it amazed her how much she was sweating. Her jog was steady, her attention on the track and the countryside around her. She was getting tired. One more hill to climb, then over the meadow and up to the peak to catch Nick.

She crested the hill and paused for a breath. To her right, the remains of a dust cloud hung over what looked like the road. She glanced up the hill, then back to where the dust had settled, and made a decision. Wrong or not, this could be help arriving. She moved down the slope.

From her view behind a small thicket of manzanita, she saw a seedy white van twenty feet away. Four men stood in a ragged assembly around Nick. She couldn't tell if he was in trouble. Her hand on her Beretta, she waited, watching.

Nick was talking to the guys. And they were listening. Although they were dressed in jeans and camos, there was a difference between them and the Covenant Family. Were they cops? They had the look, for sure. Then, Nick bent and retrieved something from the road.

Cav's Stetson.

"Nick!" She stepped from behind the bush and hailed him.

Hands flew to their holstered guns and the group looked up at her as one. She walked toward them feeling their scrutiny.

"My partner, Meredith Ryan." Nick presented her to Germain who added "Nor Cal MET," and took over introductions.

She didn't like the way Tedesco's eyes glazed into a leer. In the middle of nowhere, with an impossible mission before them, this joker was gawking at her chest. "I have a head, too."

Tedesco blinked, his face reddened, and he looked away.

"Mere, we were planning to see if the militia has Cavanaugh." Nick tipped his head toward Germain. "Sergeant Germain and his team's gonna help."

She folded her arms across her chest. "They have him. I saw them bring him in." She looked to Germain. "You have any water?"

Germain nodded to Tedesco, then half-smiled. "It's in the Beast."

"The what?"

Germain repeated, "The Beast. It looks like a van, but it's actually a pig on wheels, a gutless gas-hog, smokes like hell, and has a suspension like a carnival thrill ride."

Tedesco returned with two large bottles of water. He glanced aside as he gave Meredith hers first.

She emptied the bottle, as did Nick. She ran a knuckle under her chin to catch a drip and said, "They're holding Cav in the trailer. He's tied to a chair and they're trying to beat info out of him. It's Steiner—he looks like the one calling the shots."

Germain squinted with disbelief. "You mean Steiner, the radio geek?"

She nodded, hearing cussing behind Nick. "I never liked that guy," Tedesco hissed.

Nick asked, "Do they know about us?"

She shook her head. "Cav told them he was alone, but so far they're not buying it."

"Good man. How many guards?"

"Two big guys. When I left there was one guy working him over and a second hanging around outside. But they left because of their mission. So inside is Cav and the gorilla."

Nick nodded. "Our last count was twenty-six men."

Germain's pudgy face grew dark. "Do you have any idea where the mission is?"

Meredith fixed her stare on Nick. "I can guess. I found a panel truck that's been re-painted to look like a Sheriff's Office Evidence Van. Also, patrol units from Santa Rosa PD, the CHP, Rohnert Park and Petaluma. I also saw four big barrels of something labeled, 'poison.'" She let that information settle in. "And I found the monster truck that forced us off the road. They're working on it, pulling the winch out of the grill."

"There's our diversion," Nick said. "Set one of the sheds on fire and all hands will show up to fight it. That'll give us cover for getting Cavanaugh."

Caranica spoke up. "You two get your guy. We'll take care of the diversion."

When Nick returned from fetching the AR, Meredith cleared an area in the dirt with her shoe and squatted. "Here's the layout—" The dirt became her easel. Using an index finger, she carved out a crescent. "This is the trailer. Next to it, two barns side by side. Down here is a three-sided shed, where the monster truck is." She poked the dirt where she'd indicated the shed at the opposite end of the half moon. "Most activity is there. We'll get to the trailer along here," she pointed to where the eucalyptus trees had been marked out.

Nick took over. "Germain, the diversion should be as far away from the trailer as you can get. We don't know what shape our guy is in, so we may take some time."

CHAPTER SIXTY-TWO

Thursday, May 21, early evening

Hughes and Tedesco were making too much noise. Neither agent was in great shape, certainly not what she would expect in a marijuana eradication team. They were required to stomp all over these hills to get into illegal, isolated and hidden grows. She slowed, waiting to let the others go by. Avoiding her gaze, Hughes passed her. As Tedesco approached, she said, "Having trouble working off your winter weight gain?"

He glared at her, then hurried to catch up with Hughes. Meredith followed.

Shadows grew long in the thirty minutes it took them to get to the encampment. They would lose daylight in an hour, and she and Nick didn't have flashlights. She stepped up her pace, crowding Tedesco to quicken his stride.

Their first stop was the sentry position.

After leaving Germain's team in the trees, Nick slung the AR-15 over his shoulder and scaled the granite boulder. Meredith was grateful no replacement soldier took Curly Red's place. Loss of the sentry would have set off an alarm to the militia. From their vantage point, Meredith indicated the eucalyptus tree line. "We can follow the windbreak, then around the back of the compound, to the field where the cars are parked."

Nick nodded.

When they rejoined Germain, Nick filled him in about their next move. They set out, Meredith following the team again.

Through the trees, then, one-by-one, they snaked around the base of the cliff that framed the western boundary of the camp. At the equipment shed, Caranica posted himself where he could see most of the area.

The shed was empty, the monster truck standing alone, halogen work lights on. Nick looked at his watch and nodded to the rickety shelter near the trailer. "Dinner time," he whispered. The soldiers ate under a sagging canvas tarp on the far side of the trailer. About twenty-five men. Steiner's dark-colored Cadillac Escalade was parked next to the trailer.

Caranica held his position as the rest of the team moved toward the parking area. As Meredith passed him, he reached out and handed her an all-business tactical knife. A similar weapon was in his other hand. Her small pocket knife wouldn't open an envelope, so she assumed she'd take his place as a look-out. Now, she could join in the fun flattening tires. She half-smiled her thanks and moved out.

In the field, sat the cars and trucks of various vintages, all dusty with road dirt. None would get Nick, the car aficionado, excited.

The team spread out, crouching between vehicles—Germain and Nick going to the farthest. Meredith stooped between an oxidized Pontiac Sunbird and an 80's Dodge Ram truck. She snapped open Caranica's knife, then pointed the tip into a sidewall on the Dodge. Using the heel of her hand like a hammer, she pounded the handle. The blade sank into the rubber. When she pulled it out, she heard the satisfying whisper of air escaping. She did the same on four more tires.

When they were done, they split into their original teams, Nor Cal MET peeled off toward a barn while Nick and Meredith melted into the tree line. Germain's next task was to immobilize the "evidence" truck in the barn and start a diversion while Nick and Meredith went for Cavana-ugh.

CHAPTER SIXTY-THREE

Thursday, May 21, evening

Weaving through the trees, Nick worried that Hughes and Tedesco would slow the team down. Nick decided to let it go; let Germain deal with them. Besides, if all went well, they'd have their own man to slow them down—Cavanaugh.

There were more pressing concerns, like how to free the rancher. Plans were just that, plans. Nick had made too many operational plans to believe this would go as mapped out. While his feet pounded the hard ground, he started sorting the possible scenarios this action could take. He kept an eye on the men in the shelter eating. They were the biggest threat.

Nick stopped to check the driveway into the camp. The main road was twenty feet away. From there, a small rise hid the compound. It struck Nick how easy it was for these extremists to hide up here. And how a passerby would never think such malice could exist in this scarcely tamed wilderness. He stifled a shiver and focused on the dining area. The soldiers concentrated on eating. Nick hadn't noticed any other sentries before, but he took a moment to scan the hills around him.

Where would he put a guard? Behind the equipment shed on the hill above. Squinting, he thought he could see a figure. The man looked like he was sitting, cross-legged. Eating.

He and Mere moved, before the sentry could finish the meal and return to his duty.

After stealing across the gravel driveway, Nick found room for them both in the lean-to. Listening, he heard the low chatter of men with their attention on their meals. Boots thumped from within the trailer. Someone flung the door open. The bodyguard, stepped out, his head swiveling at his surroundings. Then he set off for the mess tent.

There were two doors at the trailer, one in front and one in back; the top half of each was a jalousie window. At the rear, Nick secured the AK strap over his shoulder and drew his Glock. He mounted the unsteady cinder-block and plank steps. He grasped the jalousie handle but found it locked. Lifting a glass slat from the frame, he reached in and twisted the knob. The door swung open with a muted squeal. He froze. Behind him, Nick heard the quiet scuff of gunmetal against nylon as Meredith pulled her Beretta out. They waited a full minute and when there was no response, they entered.

The trailer was eight feet wide, twenty-five feet long. It was open except for a bathroom bisecting the interior. In the dim light, they cleared the area with no problems. Boxes filled with gun aficionado and survivalist magazines sat among stacks of pamphlets which shouted "Christian Identity" and anarchist propaganda. These were the fodder of extremists who wanted to melt down the government—rhetoric with little real meaning, but words chosen to feed into people's fears and paranoia. Nick didn't have the time to do more than a quick scan but he'd been right about these guys.

Nick found Cavanaugh tucked in a corner in the front room—a large office space with tables, chairs and more boxes of hate. Christian, my ass, he thought.

Cavanaugh was tied to an office chair, ropes binding his wrists and ankles. His chin slumped to his chest, which rose deeply. Nick touched his shoulder.

Instantly, Cavanaugh's eyes were open and focused: He'd been faking it. Relief flooded his bruised face when he saw Nick, then a welcome smile split open a laceration on his lower lip. Blood oozed, dripping on his plaid shirt. "Evening," he mumbled.

Nick couldn't stop his own smile. He kept watch while Meredith knelt to cut the ropes with Caranica's knife.

She asked, "Are you hurt?"

"Only my ego," Cavanaugh sighed. "Twenty years ago, they would've been burying a few of their own." He flexed his shoulders and rotated his wrist, then shoved himself out of the chair. "I'm ready. Let's get the hell out of here."

"My thought, exactly," Nick smiled. Slow or not, he was proud to have this man on his side.

CHAPTER SIXTY-FOUR

Thursday, May 21, evening

Somewhere over the Pacific, the sun had set. Night falls quicker in the hills, so it was easy to see Germain's blazing diversion.

A voice from the mess tent yelled, "Fire!" The men jumped to their feet, shouting the alarm. Franks shouted orders over the uproar, while others bolted toward the shed.

Meredith went into action. She pulled Cav outside and toward the concealment of the eucalyptus, Nick on their heels. They moved to the farthest line of trees, then broke free and dashed across the meadow to the cover of the ravine.

Meredith caught her breath and slid to the dirt beside Cavanaugh. "You doing okay?" Without waiting for an answer, she reached for the flashlight Germain had given Nick. Cupping her hands around the beam, she shined it on over Cav's red plaid shirt. She mopped the blood from his lip with his shirt tail. "Any injuries? Bruises?"

"Probably got a shiner or two but that's all. I'm in good shape, considering." He sighed, leaning his head back. "Lost my hat, though."

Meredith smiled. "No. Nick found it and stashed it for you." She then flicked off the light.

"No kidding?" Cavanaugh's smile lit up the dim night. He looked at Nick. "Hey, thanks, partner."

Nick waved the thanks aside. "It's safe in the van."

Meredith put her hand on Cav's arm. "We ran into DeGraf's team. They came up in a four-wheel drive van. They're creating a diversion. As soon as we regroup, we'll go down the hill."

"Finally, some good news." Cav sighed again. "We'll be out of here tonight, then?"

"That's the plan."

"DeGraf's boys out dancing?" Cav's eyes sparkled. Meredith hadn't seen humor from him before.

"They're getting a little payback." Nick smiled, sitting next to Meredith. "If all goes as hoped, they're disabling the militia's transportation."

Except Steiner's Escalade, Meredith thought. It's too close to the mess tent.

Cavanaugh nodded. "How many guys did DeGraf have on his team?"

"Four," Meredith answered.

Cavanaugh's head bobbed. "Not enough to take on the whole group but we can foul their plans until reinforcements arrive."

Meredith smiled. "That's it."

CHAPTER SIXTY-FIVE

Thursday, May 21, evening

Even with a full moon, waiting in the dark ravine was the worst. No, hunger was the worst. No food, no water. When he got home, Nick planned on eating a big steak. *Carne asada*, with beans and rice.

Where was Germain? What took them so long?

Gunfire. Through the trees, all they could see were the flames lapping up the boards of the shed. Yes, gunfire.

"Jesus, they're getting shot at," murmured Meredith.

Tedesco and Hughes pounded across the meadow sprinting for their lives. Then, like runners sliding into base, they skidded over the lip of the ravine.

"Fuck me," Tedesco's chest heaved as he scrambled to find his balance.

Hughes huffed as he dropped next to Meredith. His thick fingers rubbed his face, then he sat back. "Germain and Caranica are on their way. They got into the barn, but these assholes managed to get some of the stuff out of the box van. They're moving the shit to the Escalade to transport the payload." He caught his breath. "They won't be using their cars, though." Hughes' smile was a grimace. Pulling his .45 from his holster, he aimed high over the shed.

From beyond the trees, the confusion continued. Nick grabbed Hughes' shoulder, whispering. "Hold it until your buddies catch up."

Hughes gave the slightest nod and settled into the dirt, gun at the ready.

Staccato shots from automatic weapons popped as the equipment shed fire died down. Through the din, Nick heard foot falls beating a frantic path across the meadow. With a grip on Curly Red's rifle, he looked, the silhouettes of Germain and Caranica raced toward him. From the trees behind the two, an engine roared and the three-sided shed walls exploded as the monster truck shot through the burning boards, the Escalade close behind.

The two vehicles thundered toward them, racing across the plateau. Back-lit by the waning flames, Nick saw three men inside the monster truck.

CHAPTER SIXTY-SIX

Thursday, May 21, late evening

The enormous Dodge chewed up turf, then swerved to the driveway, heading for the road. It paralleled the trees and was lost through the leaves. Meredith softened her eye trying to make out the truck's movement. When she spotted it, she calculated when they'd reach the intersection of the road and the ravine. Ten seconds.

Nick pulled out the AR. He propped it on the lip of the ravine, sighted his target and fired four single shots. Brass flew in an arc from his right to ten feet away. Meredith heard the metallic thunk of bullets hitting the Dodge. The truck swerved and bounced on the gravel road, the barrels in the truck bed packed tightly enough that they shuddered with every bump. Around a turn and they were gone.

Taking a calculated risk that he could disable the Escalade without hitting the payload Nick aimed at the SUV. He heard the metallic impact. Maybe the engine, but he wasn't sure where they hit. The truck wobbled, the driver steering to evade the assault. Then it straightened and spun to follow the Dodge. He hadn't set off the bomb but he hadn't stopped the Escalade from escaping, either.

Nick's muzzle flashes were a beacon for Germain and Caranica. In seconds, the two agents dropped into the ravine next to Cavanaugh, panting.

Pointing at the second truck, Germain gasped for air. "They've got explosives in back of the Escalade."

Tedesco spat, "You sure?"

Germain recovered his breath. "I saw it. Ammonium nitrate, fifteen or twenty bags of it. And they know you've freed your guy."

Someone whispered, "Shit."

Meredith spoke before she completed the thought. "We get to the van, then we can follow them."

"We can't climb to the top of the hill in the dark to call this in," Nick thought out loud. "It would be faster to get a signal from the vehicle if it's going toward Santa Rosa."

"They have too much of a head start. We can't catch up to them." Hughes' voice was sharp. "Besides, the Beast can't hit sixty mph downhill with a tail wind."

Germain looked to Nick. "Your call, brother."

Nick fixed his gaze on Meredith. Through the gray remnants of the evening, she saw the resolve in the lines around his mouth. "We take the Beast; we follow."

Germain nodded as if he'd expected Nick's answer, tossing the keys across to Caranica. "Caranica's a runner. He'll get it and pick us up on the way down the hill."

Nick nodded in approval. "We'll stay here to be sure none of these clowns follows the Escalade." Nick faced Caranica, who stood. "Just slow down when you drive by so we can hop in." There he was—Nick, her partner, coolly tossing out a bit of humor to cut the tension.

A smart salute and Caranica was off, his flashlight beam bouncing down the ravine in the darkness.

Meredith had been ready to volunteer to get the van, but was relieved Caranica was assigned. She wanted to stay with Nick. She wanted to stay together.

Shouts rose from the camp. Sounded like they'd gotten to their cars and found all the tires flat.

She asked Nick, "You think they know where we are?"

Fifty yards to their right, from the rocks, a soldier shouted to his comrades. "Over there, over there." Men with flashlights sprinted from the trees toward where Curly Red had fallen. Whoever found the sentry must have seen the detectives running toward the ravine.

"That would be a 'yes.'" Nick looked at his watch. "Caranica will be a while. We need to be close to the road so we can get the hell outta here when he shows up."

"Good call, Boss," Cavanaugh added, peering into the night.

The soldiers weren't trying to be quiet. Meredith heard a voice. "Find them. Kill them—NOW!" Gunshots shattered the night air. Only God knew what they were firing at. The muzzle flashes seemed to be aimed toward the heavens like a ragtag third-world army.

Hughes grunted as he stood. The flashlight in his hand remained dark. "I'll lead."

Meredith nudged Cavanaugh after him.

Nick waited for the rest of them to move, then touched his partner, nodding toward the road. She rose to a crouch and followed the others, Nick behind her.

No one dared to use a flashlight. Even with the rising three-quarter moon, climbing out of the ravine proved to be a challenge. She picked around rocks and boulders big enough to see, stumbling over smaller ones. She heard Nick doing the same. The ravine bottom funneled into a rocky channel, forming a drainage trough under the roadbed. Standing there, Meredith looked, hoping for enough moonlight to locate Germain, Hughes, and Cavanaugh. They'd faded into the night. With the advancing militia, she was sure they'd sought concealment. Maybe in the oaks on the other side of the road? She hated that she'd been separated from Cavanaugh.

Meredith listened past the irate shouts. Just the militia, not the hoped-for sound of an engine coming down the road.

A rustling in the trees across the road caught her attention. Muffled cries, then a shot. More rustling, then Germain burst from the shadows, Hughes and Cavanaugh on his heels. The three men took to the road, running at full speed in Caranica's direction.

With a piercing squeal, a smaller silhouette bolted from the trees. Dark, with wicked-looking tusks curling from his mouth, his short legs were a blur: A wild boar.

Nick stood, AR aimed at the pig. Without hesitating, Meredith rose behind him and used her body to block the muzzle flash from the militia men's view. Maybe they'd get lucky and the soldiers wouldn't see where the shots came from.

Nick's body jerked as a single pop echoed down the road. The first shot went wild, into the night. It wasn't a surprise, as there was no way to sight a target in the dark. Tracers would've been helpful to see where he was shooting.

Another shot, then a third.

They heard a grunt as the animal's front leg gave way beneath him. "Shit-house luck. Even with a big moon, it was a lucky shot," Nick said.

The pig stumbled, rolled head over tail, then came to his feet—three of them, anyway. He shook his head, glancing behind. Seeing Nick standing in the road, he turned and broke into a lame gallop—right at Nick.

Meredith shouted over Nick's shoulder to Cav and the agents. "Get to the van. We've got this."

Behind them, irate shouts and random gunshots filled the night. With no viable targets but plenty of adrenalin, the militia streamed in their general direction, muzzle blasts lighting their way. Meredith twisted into a crouch and fired at the flashes. In the back of her mind, she wondered where she was going to get more ammo.

Beside her, Nick fired. Two shots.

The pig slammed into Nick's body, knocking them all to the ground. She broke the fall on her hip and rolled as she'd been taught to fall off horses.

Nick grabbed the tusks, wrestling with the grunting boar. His rifle had tumbled out of arm's reach. He'd steadied the animal's head.

Meredith leaned toward the animal, put her Beretta under the jaw. Without hesitation, she pulled the trigger. Blood and tissue splattered over her arm, but the boar stopped as if he'd hit a brick wall. He dropped, stone dead.

Gotcha.

CHAPTER SIXTY-SEVEN

Thursday, May 21, late evening

Now they had murder coming at them from only one side.

Nick's relief was fleeting. His shoulder hurt like a son of a bitch. While he was on the ground, the damn boar's head or snout had rammed his arm. He couldn't see what hit him, but it felt like a sledgehammer. His knee ached, too. He couldn't tell if he was bleeding, he would have to wait to check on it. He could move, and that's what he needed to do. Move, and move fast. The militia was closing in. Across the field, then the dirt road—less than ten yards away.

Men's shouts, a vehicle with flat tires flapping against the dirt. Another sedan was dog-tracking toward them, lights off, riding on the wheel rims. Out of every window dangled bodies with rifles.

"Go, go, go."

Meredith looked back. "That way?"

Nick shook his head. "No. Those guys are headed toward the punk who tried to kill you. Someone over there saw us." Poking his head above the road, he looked for shelter. "If we can get across the road and into those trees, we can find cover." He couldn't bring himself to say hide. Nick found the AR and readied to cover her while she crossed the road.

Meredith shoved her Beretta in its holster and sprinted off.

When she was safely in the brush, he holstered his Glock and slid the rifle over his uninjured shoulder. She'd cover him as he hurried across. He prayed the militiamen hadn't seen them.

When he joined her, they slipped off the rocky edge, and stepped onto a gentle brush and old oak covered slope. The scrub was adequate concealment. For cover, the bulky tree trunks would do. He stood behind the first trunk they came to; Meredith took the next.

Almost at the edge of the road, the sedan sputtered to a stop. The occupants scattered the way cockroaches flee when a light is turned on. They fanned out in the field in a sloppy but discernible pattern. The Covenant Family was searching for them in the field.

In the cover of the trees, darkness was even deeper. Faint rays of moonlight broke through the canopy. They waited. Nick's shoulder throbbed, but he'd felt around in the dark and didn't feel any wetness. No blood.

Brush rustled nearby as a nasty looking guy with an AK-47 broke through. Nick hadn't seen him cross the road. He passed Nick's tree, then stopped, glancing around.

Nick held his breath. If the guy looked back, they'd be seen. As Nick was about to risk making noise by reaching for his Glock, the man moved on. The soldier circled around and toward the road where Caranica would bring the Beast. Nick stole after him, as silent as death.

Nick came from behind, clasped his hand over the man's mouth. Ignoring his knee pain, he swung a foot around to knock the man's legs from beneath him. On the ground, Nick wrestled the AK from the young soldier. As Nick's fingers tightened around the handle of his knife, the man threw his weight toward his rifle in an awkward move. He shifted to steady himself, then lunged for his gun again. Nick leaned into him, muffling his cries with a forearm as the knife went deep into the man's chest. With a deep sigh, the soldier stopped struggling.

Nick didn't take the time to check for a pulse. Meredith came up beside him. "Get back in the trees," his nod said.

Meredith picked up the AK and flipped the added-on clip release. She glanced at the magazine, then nodded. "What about him?" She slipped the AK's strap over a shoulder already laden with her pack.

They rolled the body under a brush.

Back in the cover of the woods, Nick's leg throbbed with pain.

"I hear the helicopter." Meredith looked upward.

Nick strained but couldn't hear anything. The militia had moved on, stomping through the meadow toward the ledge where Curly Red had met his end.

The detectives had missed their seven p.m. window hours ago. Nick's watch said ten-thirty. While he'd love to catch a ride, his concern was more about the airship's safety. These fanatics would think nothing of shooting at a helicopter. Nick expected Ferrua would have sent a chopper. In the absence of Henry One, the Highway Patrol Airship, H30, would be sent because they'd missed their prearranged meet-up. Their status would be "MIA" with the department. The administration would pool all their resources to find them; call mutual aid if necessary. It should, he thought, still doubting Ferrua.

The trouble was, Nick didn't trust Ferrua to get the facts straight. Search and Rescue Teams would be looking for the detectives, not a radical militant group ready and willing to fight. The helo would come up against the Covenant Family, and get a violent reaction.

He had to get to a cell signal to warn them. Where was Caranica and that damn van?

CHAPTER SIXTY-EIGHT

Thursday, May 21, late evening

As the noise of the helicopter faded, so did Meredith's brief spurt of hope. Pushing aside her frustration over not being picked up, she knew why Nick hadn't tried to get the pilot's attention. The soldiers were moving back toward them.

Nick grabbed her hand and pulled her down a slope. She couldn't see past him but it looked like they were heading for a creek. They slowed as Nick struggled, picking his way between rocks. The boar had gotten to him, and she was sure he'd been hurt. From his stumbling, she guessed his leg had been injured, at least. Meredith's feet got wet in the trickle between the stones, a minor irritation. They had a long way to go to escape these fanatics who were out to kill them.

Ten minutes later and still plunging through the brush, they heard yelling—the militia. Maybe they'd found the guy Nick stabbed. Alive or dead? Either way, the soldiers would be pissed off. These guys were tenacious as hell. How could they track in the dark? Meredith thought of how they'd stumbled through the bushes and glanced back. No wonder they'd been followed so easily—they'd left their trail of trampled brush.

And where the hell did Germain go with Cavanaugh? "I expect Cavanaugh stuck with Germain and Hughes. God, I hope he's safe," she whispered.

"Germain will take care of him," Nick huffed. "The sensible thing would be to meet up with Caranica in the Beast." She hoped he was right and not merely saying it to make her feel better. Cav had been their responsibility, but more than that, she didn't want the rancher to get hurt.

She figured they'd walked a mile when they stopped. The sounds of gunfire eclipsed by distance and the whisper of water rustling down the hill. A waterfall. The sound of men ramming through the brush, not trying to be quiet.

At the edge of a cliff, Nick panted beside her. In the dark, it was impossible to tell how steep the drop was. Nick sighed as they both heard men pounding through the underbrush, drawing closer. "We've gotta get down there."

To Meredith's right, were huge trees, tangled vines and bushes. The slope disappeared into the void. She glanced past him, then pointed, whispering, "It's too steep over here."

Voices, heavy boots stomping a hurried trail behind them. They were getting closer. Meredith caught a beam of a light in her peripheral view. Too close.

At the lip of the chasm, she handed off the AK, grabbed a long branch from a buckeye tree, and dropped to her butt. Straining to see beneath her dangling feet, she made out a pale boulder about six feet below. She had to do something—so she let go of the branch.

The tree branch scraped through her hands as she landed on a boulder. She stretched her arms out to balance. She called out to him, "Rifles."

In the next second, Nick handed down the rifles and followed her. But when he thudded beside her, it was with a stifled grunt. He dropped to his side, struggling to keep his ragged breathing quiet.

They'd landed in a small rock shelf created by winter runoff from the creek. A shelf. During the rains, this place would be covered by the waterfall. In this four-year drought, the spring water flow was just enough to make noise.

But now shadows obscured most of it. Meredith paced it off, her fingers feeling the stone. Ten feet by ten. If they moved to the far wall, the shelf was almost a cave. Deep enough to keep them hidden from above.

Meredith slipped her arm under his shoulder to help him move to the back. His knee had been injured before. But the fall had done more damage. He relied heavily on her strength while she leaned him against the wall. Keeping hold, she flattened herself next to him.

A flashlight beam swept across the spout of water and beyond. Meredith held her breath. Beside her, Nick had also stopped breathing.

Muffled voices drifted downward. "Where'd they go?"

"How the fuck do I know?"

Nick pulled his Glock, holding it in both hands. Meredith gripped her Beretta. The soldiers made little effort to keep quiet. They had the advantage. She hoped they couldn't hear the blood pounding through her head.

One of the men knocked a rock loose. It bounced eighteen inches away from them and off the ledge.

"Maybe they fell down—" one of the men began.

"Don't be stupid. We'd a heard 'em screaming."

"Yeah, I guess so. It sounded like a good drop. Could they be alive after a fall like that?"

Meredith held Nick's arm and pinned him to the wall.

Another man's voice. "We'd have to go around and come up the creek to be sure. Can't get down this way. Let's get the hell outta here."

"Yeah, that fire's getting too close," one of the men grumbled.

When the men stomped off, she allowed herself a shallow breath. Minutes passed, their stomping faded.

Her fingers flexed against Nick's arm, unkinking from the tension. She exhaled a long breath, still cautious. She felt Nick's eyes on her.

The fear was taking over and her focus faded into the tumult in her mind. Picturing her hand holding a wriggling mass of amygdala terror— gripping until she subdued it. Amygdala, the primitive part of the brain governing the fight or flight response. Meredith turned away. Even in the dark, he might see something in her she'd didn't want him to. The part of her that was afraid she might have to kill before this case was closed. Or worse, that she might freeze.

Her brain scrambled desperately for a way to evade this turmoil. Give up? And do what? Surrender to the militia? The Covenant Family were in deep enough now they had nothing to lose by killing more cops. No, Cav was right. They'd kill her.

Run? Where? I'd never work as a cop again, she thought. I'd never be able to lift my head again, either. Hide? Maybe. Quit?

She pictured her hand squeezing an amygdala blob. Ah, what a bunch of crap, she thought. Visualization exercises had been part of Doctor Servente's therapy. While she knew some methods of treatment worked, she didn't believe in this one. Get a grip on yourself, not pictures. She'd had four firearms at her fingertips and hadn't needed them, thankfully. She didn't have to kill anyone. Yet.

Curly Red was an accident, she told herself.

There was no acceptable way out of this mess other than to fight. Fight the militia and her ghosts, while untangling her own scrambled feelings. Everything seemed a battle these days. She was tired of this but couldn't stop. Time to move.

And now, something was happening in her. A resolve arose and pushed aside her desperate thoughts. A quiet strength flowed into her nudging out the fear. She'd do what was necessary to get out alive. She didn't need to do it alone. There was Nick. Cav was right. She'd do her job and go home in one piece. She couldn't quit.

As if nature acknowledged her sudden grasp of reality, the wind rattled the leaves of the trees. The faint scent of burning wood drifted into the waterfall's undercut.

CHAPTER SIXTY-NINE

Thursday, May 21, just before midnight

Leaning against the damp wall of the shelf, Nick tried to get comfortable. God, his shoulder hurt and now, his leg, too. His fingers felt the warmth from under the fabric of his dirty khakis. The knee joint was swollen, but no blood. He knew some of the worst injuries didn't involve bleeding. In a split second, he pictured x-rays, surgery, and walking with a cane, his career over. He fought the dark cloud that threatened.

Back to now. They would get out of this, he knew it. He had to believe it.

Where was Cavanaugh? He hoped like hell the rancher had stuck with Germain. He hated to think of what could happen to him up here. Though he lived in these hills, there were no end to the hazards. Over the past day, Nick had come to respect, no, like the guy.

The sounds of the pursuing militia had waned. The moonlight faded through the layers of trees. In the shadows, Meredith met his gaze but he felt she was far away.

Looking across the creek, she said, "Let's sit down and rest for a bit."

She never said, "I'm tired," or, "I'm hungry," like other women he knew. His ex, Angela, complained constantly. She, as a matter of fact, was extremely labor intensive. She'd been a constant problem last time he saw her. He snorted at the memory.

"Why don't you sit?" Meredith whispered. "Take the weight off your leg."

Nick braced himself against Meredith's shoulder and lowered himself to the boulder. He shivered as he leaned into damp earth of the wall. The night was cooling. He felt the influence of the fog in the distance and shivered again.

Meredith dropped beside him and asked, "You okay?"

He laid his head back and mumbled, "Um hm." He was exhausted. He'd had a few hours' sleep since he got this homicide forty-eight hours ago. He'd been almost blown up, shot at, linebackered by a wild pig, chased by domestic terrorists, and narrowly avoided a rockslide.

He'd also put his heart out on his sleeve and gotten it slapped away. That was what hurt. But he understood it. He'd spent the last two years sorting out the SIDS death of his infant daughter, Mia, and the subsequent breakdown of his marriage. After a six-month separation, he spent five days in Mexico helping to find Angela's kidnapped brother. It forced him to see his ex-wife without the veil of devotion that had obscured his vision. Before he left Mexico, he knew their split was permanent.

But he wasn't the only one facing his demons.

Meredith had worked—was still working—hard to resolve all her anxieties. She'd been through a lot in the past eighteen months. The traumatic and unexpected death of her husband would have overwhelmed most people. Add her on-duty shooting of a man inches from stabbing another deputy, and the self-defense killing of a cartel guard. He couldn't imagine her burden. But Meredith never whined. She had a tough character and the fortitude to keep punching as she worked it all out. He admired her drive because she kept it real. She had no illusions about her faltering marriage or her place at the Sheriff's Office.

So he shouldn't have been surprised she had to sort out her feeling before she could commit to their relationship.

He had a momentary flash of DeGraf's eyes just before he died. In them he saw the promises unfulfilled and precious moments that he would never see. DeGraf had no future.

Suddenly, he knew Meredith was his future. Life was too precious to squander on ifs and buts. It had to be Mere. If she wanted him to wait, he would wait.

His eyes opened and he felt the gentle thump of a heart not his own. The smell of the damp ground mingled with the sweet muskiness that was Meredith. The sound of her deep sleeping breaths filled his head as his eyes adjusted to the meager light. His chest swelled with love.

On Meredith's chest, his head rose and fell. Her arm curled around the windbreaker that covered his shoulders. He kept still, savoring the intimacy.

A whisper. "Go back to sleep."

He didn't move. "How could you tell I was awake?"

"Your breathing changed."

"I thought you were asleep."

"I slept a little. Enough." Her heart thumped a little faster.

"I like it—being together here." He sighed, glad she wasn't going to make him move.

"I—like it, too."

"Let's stay here, okay?"

He heard the smile in her words. "Deal."

He wondered what it meant. Was this her left-handed way of saying she wanted a relationship? If not, how long would she need? Would she ever want him the way he wanted her? Whatever she chose, he knew this was the woman he wanted to spend his life with.

CHAPTER SEVENTY

Thursday, May 21, just before midnight

Raymond Cavanaugh thanked God he didn't have his riding boots on. At least he could walk—and run—in work boots, even with his pea-shooter strapped to his ankle. On the dirt road, he followed Germain and Hughes. Both men made sure he kept up. In the dark the rugged dirt road was rough going. It meant a lot to him that all the cops he'd been around had cared about his safety. The image of American law enforcement had taken a beating in the media and the public in recent years. He hadn't given it much thought before but now had a new appreciation for their work.

Cav's legs moved mechanically, not real fast, but steady enough to keep up with the agents. With half his mind in survival mode, he scanned the waning darkness. He was in the middle of the shit, for sure. He was tired of being chased by maniacs, yet glad to help rid his beloved hills of the malice that crept along the ridges and canyons. But to be honest, he wanted to be home with a Scotch in his hand, matching chessboard strategies with his grandson. His nights had been solitary since Shirley's passing three months ago. The trip to Costa Rica—R and R, his son had said—hadn't helped. It emphasized his aloneness.

He was glad to be home, in these golden hills of Sonoma. Even with Jake's problems, having family close by was a comfort. He was closer to Jake than he'd been with his own son. He had to admit—his grandson had problems. If half of what Steven said was true, Cav and Jake had their work cut out for them.

He was disgusted to admit his son, Steven, tended toward hysteria. At least he recognized Jake was at a turning point in his life. To place the blame on Jake's friend, because he was born to an immigrant family was damn foolish. He wondered when Steven had lost his ability to think critically and instead paint people and ideas in broad strokes. God knew, he and Shirley hadn't taught him that.

Knowing Jake was feeling a bit lonely up here, Cav had taken it upon himself to meet Jake's friend Salvador and his family. He met them at their home in a working-class neighborhood in the Canal District of San Rafael. The meeting had gone as he suspected—Salvador wasn't the influence Steven said. In fact, Cav liked the kid.

Salvador's mother told him a cousin had lured the two boys to act as unwitting look-outs during a daylight burglary. They'd been rounded up when the police arrived, but after being questioned, both kids were released to parents. She said the detective told them the boys had been conned into being ignorant accomplices.

Cav purposely kept Steven in the dark when he allowed Salvador to come up from San Rafael last weekend. If his son didn't know, it wouldn't cause an argument. And both boys had enjoyed the Dry Creek hills. Salvador, far from the pressure of his cousin, blossomed into a decent kid, as Cav had pegged him. Jake had taken the "work-mules"—a pair of ATV's—and the boys explored the hills off-road. Cav had even set Salvador on Denver for a short trail ride. The kid preferred the ATV but logged a few hours in the saddle on the dirt roads around the ranch.

All this week, Cav had chalked up Jake's moodiness to missing his buddy, to hormones and his age. Sometimes Cav just didn't understand him.

Not like Shirley had. She could talk to Jake. She had a gift for showing people she cared and those who discerned it were blessed with a loyal friend for life. Cav was sure Jake knew both his grandparents loved him. That's what had made the ranch such a refuge for the boy. Now with Shirley gone, he wasn't sure. He hoped he could do right by the boy. His eyes stung, began watering.

Odd. He wasn't crying.

Smoke. Scanning the ridgeline before him, he saw the unmistakable glow, the pungent odor of burning brush. Feather-light ash floated by him on the up-canyon breeze. The fire was building.

CHAPTER SEVENTY-ONE

Friday, May 22, after midnight

With a certainty that resonated in her soul, Meredith decided. Then figured she better tell Nick. "I missed you."

Nick's head popped up. "Huh? I'm right here."

"After Mexico. You were so far away. It was like we'd never been—partners."

He was silent.

He didn't seem to want to address that. She gave him another thought to grab onto. "You said you wanted to stay here, didn't you?"

"Uh, yeah."

"Will you hold me?"

Nick shifted and curled an arm around her shoulder. With the reverence of a jeweler touching a priceless gem, he traced her jawline, then up her chin to her lips. She held her breath as he pulled her closer. Turning with his gentle pressure, Meredith's lips found his. Softly at first, then she pressed harder, getting nearer. Their awkward position didn't slow the kiss. His hand cupped the back of her head. He groaned as her ponytail escaped its band and his fingers tangled in her hair. He pressed his lips under her ear. "I love you," he whispered.

His lips drew a line down her throat, sending shivers to a place in her body she'd never known. At the base of her neck he lingered. She held her breath, not sure she could stand where he was taking her but unable to stop it.

His index finger followed the plane of her collarbone in a caress that made her tremble. Again, her lips met his in a deep, searching kiss. Together for time she couldn't measure, she soaked in how his body felt against hers, his heady odor, the softness of his mouth. Feeling whole in his arms, she lay her head on his chest. This was so right.

Back on earth, she looked up at his face. She touched his lips. "We belong together, Nick."

In the shadows, he found her hand and kissed her palm. She felt a tingle in that place he'd just touched—the deepest part of her. This place where no one had ever been allowed—before now. She would give Nick everything.

In a stunning insight, she realized her part in the failure of her marriage. She'd not opened enough to give herself—with an entire commitment. How could she expect her spouse to be honest when she wasn't? Somehow, Nick had seen through her barriers. He'd reached that private place long ago and she'd been a fool not to see it. He'd respected her from the moment they first met. That respect had earned her trust. With Nick, she knew there was no other way. It was everything, or nothing. They'd tried "nothing" and it hadn't worked. They had to be together.

Meredith sighed, hating the words she had to say. "I still have problems to solve. God knows having a relationship with a co-worker will be tough enough. I can't do any of the things I've got to do without you."

She hushed his protest and said, "Well, the truth is—yes, I can. But I don't want to. I want to be with you." She considered her words, then continued. "We can figure the rest out as we go along. But I need to be with you."

Nick turned to face her. Moving a stiff shoulder, he wrapped his arms around her and she melted into him.

CHAPTER SEVENTY-TWO

Friday, May 22, pre-dawn

The back of the hill was ablaze from the glow a hundred yards ahead. Smoke billowed upward blending in with the early morning sky. Cav had seen fires like this in these hills. This time of year, in a four-year drought, with nothing to stop it, they were in trouble. Unless they could get out of here—fast. In front of him, the two agents trooped on, hiking toward Caranica and the van. They slowed as the smoke restricted their breathing. He didn't know where their van was parked but he had doubts the agents' vehicle would make it through this.

Clouds reflected the light and he began to feel the radiant heat from the fire. To his right, the flames jumped a small ravine to a dry coyote brush. It erupted like a torch, crackles of moisture popping as the fire consumed it. "Hey," he yelled at Germain.

Without looking at him, Germain shouted, "The van is around the next turn."

So is the fire, Cav thought. He followed anyway, his mind mapping several paths out if they couldn't get to the van.

He wrapped his bandana around his nose and mouth but still the smoke was a problem. His eyes watered and his throat was raw. His lungs felt like they were filling with concrete. Ash the size of golf balls drifted past him, some settling on his sleeve. Tedesco coughed, stumbled, but kept on. Germain, too.

Cavanaugh looked behind him and saw Hughes urging Tedesco along. They would all be together, except for Meredith and Nick.

As the road twisted around the hill, they ran head long into Caranica driving the van they called the Beast. It was going to be Barbequed Beast if they didn't get it out of there—right now. The van slowed to pick them up.

Cav's watery eyes were riveted on the flames that guzzled fuel as he scrambled to get into the vehicle. The fire approached from the north, across a meadow. The early dawn brightened to a sepia, the smoke dulled the scene. From the grass to a half-dead manzanita bush, the fire skipped to the top of the oak above the vehicle.

They had seconds to get out.

"Move, move, move," Germain shouted.

Through the window, Cav watched the flames leaping from bush to tree then rushing down the hillside. Like it was the devil incarnate seeking the easiest path. It had been two hours since Cav had seen Meredith and Nick, the fire was racing toward where he'd seen them last. He was sure they'd moved on, away from danger. Though they were running from overwhelming numbers of the Covenant Family soldiers, both deputies were sharp enough to realize the threat from the wildland fire.

They would be safe. Wouldn't they?

CHAPTER SEVENTY-THREE

Friday, May 22, pre-dawn

Nick sighed, finally admitting the truth. He hadn't realized how lost he had been until yesterday when he'd finally realized Meredith owned his heart and soul. The past year's struggle to relieve the grief that saturated him began to fade. For the first time since Mia died, he looked to the future with excitement. The promotion hadn't given him this sense of anticipation, which should have told him something. Now he knew how important she was in his life. She came first.

"Mere—" he began. The early rays of sun illuminated her face enough to see her expression. She loved him. It was in the softness of her eyes. But he wanted to hear her say the words.

Then his warrior mind caught something. Wood smoke. Damn, the wildland fire.

Damn.

"We need to move." He grabbed her hand and stumbled to his feet. They each took a rifle, securing as best they could. Scanning the terrain, he looked for a way up to the road. "Can't go down, there's no place to get out of this creek bed." He pointed to a rocky outcropping beside the trickle of water. "Can we make it up that side?"

"With your messed-up knee and shoulder, we'd need a rope or something."

The hillside was an exposed tangle of tree roots, the longest extending toward them. Stretching across, Meredith grabbed a thick one. Pushing it to his chest, she asked, "Can you pull yourself up?"

Of course he could, shoulder be damned.

The morning dawned with a diffused light. The air temperature was comfortable—Nick estimated it in the mid-60's. Warm for spring. Meredith picked her way along the rocky slope, paralleling Nick upward. She kept within arm's reach. God bless her, he thought, his anchor. The idea of courting the woman who'd saved his ass so many times almost made him laugh.

Gripping the root, he pulled himself upward, an inch at a time. Biceps, triceps, pecs and lats strained pulling his body weight. Ignoring the strain on his shoulder, he worked hand over hand, breaking a sweat. He'd done it many times in rescue training, more at the gym, to be ready for this moment. Dirt turned to mud in his sweaty hands. He wrenched himself upward, legs dangling against the rock. His knee felt like he had a kettle ball strapped to it, weighing him down.

Glancing up, he saw the top of the slope fade into the smoke. He anchored himself on a rock as he coughed—several times. Five feet more.

"I'm going to swing you over to this ledge," Meredith said. "Will your knee support you?"

Nick grunted a "yes." She grabbed his forearm. He was shaky at first, balance off, but Meredith's grip was solid.

The air was thicker here—visible. Ten feet away, yellowish-gray smoke shrouded the road. With Meredith's help, he scrambled from the edge of the cliff into the grass where the militia had stood sometime during the night. When was that? How long have they been on the ledge?

Rolling over onto his back, he sucked in a gulp of air—and fell into frenzy of coughing. His eyes and nose ran. It was difficult to take a full breath.

"C'mon." Meredith pulled his arm. "Let's go." Gunfire echoed across the distance. Who knew how far away the shooter was? Who was it? Who were they shooting at?

CHAPTER SEVENTY-FOUR

Friday, May 22, dawn

Fuck those guys, Steiner thought. If they couldn't defend their own backyard, they deserved the misery that fell around their ears. They weren't so bright, anyway. But he'd thought they had more fight in them. They were supposed to be soldiers.

Some of the goddam cops must have survived the assault on the base. He'd been in too much of a hurry to count corpses, and this was the result. Unlike others in his cadre, he would learn from this mistake. The cops and his fuckin' boys had created a shit load of trouble for him.

Because of DeGraf's fucking buddies, Steiner had to scale back their attack on police stations. The detectives had set the barns on fire and destroyed the vehicles designed to hold the explosives. An "evidence van" parked next to a police building would have caused no suspicion.

Because the cars and trucks had been burned, Steiner told Lampson to steal a pick-up truck. It would be easy enough in this agricultural area. They'd load a truck with a few bags of the chemicals from the back of the Escalade, park it as close to a cop building as possible, set the detonator, then move to the next target. Even the reduced amount of ammonium nitrate would cause enough damage to knock out department resources. Using pick-ups made it riskier to deliver the bombs, but they would have to make it work.

Steiner targeted communications centers to disrupt the pigs' response. He and Lampson would repeat the process until they emptied the Escalade in Rohnert Park. Steiner was confident he could seriously damage the Sheriff's Office, the Santa Rosa Police station and the Highway Patrol office in Rohnert Park—all three within an hour of each other. The bombings would overwhelm the cops, making Steiner and Lampson's getaway easier.

For the crypto operation, he'd sent Franks and the Lewis brothers out an hour ago to Santa Rosa while he and Lampson would set the bombs at the cop shops. A barrel for every target was in the back of Franks' 1985 Chevy Suburban. Franks would go to the water tanks in Santa Rosa's Rolling Hills Estates to wait for Steiner's call to dump the bacterium. Steiner made no secret of the fact that the dump would take place, regardless of the county's response. Franks' secondary order was to keep the two Lewis idiots in line long enough to complete the task. He needed the Lewises' muscle to dump the toxin. What Franks didn't know was he, along with the Lewis brothers, was expendable.

Steiner thought his plan to dump the barrels of toxin into Santa Rosa Water system was brilliant. Starting in Rolling Hills Estates, an exclusive senior community, he arranged to contaminate all five system-wide storage tanks. The Estates had an elderly population, thus more susceptible to contaminants. Many Hills residents were affluent as well as influential, which meant more pressure on local government. Steiner thought it the best place to start the toxin release. From there, the rest of the county would fall as the pathogen made its way south on the water supply route along densely populated Highway 101. Cryptosporidium would infect anyone consuming water within two days. Some would feel it sooner than others. It should have a tremendous impact on the Tour of California bicyclists and spectators.

The clock would start ticking soon when Steiner called Franks' satellite phone. Franks would send the extortion email to the County Supervisors. The message told Healy if he paid the two-million-dollar payment, the crypto would be stopped from entering the water system. The three P.M. deadline would arrive after the last police station, Highway Patrol Office in Rohnert Park, was in ruins. Healy and the board would know how serious the Black Corp Team was. They'd know they couldn't depend on the cops to help. The Black Corps Team meant business: Pay up or we contaminate your water supply.

Steiner's gut jumped with anticipation every time he thought about the County Supervisors reaction. Cryptosporidium? In his emailed message to Ted Healy, the Chairman, he included a video of an incident in Wisconsin so they could see what they were facing if they didn't pay up. In Milwaukee, 1993, the outbreak killed a mere 104 but sickened half a million, quickly overloading medical services for hundreds of miles. The video showed the chaos of thousands of people ill with stomach cramps, fever, diarrhea and dehydration. In Sonoma County, as in Wisconsin, this kind of disaster would quickly burden all resources.

He'd use the crypto again, in the future. He hadn't slogged through all that cow shit for one incident. It was a good scheme, and the half dozen barrels containing the pathogen still sat in a Santa Rosa storage unit. He and his chemist, a sympathetic research assistant from a nearby university, had found a small group of infected calves at a local dairy. The chemist tested the pathogen to ensure it was strong enough to cause illness in humans. Unfortunately for Steiner, culling the microscopic parasite meant shoveling calf diarrhea into a half dozen fifty-five gallon drums. A nasty job, even with protective clothing.

The Tour of California bike race had been an irresistible distraction. The population of Santa Rosa, 160,000 people and the 40,000 spectators from the Amgen Tour of California, was tailor-made to bolster his plans. He'd moved up his timetable by two weeks when he read in the paper about the Tour coming to Santa Rosa. It was the perfect diversion. Many of the county's officers would be directing traffic around the Tour route. Even if the race stopped, cyclists and spectators would be on the road. The cops would have to remain to control the crowd. The priority would be to manage 200,000 people, some of them hysterical from the bombings. The insidious threat from that innocent drink of water wouldn't yet be on the radar. Although the symptoms take two days to appear, almost everyone would feel its ill-effects.

With cops in chaos there would be no one to come to the aid of the Board of Supervisors. The Board had no choice but to pay.

Steiner planned to use the Escalade for their escape vehicle. He and Lampson had to get from the last bomb set in Rohnert Park to the ransom drop—the newspaper rack outside the entrance of the Charles Schultz Airport in Santa Rosa. Then, with a suitcase of cash, to their plane at Cloverdale Airport for a chartered airplane ride out of here—to freedom. He'd be able to fulfill his dreams of power and money. He'd raise his own army and—he flushed with anger when he thought of them.

Those fuckin' Lewis brothers—he'd have their hides when he—

No, he wouldn't. Fools like them wouldn't survive without him. He didn't give a rat's ass about those two, nor did he expect them to make it out this operation alive. And Steiner wouldn't return to the Dry Creek hills. Any Covenant Family survivors would have to find their own way back to the main camp in Susanville. He'd be more selective when picking his new soldiers for his next operation.

Steiner glanced at his bodyguard behind the wheel. Lampson was amped and driving too fast, fighting to keep the Escalade on the road.

A large black-tailed buck darted across the road.

The truck zigzagged across the asphalt and came to a ragged stop. The driver side front bumper mashed into the guard rail with a sickening metallic sound. The Escalade tipped like it was hung up. "You fucking idiot," Steiner yelled.

Another foot and they'd have been on their way to the bottom of Lake Sonoma.

CHAPTER SEVENTY-FIVE

Friday, May 22, early morning

Meredith heard an engine. She looked to Nick, and his expression said he'd heard it, too. Two long minutes later, the Beast swayed down the road toward them, its off-white color blending into the dim pre-dawn light.

The shooting had stopped.

The motor was muffled, but audible. In the deadened silence, the soldiers would soon hear a vehicle coming. Meredith hoped Caranica would keep the lights off.

When the Beast was a moving blotch fifty-feet away, Nick limped out of the trees, the AR-15 in ready position pointed toward the hills. Meredith followed and crossed the road to the passenger side. She barely made out Caranica behind the wheel. Nick pointed the rifle upward to signal them then limped his way next to Meredith. The van slowed, and she heard a door sliding open.

The Beast pulled up. Nick handed the rifle to Germain while Tedesco and Cavanaugh jerked him inside. Then, they grabbed the AK and latched onto Meredith dragging her on top of Nick.

A spray of bullets thumped dully into the body of the vehicle. It sounded low and lethal to the tires. But the van kept rolling. She fell onto the floor next to Nick. Her heart was beating wildly and it was Cavanaugh who pulled her upright in a tight embrace. When the van swerved, and jerked her away from him, Cav said, "Glad to see you."

Her reply was cut off as Caranica pushed the gear down to second to slow the van for an upcoming curve. Germain yelled over the grinding engine. "Everyone in one piece? Nobody hurt?"

Muttered answers amounted to no.

Meredith grabbed a headrest and got to her knees behind Caranica. "You know where we are?" It looked like the Greek had steered them past the worst of the trouble. She couldn't hear gunfire, but the smoke seemed heavier.

"Near as I can tell, we got about five miles until we hit pavement at Rockpile Road." Caranica coughed, but riveted his attention on the road. The Beast leaned around the next sharp turn and slowed. "At this rate, it'll take forever. I can't go too fast because I can't see with all this smoke."

Nick helped Cavanaugh seatbelt into a bench seat then sat on the floor next to him. They braced against another turn. "It won't help if we crash," the rancher muttered.

Caranica used his sleeve to wipe his nose and kept his eyes forward. Meredith squinted past the dash lights, trying to see into the washed-out morning. The van slowed, but still took a corner on two wheels.

"Holy shit, dude." Germain groused from the front passenger seat, holding the AR. "We'll never make it at this rate."

"Fuck it," Caranica said, flicking on the headlights. It helped—a little. Germain blew out a tense breath. Nick tagged Meredith's elbow. "Hang on."

She sat on the floor beside Nick, drawing her long legs in to her chest. Swaying side to side, she cringed, sure they were going to crash. No seat belts, nothing to hold onto.

Nick said, "Caranica, give your phone to Mere. While you drive, she'll try calling for help. Germain, keep helping Caranica." He turned to Tedesco and Hughes in the back seat. "Tedesco, watch the passenger side. Hughes, keep an eye on the fire and watch for trouble from behind. I'll watch the driver side. Ryan, yell when you're able to get through to dispatch."

"Germain, get my cell out." Caranica nodded toward his back pocket. "And no funny business." The driver glanced at his boss. Germain's face was blank as his index finger shoved glasses up the bridge of his nose. He reached for the phone.

Caranica's phone was the same model as Meredith's—making it easy for her to navigate. But only one bar. She punched in the private number for dispatch, her finger jabbed the 'send' button.

The recorded voice said she was sorry but all circuits were busy and there was no way in hell she'd be able to make a call. Meredith would keep trying until she got through. A glance out the window revealed little, gray shadows of trees or a ghostly hillside.

The display on the phone read 6:15 A.M. Department staffing was surely depleted at the moment. Graveyard patrol units would remain on duty after any major incident. Assuming whatever event was resolved, their numbers could dip below minimum staffing. Deputies had to recover from huge events. The brass had to give them some rest. Meredith worried about getting enough help into the hills to deal with all these militants. The soldiers might scatter once they smelled trouble. Or worse, they wouldn't. Maybe they'd rally, re-group and attack.

It didn't matter. Right now, she had to stop the mobile bomb before it did its job. She scanned the phone's screen and bit her lip.

No signal.

CHAPTER SEVENTY-SIX

Friday, May 22, early morning

The Escalade stopped with a jolt. They'd hit a guardrail separating the road shoulder from the slope to the lake. Steiner's head snapped against the head rest. He and Lampson looked out over Lake Sonoma. A weak sun rising over the eastern hills did little to illuminate their world. On the edge of the precipice, Steiner couldn't see the ground beneath them.

Lampson hit the steering wheel with his hand. "Muthafucka"

Steiner punched Lampson's ear before he could stop himself. The enforcer's head snapped sideways, then whipped back. Lampson's vicious glare told Steiner he'd screwed up. Beneath the bodyguard's shirt, muscles flexed. Uh oh.

"Sorry, big guy," he said, knowing that wouldn't be enough remorse for Lampson. He couldn't show fear to this animal. Steiner opened the door and leaned out, grasping his MAC 10. He didn't trust Lampson, ever, but especially when he got like this. "You try pulling this heap from the rail. I'm going to check up front. Maybe I can figure a way to—"

Lampson growled and slammed the truck into reverse. Steiner jumped from the running board. His feet barely touched the asphalt as the tires chirped in refusal. "Wait a minute, will ya?" Steiner's words were lost in the screeching tires.

He stomped around to where the Escalade and the guardrail met. The plastic skirting below the bumper had jumped the rail and came to rest on it. If Steiner rocked the pick-up hard enough sideways, he might shift it free. A glance over the side told Steiner the truck was in trouble. The shoulder angled to a steep drop into Lake Sonoma, three-hundred-fifty feet below. Lampson kept up his furious attempts to reverse.

Steiner didn't bother telling Lampson what he was going to do. The guy was in a 'roid rage' and wouldn't listen to him anyway. Steiner leaned a shoulder against the front quarter panel and pushed with all his strength. The truck budged, but it was hard to tell if it was enough. It wasn't. He heard a thump from underneath.

"Fuck, that's all I need," he said out loud. Slinging the MAC out of the way, he dropped to his knees to see how damaged the Escalade was.

Bad news: The bumper cowling hooked onto the guardrail. Fuck. They'd have to muscle it off. Any other damage? He looked around but saw nothing out of the ordinary.

Then, from under the Escalade, Steiner saw the dim glow of headlights in the distance. A beat-up van was on the bridge—waiting.

CHAPTER SEVENTY-SEVEN

Friday, May 22, morning

Dropping in elevation, the agents drove through the fire, running the dilapidated van at the highest RPMs it could grind out. On a dirt and gravel road, traction was a problem. Caranica constantly adjusted his speed, his eyes watering and nose running. His focus was like a living, breathing, being—the most powerful influence in the van.

Fire on the uphill side raced down a slope to lap at the tree trunks like the tentacles of an evil spirit. The inferno threatened to jump the road at every tree. Glowing embers blustered on the firestorm current. The day looked dull, as if viewing through a dirty lens.

Inside, the van was silent, everyone following their assigned task. Riding shotgun, Germain spoke up now and then, giving Caranica updates about a deer darting out in their path or a turn coming up. Occasionally, someone would mutter an astonished, "Fuck," at the fire.

Five miles took an eternity. By the time they reached the asphalt, Nick's nerves were stretched to breaking. It was past time when they could let these militants go and round them up later with more back-up units. Not viable. The Black Corps Team members were committed radicals out to kill and terrorize the population, somewhere close. They had to be stopped—now.

The day broke into a sepia tableau of burning, airless devastation. The fire sucked the oxygen from the air, making it difficult to take a full breath. Nick thought the blaze would follow them, and they could outrun it, no? He hadn't dreamed it would burn around to the southeast and jump in front of them.

The van plodded on as the road dropped in elevation. To their right, they came to an area where homes nestled in the trees, vineyards at their backs. The fire skipped acres, then incinerated a country home, now a flaming skeleton of framing and joists. The blaze licked from redwoods to scrub to parched grass, missing the irrigated grapevines. Ash blew violently along the fire's windstorm. Barely outrunning the inferno, the van sped on, the destruction registered fully in Nick's tired mind. Brush was devoured, giving a glimpse into the forest: flames as far as he could see on one side, trunks standing resolute against the assault. Is this what hell was like?

"The fire's moving too fast," Cavanaugh breathed beside him.

The rancher was right. For the first time, Nick wondered if they would get out.

Germain shouted over the crackling firestorm. "We're close to the Warm Springs Bridge—less than a mile." Caranica grimaced as he hunched over the wheel. The van slowed for a turn and Nick looked out the side window. Ahead, a burning pine leaned over the road, flames tracking under the bark. As the van drew closer, the tree exploded.

Shouts of alarm filled the vehicle. A blazing branch dropped onto the asphalt in front of them, spewing sparks across the windshield. Caranica swerved, dodging the falling limb.

Then, as if guided by a capricious hand, the fire steered away from them. It traveled down a ravine, trailing heavy smoke.

With a sigh of relief, Caranica slowed at Lake Sonoma. They entered the Warm Springs Creek Bridge. The 355-foot-high, 752-foot-long gold and concrete cantilever structure was formed with a crest in the middle. The gradient was such that one standing on the end of the bridge couldn't see the other side. The smoke cleared as they pulled to a stop short of the rise.

Germain grabbed the dashboard as the van halted. "I see tail lights." He pointed to far end of the bridge. Flinging the door open, he leaned out, stretched to his full height. "It's the Escalade. They're not moving."

From behind, Hughes said, "They wrecked."

The occupants of the Escalade would be able to see them from their present position, but they were out of range to take a shot. "Can you tell how far ahead they are?"

Germain shook his head. "A quarter mile. With the smoke, it's hard to tell." Over his shoulder, he spoke to Hughes, who crawled back inside. In a moment, Hughes handed Nick something resembling binoculars, but heavier. "Use these. They help."

Night vision binoculars. Sweet.

Nick flicked them on and fought to relax his focus as his eyes became accustomed to the unusual green light. Through the smoke, he sighted on the figures—two men, a driver and passenger.

The truck had jumped the guardrail, as Hughes guessed. It was half off the asphalt, but at a 45-degree angle. The front bumper rested on the mangled guardrail at the edge of the dirt shoulder. The passenger-side tire spun a rooster-tail cloud of dust. The bodyguard sat behind the wheel, one leg dangling over the running board as he concentrated on rolling the truck off the obstacle. He revved the engine, then slipped the Escalade into a low gear. The back tires ratcheted against the asphalt in a futile crabwalk.

Despite the goggles' weird illumination, Nick saw Steiner's profile outside the passenger door of the oddly rocking truck. Then, Steiner dropped from sight.

Nick handed off the binoculars. He was able to judge the distance more accurately bare-eyed. "Okay, I know this area." Nick felt his adrenalin building. "A turn-off leads to a parking lot over there. Looks like they've chosen the place. We choose the time—let's finish this."

Caranica shifted the van in park. Germain's voice was low. "They'll have heard our engine. They know we're coming."

Nick said, "If they get that Escalade shaking the wrong way, the explosives might ignite. We've got to be careful how we approach them."

Meredith said, "Listen. A siren."

Nick heard a muffled wail in the distance coming from down canyon beyond the dam. Dropping the binoculars to the driver's console, he thought—the local deputy coming to check on the fire? Fire department? Cal Fire's nearest station was miles away in Healdsburg. No, volunteers covered this area. Whoever got here first was in for a big surprise. He'd be coming from the opposite direction to the bridge and into Steiner's path.

"Get moving. Someone's going to drive into it. Set up for a felony car stop." Since there were two sergeants, Nick needed to make it clear he was directing this operation. "I'm OIC." Officer in charge.

Germain bellowed to his men, "You all get that?"

They answered as one. Germain ran a tight ship.

Nick set out a tactic for approaching the SUV. Caranica would announce the warning. Hughes would position outside the van's driver door. Germain and Nick at the passenger side would cover Steiner, and Tedesco at the back. The scene of the stop had exposures on all sides, but it couldn't be helped. Meredith was to stay mobile and keep Cavanaugh safe.

Nick scanned the area around the Escalade. The air was still murky, but visibility was better than it had been higher up Rockpile Road. He studied the two men. The big guy behind the wheel had the gas pedal jammed to the floor, while the other was on the passenger side, leaning into the fender. Both men moved with jerks of frantic impatience, betraying their desperation.

Caranica steered below the crest of the bridge so they wouldn't be profiled against the glow from the fire. At twenty feet from the Escalade's taillights, he turned the steering wheel. The van was at a forty-five-degree angle to the truck when he killed the engine. Nick tagged Caranica's shoulder with a fist. "Perfect."

It was time. The siren's wailing grew closer, making the need for action more urgent. As for taking Steiner, the odds would never be better—six against two. If done right, Nick hoped to get the leader in custody. They had to know where the cryptosporidium was.

Shrubs and bare dirt made the scene barely manageable. A pair of coyote brush bushes on the hillside could hide someone. But through the smoke there wasn't much concealment, and no cover. The other side, below the guardrail, was a sheer 350 foot drop to the lake.

The SUV broke free, swinging wildly sideways. Then, recovering, it swung backward. Lampson slammed it into gear and plunged toward the road—without waiting for Steiner.

Steiner ran after it, but after a few steps, he stopped. "Muthafucka," he screamed. Bracing his hips, he pulled a MAC-10, out of his jacket and fired four rounds at the Escalade.

Lampson lurched, falling forward. The Escalade began an uncontrolled turn, the driver's body convulsing. The SUV swung around, tires scattering gravel as the motor accelerated.

Steiner fired again. The driver jerked sideways, then fell forward across the steering wheel as the Escalade completed a 180 degree turn. It continued accelerating, the driver's foot must have been on the gas pedal.

Steiner dropped the MAC-10. He clutched a cell phone in his fist. Holding it up, his thumb pressed the keypad. He whirled and sprinted to the opposite of the road.

The Escalade plowed past the guard rail at a severe angle, slowing but still in motion. Someone shouted, "He's going over." The Escalade pitched forward, the driver's body slamming inside like a loose rock.

Nick swore he heard a tic. "Take cover," he shouted. Then, the taillights vaporized in a cloud. Before he could duck, the world exploded. The air was sucked from his lungs. The van bucked as the road beneath them folded, then swayed. A second later, the sound wave hit along with a superheated cloud of dust, dirt and rock. The van tipped over and with wail of screeching aluminum, skidded eight feet sideways to the bridge railing. It came to a sudden stop.

Nick was blinded, his pulse pounding in his ears. Breathing smoke and dust, he fought for stability as bodies jammed into his. With nothing firm to grab onto, he let gravity do its job and sank to his hip.

Coughing and groans filled the Beast. Nick was wedged on top of Germain and beneath Caranica. He shouted. The blast had reduced his hearing. "Meredith?"

"Yeah?" Her voice sounded shaky. She could've been thrown anywhere in the back of the van. She could've been hurt.

"You okay?" He pushed out the words, mashed into one two-syllable question, in the language they understood. He hoped she could hear him.

"Yeah." She sounded disgusted like she'd been caught lying.

When he could breathe evenly, Nick shouted, "Mr. Cavanaugh?"

His voice was strained, "I'm fine."

Germain's chest heaved and he snapped, "My guys—roll call."

Coughing, Tedesco answered up, saying he was in one piece. Then, Hughes did the same. Caranica moaned, shaking off broken window glass, scattering it over the three men. Caranica moved away from Nick. "Yo. No injuries, sir."

Now that Caranica's weight was off him, he brushed off glass shards and shifted. Damn, his shoulder was jammed between Germain's back and the seat. Nick heard the unmistakable sound of a switchblade sawing through the seat belt fabric. With a jolt, Germain bounced into the dashboard. Holding the vinyl seat, Nick pushed himself upright. He helped Germain get up and the two bent to look through the open windshield.

The firestorm they'd just been through paled to the dust from the explosion. Although it was drifting away, it obscured where the Escalade had gone off the road.

And where the hell was Steiner?

CHAPTER SEVENTY-EIGHT

Friday, May 22, morning

Meredith coughed and sputtered the dust out of her mouth. Her fingertips rubbed her eyes until they cleared enough to see. Knowing that weasel Steiner would bail if he was still alive, she scanned the hillside opposite where the SUV exploded.

Through the dust, she made out a figure moving on the slope. He'd been running but stopped and turned toward the Beast. "Look." She couldn't take a full breath.

From the front of the van, Caranica pulled a Glock and backed behind the engine compartment for cover. Nick put a hand on Caranica's shoulder. "Wait. He's out of range." They watched as Steiner turned, aiming at the Beast. He fired a short, futile blast. Bullets drove into the ground between them. Steiner bolted up the hillside.

Nick was the first out of the demolished van, Caranica following. Meredith reached a hand toward Cavanaugh, but he waved it away and said, "Go." She shoved the AK-47 into his arms.

He pushed it back to her. "You need it more than I do. Besides, I got my pea-shooter."

The hot zone was over thirty feet away and she knew he could defend himself if needed. She took the rifle and used the butt to knock out the rest of the glass in the window above her, she stood on the armrest of the back seat and boosted herself out the window. Once on the asphalt, she slipped the AK strap over her shoulder.

Following Nick and Caranica, Meredith watched the hillside. The detectives hunched behind the bridge railing at an angle that Steiner couldn't fire at. A few more feet until they ran out of cover. Then what?

They passed the bridge railing and hugged the base of the hillside. She couldn't see Steiner. Maybe he couldn't see them. Her eyes burned as she strained to find the anarchist against the slope. With dismay, she knew they couldn't just shoot him. "We need him alive so he can tell us where the toxin is."

Nick grunted in agreement.

From the hill above the roadway came a shout. "You assholes, drop your weapons."

Steiner's small stature was suddenly imposing, as the MAC-10 in his arms pointed downslope at Caranica, Meredith, and Nick—with no cover.

Crap.

CHAPTER SEVENTY-NINE

Friday, May 22, morning

Cavanaugh struggled against the van's worn rubber floor mat. Bracing himself against a seat, he looked out the windshield. Germain and Tedesco had gotten out of the van, but Hughes stayed behind to give Cavanaugh a hand.

Across the bridge and a quarter-mile up the road, a sheriff's patrol car parked blocking the S-curve. Red and blue lights rotated from the rooftop lightbar while the deputy watched from behind an open car door.

"Stay on the pavement. He can't get out that way. It's a dead end," Cavanaugh shouted. Fire roads networked up and into the hills. Most weren't maintained enough to manage, even with a four-wheel drive. *Now we'll get him.*

The familiar drone of a small engine laboring over the road caught Cav's attention. It came from behind, the engine straining, then coasting. Germain shouted, "Lucky, check that out." He nodded to the noise coming behind him. Germain and Tedesco moved up, keeping their attention on Steiner.

Cavanaugh's work-mule ATV paused at the crest of the hill west of where Steiner stood. A tall, wiry figure stood on the seat, looking down at the stand-off. A young man, almost a copy of himself as a youth.

Jake.

Steiner fired a short burst, turned and raced up the slope to the ATV, a panther still stalking prey.

Cavanaugh fought the fear rising in his chest. A pissed-off anarchist holding a MAC-10 climbed toward his grandson. He came as close to panic as he'd ever been, including in Southeast Asia. There, he been a scared boy. Here—everything was at stake. At the top of the hill, Jake froze, his face white with shock.

"Jake!" Cavanaugh shouted but couldn't hear his own voice over the shooting. There—a cut in the hillside. He could get up the slope to Jake and Steiner wouldn't see him until the last minute. He'd think of something once he got there. He was running before he knew it, faster than he thought possible.

Steiner reached the ATV, still sporadically firing downhill at the agents. Turning, he kicked the stunned teen from the saddle, then jumped on it. Shoving the rifle under his arm, he fired another few shots downhill. Twisting the handlebar into gear, he whipped the ATV around and sped off the way Jake had come.

When Cav reached Jake, he was lying in the dirt. The rancher skidded to his knees, praying that his grandson was in one piece. He grabbed the kid's arm. "You okay?"

"Uh, I think so." Jake shook his head, dirt flying from his hair. "Hey, that guy took our work-mule."

"Yep." Relief washed over Cav as he answered. "And I'm gonna get it back."

Jake was okay. That was most important. But now, Steiner was mobile again and headed back on a trail that would take him away. He'd be lost in the hills, for sure, but he wouldn't be in police custody.

They had to get him. Cav believed Steiner had the means to release the toxin with a remote detonator.

"Jake, you stay with these guys. I'll be back soon."

CHAPTER EIGHTY

Friday, May 22, noon

Meredith was vulnerable, as they all were. That freakin' Steiner was on the hillside firing at them. She barely made out the muzzle flashes from the MAC-10. But the streaks of light looked dead on. Beside her, the DEA agents dropped to the ground and took aim.

Steiner swung around, the MAC's rounds thunking into the roadway. Nick grabbed her arm to pull her out of range just as she felt a chunk of asphalt slam into her left shoulder. She fell backward. Her mind shuddered, unable to comprehend what happened. When the shooting stopped, the shock disoriented her.

"I'm hit, I'm hit," Tedesco shouted, then grunted in anger and pain.

Nick and Caranica dragged her back to the cover of the bridge. She knew because she felt the gravel cutting into her hip. Germain and Hughes did the same with Tedesco, only pulled him farther back behind the van.

Was that Cavanaugh running up the hill? Then, the smoke fell like a veil covering her eyes. She couldn't see. She couldn't feel. Her head dropped into Caranica's lap. Nick hovered over her. Nick. She heard the two men shouting at each other. Then Nick was gone.

The siren had stopped, too. She'd seen the deputy on the opposite side of the bridge. Meredith knew he'd call for help. She felt a hint of hope that back-up was on the way. She hoped they'd arrive soon. She and Nick needed support now.

CHAPTER EIGHTY-ONE

Friday, May 22, early afternoon

Cavanaugh ducked behind a blackberry thicket. The work-mule engine revved but wasn't moving. The vehicle lay on its side. Steiner pushed to shift it upright. Twisting the right-hand grip, he gave it gas to engage the wheels. They spun, kicking up dust and rocks, but the ATV didn't move.

Steiner yelled, cussing as if the machine was stalling his escape on purpose. He didn't hear Cavanaugh until the last moment. When the rancher was ten feet away, Steiner's hand went to the MAC-10 slung across his chest as he whirled to face Cavanaugh.

Cav dove sideways, .38 in hand. Steiner was a small target. With a grip on the 32 round box magazine, he wasn't fast enough at bracing the stock of the automatic submachine gun while swinging it up to firing position.

Without sighting him in, Cavanaugh squeezed the trigger. One shot was all he needed. He had to keep Steiner alive. The .38 round punched through the chamber of the MAC-10. Steiner's eyes sparked in surprise behind the faintest wisp of smoke. The MAC-10 dropped on its strap as Steiner stumbled backwards, tossing the useless rifle to the ground.

Cav covered the ten feet to the Black Team leader before he could fully recover. Cavanaugh made quick work of disabling Steiner even though he was decades older. A forearm across Steiner's throat took him down and a knee to his groin incapacitated him. Steiner writhed in anguish, as Cavanaugh retrieved a sun-bleached bungee cord from the ATV.

After he bound Steiner's wrists, Cavanaugh straightened. Still feeling the warmth of the gun barrel in his pocket, Cavanaugh pressed a boot on Steiner's neck as he flipped open the pistol's cylinder. Five rounds left and ready to shoot. He slipped it closed and snapped it into his ankle holster.

Cav heard movement from behind him. Reaching for his gun, he was ready when Nick scrambled around the side of the hill, his Glock out.

A slow smile spread across the detective's face. "Aren't too many reporting parties who tie up bad guys for us."

Cav hmphed. "This guy made it personal."

"Yep." Nick frisked Steiner, recovering a switchblade knife. "Big mistake."

Leaving the groaning prisoner, Cavanaugh went to the ATV and jumped on one of the upended tires. The vehicle snapped upright, tires bouncing. Nick pulled Steiner to his feet and pushed him in toward the path. When the man hesitated, he gave him another shove. "Back down to the bridge."

Steiner recovered enough to glare at the detective.

"March!" Even to his own ears, Cav thought he sounded like a DI. No matter, it had the desired effect: the anarchist turned and shuffled down the track. Cavanaugh straddled the seat and followed Nick and Steiner.

Meredith. He wanted to be sure she was okay.

CHAPTER EIGHTY-TWO

Friday, May 22, early afternoon

Steiner thought this through as he'd walked down the hill. He'd gamble that the cops didn't know his plans. If he could get close enough to a gun, he'd show them all. The hayseed rancher was packing in an ankle holster. With his hands tied in front, he'd grab it or the deputy's Glock, depending on who was closer. Then, he'd kill them—all. To hell with worrying about the fall out. These assholes have been a pain in the ass since they showed up. The crypto arrangement was already in motion, so he had one last bargaining chip. The cops didn't know about it—yet.

The Escalade was dust and so was Lampson. And he still had to find some wheels to get to the ransom money. He looked from side to side to see how many cops were at the bridge. He counted six, including the uniformed deputy on the road. Three of DeGraf's guys were huddled on the bridge and that bitch cop was on the ground nearby with an agent. Looked like he'd hit a few of them. Good.

Steiner was beside him as the detective stumbled the last few steps down to the asphalt. Steiner reached his bound hands to the Glock's grip. The scabbard style holster didn't have a safety snap and faked Steiner into thinking he could get the gun out easily. The black leather had been molded to accommodate only the Glock 17. He'd heard about these, but damn. This wasn't the time to figure them out.

Steiner yanked again, loosening the Glock.

Time to kill these cops and get off this godforsaken hill.

CHAPTER EIGHTY-THREE

Friday, May 22, afternoon

Caranica was hovering over Meredith trying to get her comfortable. Meredith's shoulder was numb. She'd have a hell of a bruise tomorrow. Aside from the increasing pressure on her shoulder, she wasn't so bad. Her brain was a bit cloudy, though.

Not too far away, Nick shouted, "Get away from the gun." Twisted into an impossible angle, Nick wrestled with Steiner. The smaller man had both hands in the area of Nick's gun. Her vision suddenly cleared. She rolled away from Caranica who managed to support her.

On their feet, Caranica drew his handgun. His left arm wrapped around Meredith's waist. The two stood ready as Nick and Steiner fought so close that there wasn't a clear shot. Meredith strained for a better angle on her target.

Suddenly, Steiner pushed Nick on the ground. The militia leader anchored himself on the hillside. He lifted his hand, the Glock in his fist, aimed at Nick.

A shot echoed down the canyon at the same second Meredith squeezed the trigger. Next to her, Caranica fired. Steiner's hand exploded, blood blossomed on his chest as the Glock flew like an injured bird in the dirt. With a howl of pain and outrage, he sank to his knees and fell sideways. His screams reduced to a curse as his breath left him.

Where did the first shot come from? She scanned the hillside above her. Cav? Yes, Cav. With his snub-nosed .38—his pea-shooter—he stood ten feet above Steiner. Movement caught her eye across the road. What now? The uniformed deputy from the road dashed towards Steiner, shouting to Cavanaugh. "Drop the gun."

Then Nick was on his feet, sprinting to the deputy. He must have recognized Nick because the detective broke off and went to Steiner's body. Caranica was behind him. Kicking the Glock aside, Nick checked for a pulse. He shook his head, picked up his pistol and skidded down the hill, leaving the deputy, Cavanaugh and Caranica at the corpse.

Too much was going on. Meredith blinked to clear the fog of confusion threatening, an input overload. She dropped her Beretta to a low ready position. All ten fingers pressed tighter around the Beretta's grip and she shoved the mist back. She had shot Steiner—no, all three of them had shot him. Cavanaugh, Caranica, and she had taken the shot.

Nick was beside her. He put his hand over her gun, his eyes holding such compassion that it jolted her back to reality. She held the gun but allowed him to cover the trigger guard. The dregs of panic gave way to a sense of trust she hadn't known existed.

He knew what was happening to her.

She searched Nick's tired face. What next?

He whispered. "You did what you had to do." His eyes said, "You had this."

The mist fell away. She felt resolve rushing in to sweep aside her doubts. She knew, again, what she could do.

CHAPTER EIGHTY-FOUR

Friday, May 22, afternoon

Movement on the hillside beyond Steiner's body caught her eye. Nick called to the deputy who lowered his handgun.

A teen-aged boy stepped out of the bushes and walked to where Steiner lay. He was tall, thin but with broad shoulders and a shock of blond wavy hair that stuck out from under his ball cap. In jeans and a faded red T-shirt, the young man stood, staring at the corpse as Cav met him.

Meredith's knees shook as she watched Cavanaugh with the boy. The rancher gently steered him away from the body and off the hillside. She saw what Cav had been like two generations ago. They had to be related—a grandson? The likeness between the two hinted at a deep tie.

It dawned on her—this is what Cavanaugh had been hiding. The kid was involved in the murder.

As the two walked towards them, Cav said, "Steiner is no longer a threat." His eyes met Meredith's.

It was over. Although she knew Steiner was dead, it felt like someone had punched her in the gut.

Exhausted and still shaking, Nick steered her to a boulder. She hadn't slept for more than a few hours in three days. She was tired from stomping around these hills, chasing criminals. Tired of doubting herself and wondering what she'd do in a tough spot.

She'd found out, hadn't she?

Afternoon light filtered through the oaks, diffused by the pallor of smoke. Meredith looked up at the sky, wishing she was up there in the cool, open atmosphere instead of here where she always had to make choices between bad and worse.

***

When he touched her, Meredith knew it was Nick. Wiping a sudden gush of moisture from her eyes, she cleared the gravel from her throat. His hand spread out on her back, avoiding her injured shoulder.

In the distance, a fire truck lumbered up the hill, straining against the grade. Caranica trotted to the shoulder of the road and flashed four fingers, the hand signal for 'sufficient units on scene,' a code used to convey no more help needed. Tedesco was okay. Then, Cav and Jake walked toward them.

Nick did a strange thing. He didn't move his hand away when Cav and the youth approached. Meredith thought he'd return to 'all business' mode, but he kept his comforting hand on her. Caranica briefed Nick on the agents' injuries. Germain had minor scratches from ducking flying bullets. Hughes cut open his forearm when he dove for cover, and wrenched his knee. Tedesco would live; he'd fallen, maybe broken his forearm. Hughes had splinted it with a T-shirt and some straight branches he'd found.

"Hey, someone go check in with the deputy," Nick said. "See if he's got an ETA for help on this cluster-fuck." Caranica trotted over to the uniform staged at Steiner's body. He was back in a minute.

"Nick, you need to hear this." Caranica pursed his lips, looking at them both. "So you know, the cavalry is on the way, about ten minutes out. The young man here called for help. This is Cavanaugh's grandson, Jake."

Nick nodded. "Thanks." He eyed the boy, just inches shorter than he.

"Sir," Jake said with the same thin-lipped grimace as his grandfather. Clearly, the boy dreaded what was coming.

Meredith asked, "You have something to tell us?"

Jake's face twisted in an embarrassed frown. "Yes, ma'am. I was up here a couple days back." Meredith wanted to know exactly when, but had learned from Nick to let people tell their stories, then go back and question them.

"I wasn't s'posed to be so far out." He glanced at his grandfather. "I found these soldier guys last week, right after I got here. When I could, I came out here to watch these guys in their camp. At first I thought they were, like, Army or something, because they had all these guns and stuff. Then I figured out they weren't real soldiers. I went down a-ways and got a cell signal, I called my buddy, Salvador. He thought they were some kind of secret army. I wasn't sure what to do."

The young man's eyes opened wide with dread as he met Nick's gaze. "Last weekend, Salvador came up to stay with us. We drove out here on ATVs. We walked around a corner and came face to face with one of them." He squinted with anguish. "The guy pointed his gun at me."

Jake looked from Cav to Nick and back to his grandfather. "He was gonna take me to their camp. I knew I was gonna be in shit, no matter what. So I told him no way. He pointed his rifle at us and shot at us."

Jake's eyes glazed over, lost in the nightmare of the moment. He cleared his throat. "I had Grandpa's old .22 revolver, so I pulled it out and shot him." The boy's eyes moistened when he looked at his grandfather. "He looked so surprised."

Like the weight of a feather falling, Cavanaugh's voice encouraged him. "Go on, son."

"I knew there was no way these Army guys would understand self-defense, so Salvador and I pushed him off the road, piled some dirt on him." He paused. "I figured I'd tell Grandpa about it, but the words kept getting stuck." Jake faced his grandfather. "I know I let you down. I'm really sorry."

Raymond Cavanaugh grabbed the boy by his shoulders, pulling him close. Without words, Cav had said just the right thing.

Nick spoke first. "Mr. Cavanaugh, is this what you concealed from us?"

The brim of the Stetson dipped over Jake's shoulder. Cavanaugh put his grandson aside as he explained. "Jake thinks he can keep things from me, but I been around too long. I knew he was involved in the death of that man—but I didn't know how. I wanted to give him a chance to tell me straight before I talked to you folks."

Meredith's insides unclenched. She'd believed the worst—that Cavanaugh had killed the soldier. It hadn't dawned on her he was protecting someone else. But now, with everything revealed, she saw that it fit so neatly into his character.

"It would've been easier if we'd known the truth from the start." Nick's tone was bordering on a reprimand.

"But it was self-defense," Cavanaugh snapped.

"If we believe Jake's story—"

Cavanaugh stepped toward Nick, his head in an angle. "What do you mean—?"

"I mean how and why he shot the victim. Because he popped off a round at him? Would a reasonable person believe the victim intended to use the deadly weapon against him, to kill, or injure him? Probably. Then it would be self-defense."

"That's what he told you," Cavanaugh insisted. "That's not murder."

"That's true—"

Meredith spoke up. "A homicide is any killing of a human being by another. Murder is an unlawful killing. All homicides are not murder but all murders are homicides. A self-defense homicide is justifiable homicide. But the burden of proving that it was justifiable is on the defendant, not the State."

"The only ones who acted with malice aforethought are the Covenant Family, not Jake." Nick sighed. "Right now, we'll take information for the report. The Juvenile DA will decide about prosecution, but with the buddy's statement, there may not be any charges at all. If the crime scene techs match that bullet, that would support your story."

"It's not a story," Jake insisted. "It's the truth."

"Relax," Nick said. "I believe you."

Meredith had to ask. "And where's the soldier's rifle?"

"We pushed it down the hill," Jake answered. "After that, I didn't want anything to do with guns."

Cavanaugh's shoulders relaxed, and Nick half-smiled at the rancher and his grandson. To anyone else, his smile would appear as a polite reaction but she knew he was pleased with the outcome.

An ambulance parked near the end of the bridge. The driver got out, looking for his patients. Caranica hailed the paramedic, "Over here."

No way could she quit this life. Now, she didn't have to. Meredith felt the first aches in her chest from all the running she'd done. She pushed it aside and relaxed for the first time since Monday.

Quit? No way.

CHAPTER EIGHTY-FIVE

Friday, May 22, late afternoon

A strike team of fire engines roared past, the sirens silent but the rotator lights reflected in the van windows. With a sigh, Nick slumped against a rock. This stuff never goes away. Activists clamored about their idea of a warm fuzzy police force. But with the chips down, they wanted someone who would do the job—whatever it was. From bar fights to evacuations, domestics to abandoned children, only decisive action got things done. The trick? To get it right the first time. There were no do-overs in this line of work.

A pair of Sonoma Sheriff's SUVs followed the caravan of fire trucks. The last patrol unit screeched to a halt next to the Beast. A voice shouted, "Sarge. Nick." Detective Joey Willis jumped from the back seat and jogged toward him. "Sarge," he panted as he reached Nick and Meredith.

Nick was so tired he couldn't answer. What could this guy want now?

"Glad you two are okay." Willis squinted in the dull afternoon sun. Shoving his sunglasses into his collar, he looked to Meredith.

Beside Nick, she had a faint smile on her face. "Joey," she said, by way of a greeting.

Willis glanced back to Nick. Then his gaze followed the fire engines moving down the road. He smiled with even, white teeth. "Santa Rosa PD already got the clowns headed to the water tower. Their truck broke down at Rolling Hills front gates. Enough residents called in the suspicious-looking truck that the PD sent some State Park Rangers from Jack London Park over to detain them. Two of the three are talking like crazy. They're all in custody."

Nick asked, "How about the toxin?"

"That's the good news: none of the contaminant was released. They never even got close to the tanks."

Willis' portable radio crackled with dispatch relaying reports from other agencies that more of Steiner's accomplices have been caught. Based on phony emergency vehicles Meredith had seen, Nick had radioed in to warn the targeted agencies. Within minutes, Santa Rosa broadcast two in custody—tattoos made white supremacists easy to spot if one knew what to look for. Two more outside the Sheriff's Office, then more.

Willis said Lassen County Sheriff's Office was headed to the Covenant Family compound in Susanville. "They'll look for weapons, drugs, and outstanding warrants." Willis' smiled like a first grader going to recess. "I'm going to help round up these idiots left up here. Want to come?"

Groaning simultaneously, Nick and Meredith glared at Willis. She shoved him toward the patrol car. "No, we're done here. You go on and save the world, Joey."

Looking over his shoulder, Willis' face scrunched in a quizzical twist. Then he relaxed. Shrugging, Willis walked away. "Guess that's how things are."

CHAPTER EIGHTY-SIX

Friday, May 22, evening

Sitting on a bench tucked in a corner of the crowded ER waiting area, Meredith whispered, "Nick." She put her hand on his chest. Even in the middle of the bustle, she heard the throb of his beating heart. That strong heart was always near hers.

But she had to find out.

Whispering, she asked, "What do you want out of this? Romance, marriage, kids?" Holy crap, why was she asking this? She didn't have any of those answers for herself.

Without hesitation, Nick sat up. "Yes. All of it."

Meredith considered his answer. "Well, I don't know about marriage and kids right now. I don't think I can wrap my mind around that yet."

She felt his shrug. "We've got a good start."

Sitting there with his arms around her shoulders, she felt some of her burden evaporate. Nick was—and would always be—there, beside her. The shadows of her violent father and her unfaithful husband drifted out of her mind. She still had issues, but she knew that would always be part of her life. There was no "happy ever after." But she knew life would be so much better with Nick as her partner.

Epilogue

The autumn sunshine burned the top of his head. Dressed in a short-sleeved shirt and slacks, Nick leaned against his new Chevy pick-up parked at the curb. He sighed with contentment when he saw Meredith push through the exit door. She was beautiful in a way that the Hollywood could never capture. Her simple sheath dress accentuated her athletic physique. She squinted as she strode into the sunlight, tucking a wisp of her chestnut hair behind her ear. He knew that gesture so well. Yet, she had changed in the past few months. Being away from work suited her. She'd never worn dresses before. She smiled and laughed a lot more, too.

"Hey, how'd it go?" He couldn't help but smile. "How'd she take the news that you're breaking up?"

"Very funny." Meredith smiled. "I graduated; don't need therapy anymore. That's not exactly a break-up."

He opened the door and held it while she got in. "So, do I come out looking bad when you're in there talking?"

She laughed outright. "She and I are having lunch next week. Come along and ask her yourself."

Nick couldn't help himself. He leaned in, kissing her. He left one hand on the rising bump that was her stomach. "Okay, Mommy," he said. "Maybe I will."

The End

About the Author

Thonie Hevron worked in California law enforcement for 35 years. Retired, she uses her experience to write suspense novels based on the richly textured lives of the people behind the badge. Hosting a bi-weekly blog on Just the Facts, Ma'am, Thonie posts stories from law enforcement veterans to accurately portray the police character for fiction writers. She also writes and hosts guests on Writer's Notes. Her first suspense/thriller, By Force or Fear, placed third in the Public Safety Writers Association (PSWA) 2012 Fiction Competition. It is set in the Sonoma County Wine Country where she lives. Home for Thonie is in Petaluma, California with her husband, Danny. The second Nick and Meredith story called Intent to Hold placed first in Oak Tree Press' Cop Tales contest and third in PSWA Annual (2014) Fiction Competition. With Malice Aforethought is her third book and, while unpublished, won 2nd Place in the PSWA 2016 competition. Her next book, Walls of Jericho, is a standalone police thriller. Thonie's story, Johnny Walker appeared in the PSWA anthology, Felons, Flames and Ambulance Rides. Website: Thonie Hevron blog: Just the Facts, Ma'am. Facebook page: https://www.facebook.com/thoniehevronauthorpage/

Thanks for reading With Malice Aforethought. If you have a moment, please go to Amazon.com and rate this book. Authors depend on reviews for a number of things, not the least of which is to indicate they are on the right track with their readers. If you liked it, say so. If there was something that bugged you, let me know. Maybe it's fixable, or maybe not. At any rate, no matter what you have to say, a review would be most welcome!

Thonie Hevron

28414614R00188

Made in the USA
Columbia, SC
15 October 2018